UNFIN

SAVING JUNEAU

BY MELVIN BROWN AND SCOTT WATTS

This is the first book in the Vlad and Jim action series.

Thank you
Melvin Brown
#1

TABLE OF CONTENTS

PROLOGUE

Grant Bismarck (ex-CEO of PEDEI Corporation) downed his drink and waved for the stewardess to bring another. He was so scared and elated, all at the same time. How could a person go from being fired from a million dollar job and get rich beyond belief all in one fell swoop? Grant leaned back in the first class seat and mentally patted himself on the back. He ran the last few days' events through his mind. The rollercoaster ride, from total failure, to possible life incarceration, to now having the potential to be one of the wealthiest men alive, was very exciting, to say the least. Grant chuckled every time he thought about the entire situation. Every American law enforcement officer, or official was out to get him, but he had walked away and would land in a country with no extradition and a government easily swayed by large amounts of money. The only thing that would make the entire thing better, was finding a way to kill the bitch that sold him out to the federal government. 'Leah Swain.' Even saying the name pissed him off to no end.

Who would have thought, a simple executive secretary could destroy a perfect plan! Grant had set up the entire operation to insure that his security chief would end up taking the entire fall, if the operation went bad. It still amazed and excited him that he was responsible for the largest attempted terrorist attack in American history! The funny thing was Leah had been his trusted assistant for over seven years and he believed she was totally loyal to him. Who would have thought, the woman was having an affair with the man he had kidnapped? That was just bad luck. The entire plan had gone off like clockwork, right up to the end. Even when the final stages of the plan fell apart, everything would have been fine, if she had not had all of the evidence linking him personally to the crazy guy (Brenner).

Brenner had been an old army contact of Maris, his chief of security, and had a lot of experience with covert operations with the CIA. Grant ordered his third drink of the flight; but, if he thought about it, he had pretty much been drinking steadily ever since his contact in the CIA had called and told him the feds were going to arrest him. He had been so careful to insure he had no trail to himself.

Everything led to his security guy, Maris, but the bitch had been taping his meetings and even had photos of Maris and himself, meeting with the mercenary Brenner. Who would have thought that a woman would bring him down? Granted; choosing her based solely on her movie star looks: blond hair, true blue eyes, and a perfect body, wasn't the best decision he had ever made. She had been a little tall, at five-ten, but she had even been a very good assistant, right up to the betrayal.

As Grant reviewed the last couple of days, starting when he got the call, he still had to be pleased with the entire event. The scientist had been kidnapped, along with several international representatives, including the senator from the state of Alaska, who just happened to be the only daughter of the current President of the United States. 'Maybe that was a bit of a mistake,' he thought to himself. Nothing was easy when you were stealing something worth a billion dollars. Grant patted the briefcase he had in his lap! The research notes and formula in the case, were his ticket to the life he had always seen in his future (Money and power beyond belief). He would be able to buy guys like Brenner and Maris any time he wanted something done, or someone eliminated. That was power! The country he had cut a quick deal with, was meeting him in one day, with the final installment on his billion dollar payday. They had already deposited half in his numbered account. Things couldn't get much better!

Grant had a little difficulty walking down the stairs, when the plane landed. He knew he should have stopped drinking a bit sooner. Of course that had not kept him from stuffing his pockets with more bottles of airline booze. The plane would only be on the ground for his short meeting, and then on to his country of choice. He had the case under his arm, as he walked towards the small office, close to where the private jet had landed. He glanced around the area and was surprised that there was only one building in sight. His contact had supplied the coordinates, but no more information. Crazy way to do business, but you can't be too choosy when time is running out. He could see two men waiting for him. He had expected some oriental men, but as long as they had the money, he didn't much care. He had used up every covert contact he had in the government and a few corporate people he had aided along the way as well, to get out of the states with the case.

His state department friend had been able to delay the arrest, but had assured him, it would only be a delay. Grant had not wasted any time crying over spilt milk (or blood). He had made his escape plans and set the sale of the research data right away.

From the very beginning, he had known this would end his career with the corporation, but had seen that as a positive. After spending most of his adult life climbing to the top, he had become bored. Getting there had been a lot of fun and the thrill of doing whatever it took to move up, had been a kind of addiction to him. The first time he had a man killed so he could advance, had been the turning point in his life. It had been so easy, a simple call and a few days later, the man was gone! Now that was the ultimate use of power. When he set up the current operation, he had purposely hired a man known for his bloody approach. Brenner had been kicked out of the Army for abuses of power and even the CIA had washed its bureaucratic hands of him. Every report, from the first exploding boat, had been like a total orgasmic experience for Grant. Even when he knew that the President knew he was involved, he was just that more excited. Too bad he had to wait so long to discover the thrill of this kind of power!

When Grant reached the shack, he could see two more men through the open door, both Oriental, sitting inside. As he walked up, the two men outside just looked at him and gestured to him to enter. As he walked through the door, he was surprised to see the two men enter behind him. The first real surprise happened when one grabbed him from behind and sat him down.

"What the hell is going on here? I expect to be treated properly, or I will sell this to someone else." The fear and bile rose in his throat, when the other man just slapped him in the face.

"Listen shithead, just sit down and be quite. You may live longer that way!"

Grant finally glanced at the two others seated and noticed that each had their hands strapped to the chairs and had a gag in their mouths. The man that had grabbed him from the back, pulled his hands down to his sides and used plastic ties to secure his wrists to the chair. He then did the same for his feet. Grant could feel his loss of control and urinated down his leg. The older of the two men, sat down in front of him and slapped his face before beginning to talk.

"I guess you thought the President of the United States, was going to let you walk out, after trying to kill her daughter and let you get rich? The funny thing is, if you had not involved the senator, you may have been able to buy your way out of the country. When you did that though, there was no way. You should have studied the President a little closer. She would charge Normandy Beach by herself, to protect her daughter and she feels just as strongly about the entire country."

Grant finally controlled his own fear, enough to try and control the situation. "Look, I can make both of you wealthy men, beyond your imaginations. Do you have any idea what this case is worth?" The older man smiled and just reached over and picked up the case that Grant had dropped.

"Let me guess, about a billion dollars!" The man smiled again and looked at the other guy. "What do you think the case is worth Jim?" Before Jim could answer, the first man spoke again. "Where are my manners? I should introduce myself and my quiet partner. Jim is the man who shut down your mercenary operation, and by the way, is engaged to the Senator from Alaska. I'm Vladimir Choskey. I work for the CIA, and in this case, directly for the President of the United States." Grant sank lower in the chair. It took him a minute to gather enough strength to continue.

"So I am headed back to face trial?"

Choskey just looked at him with the same sad smile. "No, the president is afraid that you could buy your way out of that, and possibly stay alive. That's not an option! This will end right here." Choskey grabbed one of the Chinese men and the man called Jim grabbed the other. As he was walking past Grant, he leaned down and whispered in his ear.

"I wanted to put a fifty-caliber bullet in your head, but Vladimir wouldn't let me. You may believe he did you a favor but think again. We are going to leave you here. There is no water, and no way to call for help. Have a nice couple of day's scumbag!"

Jim pulled the man he had by the arm out the door, following Choskey. Jim took hold of both men and walked them towards the flight line. The plane, they had come on, was waiting. The men were escorted up the boarding ladder and walked to seats. Jim sat each one down and left the plane. He was back quickly with the brief case the men had brought with them. He cut the gags off both men and released their hands.

"You are two very lucky men. You get to go home and talk to your Boss." Not a sound came out of either of them. They just watched, as Jim took his knife and broke the locks to open it. Inside, was a pile of bearer bonds, worth a half-billion dollars, Jim thumbed through the bonds and smiled. "I bet you think I am going to take these, that would make me quite happy, but the president said to let you go."

"I do have one demand through." He reached into his back pocket and removed an envelope. It had the President's name on the front. "You need to make sure your scumbag boss gets this letter from my President. If she doesn't receive a call from him after a few days, the information about this entire episode will be on the nightly news. I don't know what the note says, but I think you can plan on being out of the industrial espionage business for good in the United States." Jim dumped the brief case in their laps and walked towards the exit. At the last minute, before departing, he couldn't resist one last stab. "You boys have a nice ride back to China. I wonder if you will be put in prison or just shot?" On that note, he signaled the crew to depart. Jim had to hurry, or miss all of the fun with Vladimir.

Choskey waited until he saw Jim leaving the jet from China and then turned back to the primary reason for being at this vacation spot. He walked back into the room and sat down. "I have to apologize for my good friend. He is quite intense when he sees friends killed and nearly loses the love of his life. He is a direct action kind of guy where I'm more a planner and a thinker. So let me explain how we've played you. The crew of the jet that brought you here, works with me for the CIA. The President knew you'd been warned, and so we were on to you from the moment you called your Chinese contact to sell the formula. The half-billion dollar down-payment, has already been transferred from your account to the government. I suspect that money will go towards fixing the damage you caused in Alaska. I guess the rest will stay with China. I was afraid that trying to collect that, could cause some problems."

"I have to tell you a bit about this building. It is linked to a very large air-fuel bomb. You know that is the same thing your man was going to use in Juneau." Grant just sat there and cried, as he heard everything.

"The bomb will not explode, unless you open the door. You have two choices: sit here and die of dehydration, or open the door. That will be quicker for sure. I kind of hope you wait it out; but, by the smell from your pants and the puddle under your chair, you will open the door. It would take quite a man to sit here and die! You could try and find the bomb and defuse it? That might be fun! Well time to go, I can hear the airplane warming up." Grant heard him get up and walk towards the door. He was crying and begging, but knew there was not going to be any last minute reprieve.

Choskey hesitated at the door, and turned for one last statement. "The President told me to mention, that she would personally destroy your corporation and any person who has made a penny, working for you. Have a nice day!" Grant kept screaming and begging, until he heard the jet take off.

Grant spent the first several hours alone, figuring out how to get untied. He finally just stood and dropped backwards on the chair. It broke easily. When he was free, he checked it, and found that it had been rigged to break just right, to let him get loose. It took another hour to convince him that the only way out of the building, was through the door. The shack was built out of cinder block and concrete. There were no windows at all. The roof was also a concrete slab. He finally gave up and sat down. The first night he slept but the next day the heat got unbearable. The only thing he had to drink, was the airplane booze he had in his pocket. He forced himself to ration that. He had a lot of time to think about everything. The crazy thing was he didn't even know where he was. Thinking about the entire thing, he finally remembered where he had heard the name of Choskey. Brenner had mentioned that the CIA guy was in Juneau and that he would kill him for free, along with an Army friend named Jim, something like Walker, or Walters. Grant had to laugh about that. "He was brought down by a couple of government stooges. Nothing men, without any personal drive at all."

Grant spent the second day, thinking about the events that brought him to this shack in the desert. It had all started when he interviewed a scientist (Robert Westlake) for employment. The man had some emerging ideas that could prove to be huge. Grant had seen the possibilities almost right away. He had planned to control the man from the first day he started work.

When the man had quit the corporation, Grant had realized that he could have it all, without the corporation getting anything. Even now, the thought of the operation excited him beyond belief. Grant spent the third day thinking of how he would personally kill both men and the President. That evening, as it began to cool, after drinking his last bottle of booze, he didn't even know what it was, he opened the door.

Chapter One - THE SCIENTIST

(One hundred-twenty days to start.)

Robert (Rob) Westlake was as happy as he had ever been in his life. He could count the millions he was going to make, now that his research had proven out his theory had worked! Interestingly, today was his four year anniversary, from officially ending his employment with Petroleum development and exploration International (PEDEI). When he first went to work for the company, he had expected to stay there, until he reached retirement. Rob's father had worked for the same company his entire working life and had instilled that idea of loyalty to his son. Rob had quickly realized that PEDEI Corp., instilled no loyalty in any employees. Four years ago, it took all of his energy, to keep from quitting, with no hopes for other employment. He knew the corporation would blackball him in the industry and there were not so many jobs that paid as well, for a fish biologist/chemist. He had contained himself, but started planning for a way to get out. The only person with the Corporation that knew about his disgruntlement, was Leah, the love of his life, and surprisingly the special assistant to the CEO of the corporation. She was the only thing that kept him from quitting and just walking away.

Thinking about Leah, made him flash back to the start of his disillusionment for his job. The problems started soon after he was hired, right out of graduate school. The research was interesting enough, but seemed aimed at keeping the EPA happy and not the kind of research he had worked hard to get to do. Every study seemed aimed at finding ways to cover up mistakes, or spills in the field. Even his own research focused on cover-up for the corporation. Rob had developed a new dispersant for oil spills. The problem with it, was it worked wonders in making the spill disappear, but in reality, just caused the crude oil to settle out of suspension, faster than normal. That was not so bad in itself, but the oil would not break down and remained on the ocean floor in globs of poison for the ecosystem. PEDEI had rushed the new dispersant into production, even when he had described the negative result. That was when he decided he had to find a way to move on.

He had started in college, to become a research scientist in fisheries, but had gotten interested in the chemistry side of the oceans, and how this affected the fish habitats. He had stayed in graduate school, to work on a second Ph.D. in chemistry. He was surprised when PEDEI (called 'petty' by most employees) recruited him in his last term, when he was finishing his dissertation. He had expected to have to claw his way to a research position through the academic world! PEDEI offered him a great salary and his own lab. Unfortunately, their idea of research was not his idea. Rob seemed to be in trouble, most of the first year, over not staying within company guidelines for proper research. Rob saw a lot of other researchers come and go over the five years of his employment. He began planning a way to move on. The one problem with leaving the company, was his relationship with Leah Swain.

They had met when he was working summers as a deck crewman, on her uncle's fishing boat, based out of Juneau Alaska. He had gotten the job with the assistance of his academic advisor, who was a close friend with her uncle. He had taken the job as a way to spend time in Alaskan waters during his summer break from school. It had been a bonus to get paid for his work. He had been part of the crew for a month, when the skipper's niece had come aboard to help out, since the cook had quit. She was the most beautiful woman Rob had ever been close to. Her blue eyes could melt him on the spot. She had long blond hair and a gorgeous body. She moved like a gymnast. The real surprise, was her incredible personality that was totally at odds with her looks. Leah was just finishing her own schooling and waiting for a job offer from several companies she had applied to. They had hit it off, right from the first time they met. He spent as much time with her as possible, when in port and on board, as much as the captain would allow.

Just before Rob was scheduled to leave the boat, Leah accepted a position with a large company located in the lower forty-eight. She was gone before he even had a chance to say goodbye. Rob was sure he would never see her again, but several years later, when he started at PEDEI, he was totally surprised to literally run into her in the staff cafeteria. He had hoped to see her and he probably took the position because she worked there, as much as for the job itself.

Leah was more surprised than him; of course she had not had any advanced notice. When she recognized him, she acted quite cold, until he was able to get her to sit down and talk. Leah had admitted that she was still angry that he had not bothered to even say goodbye when she had left. Rob had spent the entire lunch break, convincing her he had tried, but had been told she had left without trying to contact him.

Rob and Leah had taken several days of lunches and finally a dinner date, to decide that her uncle had fooled both of them. He had been afraid she would not have taken the great job in New York, and instead, stayed in Juneau, to be close to Rob. The real surprise to Rob, came when he found out that she was the special assistant to the CEO. The corporation had a policy that frowned on executives and employees dating, and even though Rob was a research scientist, they decided to keep their relationship secret from anyone in PEDEI. He and Leah quickly realized that the summer fling for both, could grow into a long-term commitment.

Over the next year, their feelings got more intense and the need to keep the relationship quiet, added to his need to get out of the Corporation Rob knew that any future plans, would include Leah. Rob would have to find a way to replace both incomes, before they could be together. That was the motivation to make a commercially sellable discovery. Rob spent most of his free time away from the company, reviewing his early research from his dissertation. The original idea for his compound (discovery) came from a fish he caught in Alaska and had been studying off and on ever since.

He had become interested in the fish, when he had taken it off a hook and the captain had told him to toss it overboard. Since it looked like a flounder, with unusual coloring he had been surprised by the order. He had asked why this flounder was not kept, when the others were, since the crew ate flounder on several occasions. The captain had told him it was a fibrous flounder and inedible. As he moved over to the rail, he noticed the slime he got on his gloves was very thick, almost like grease. He pitched the fish, then grabbed a rag to wipe off the slimy stuff. As he cleaned his gloves, he realized he had, in his haste, grabbed an oily rag from the bilge. Rob had taken the rag to the garbage, when he noticed that the rag appeared cleaner in spots.

He went down to the head and rinsed the rag in plain, cold water. Almost all of the oil and grease rinsed out. The only reasonable explanation, was the introduction of the fish slime.

Rob tried to research the fish when he got back to Juneau, but couldn't find any information locally at all. He was able, during the remaining season, to collect several samples. Rob asked around other fishing boats, and a lot of locals recognized the fish, but only as a real pain that had started showing up over the last few seasons. Rob decided on the spot, that this fish would be his dissertation research. A new species would be an easy ticket to his Ph.D. Back at the University, he was unable to find any more information about the strange fish. He did find a short side-note, in a marine biology periodical that mentioned the fish and the fibrous texture. When he contacted the author about the note, the man had similar contact with the fish as Rob had. That researcher had never followed up on the study, since it did not fit into his work at the time. Rob wrote up a prospectus to present to his dissertation advisor. He was given approval to do preliminary research that could lead to funding grants.

When Rob presented his finding to his advisor, the funds for an onsite study were found, and he was back in Juneau a few months after leaving. The Flounder slime had interesting chemistry that did a couple of important things for the fish. It produced an oily substance that aided in temperature control and protection from predators. The way the slime, or oil acted, when in contact with petroleum-based substances, was the most interesting effect. The findings led to several published papers and his Ph.D. The final success, was his landing the research position with PEDEI. Rob would never regret taking the position, since it brought Leah back into his life.

When he interviewed for several research companies, PEDEI had been one of them. He recognized the name, but had to go to his journal from his fishing experience, to recall that, that had been the corporation Leah had gone to work for. The simple link to his past, was enough to make him choose PEDEI. Rob had shown Leah his fish research, the first time she spent the night at his home. He had already started studying possible commercial applications, if he could find a way to duplicate the compound in the lab.

Leah immediately saw the risk to his research, if the Corporation ever found out. She had no illusions about her boss. The biggest surprise to Rob, was how unhappy she was with her job. Her unhappiness was just as strong as his. When the corporation misrepresented his dispersant to the general public, she was more upset than he had been.

Rob was almost afraid to even think about the project, let alone talk about it. He had become a bit of a problem for the company, when he published a paper, condemning the new dispersant he had developed (the article had been Leah's idea). This led to his being asked to leave the Corporation, which was perfect, as far as he was concerned. He couldn't be happier about it. Rob and Leah decided that he would pursue his research in his private lab and she would support them, until he had his compound ready for the public. That meant that she had to keep her job and not be linked to him.

Rob worked alone for the next year, but finally had enough research data to try and find some outside money. While with PEDEI, he had met a man who had been very interested in possible applications for the dispersant he had fabricated for the corporation. Rob had spent a couple of hours with the man in a bar during the conference they were attending. Rob had forgotten the entire thing, until he was trying to find a way to raise the money he needed. The man had given him a business card and surprisingly Rob found it in the jacket pocked of the suit he had worn that night, three years before. As a last ditch try, Rob called the man. He was surprised when he recognized the number as Juneau Alaska number. Rob only reached an answering machine, but was surprised when he received a return call the next day. The man's name was Vladimir Choskey and he lived in Juneau. The crazy thing was, that Vladimir was so interested in the research, he flew down to Los Angeles, to meet with Rob in person.

Rob was able to impress Choskey enough, that he wrote an impressive check on the spot. Rob was sure the discovery was going to change the world. The applications were staggering. The product was biodegradable, both on land and in the sea. What it could do, was act as an extraction catalyst. Injected into a well, it would draw the crude, or natural gas out of the surrounding rock, without having to use controversial fracking.

The beauty of the compound, was that once the crude was attached to the compound, it became safe in the environment. Natural gas separated, as soon as exposed to the light. If a spill happened in the ocean, the compound kept the crude from separating, making recovery quite easy and environmentally stable. On land, the crude could be literally pumped in an open reservoir, with little special need for expensive containment facilities.

The best part of the entire project, was how simple the compound was to manufacture. Rob had found a way to produce the compound, with relatively simple lab facilities. Why he was so happy today, was the patent had come through, on his compound. He owned it, lock, stock, and barrel. He had made sure that his early studies had no ties to the work he had done for PEDEI Corporation. The corporation would have no ability to make any claims on this compound.

During his academic career, and later, with PEDEI, he had published several papers, dealing with fisheries, sustainability, and how chemistry could help. He had been invited to speak at a fisheries conference for the Pacific Rim. He had accepted, but now he planned on breaking his news to the world at the conference. Rob had discussed this with both Vladimir, his money partner, and with Leah. Representatives from several countries would be present and that meant press coverage for him. His only decision, remaining in his mind, was take the money he would be offered, to sell the research, or do the development himself. Better yet, maybe a combination of both!

Unbeknownst to Rob, several organizations were already aware of his discovery, and were deciding how to best exploit it. PEDEI had been aware from the onset, about his early research, and had kept abreast of his continuing research, after leaving the corporation. They knew he had carefully separated the research from his earlier company study, and that they would have no legal approach to the results. The United States Government had gotten very interested, as soon as his patent data had become known. Russia had decided to send representatives to the fisheries conference, only when it was announced that he would speak. Rob thought he was the only person in the world that knew about the compound. This couldn't be further from the truth.

Chapter Two - PEDEI

(Sixty days to start.)

Grant Bismarck (CEO of PEDEI corp.) was waiting for his chief of security to deliver the update on the research scientist (Rob Westlake). Grant had begun surveillance on the scientist, the moment he had left the corporation, several years before. He was sure the man was onto something special, but had decided to let him think he was out of sight of the corporation. Westlake had done a good job, in insuring there was no legal recourse on the discovery, so Grant knew the only way, was to regain total control of the man and his research. The security men watching him, had kept Grant fully informed on early successes and setbacks. He expected the coming update, to verify the completion. His secretary buzzed him "Sir, Steve Maris is here, for his appointment." "Bring him in and then why don't you take an early lunch Leah," Grant added. He didn't want any disturbances and especially didn't want her walking in on this meeting!

Grant enjoyed the view as she walked out. One of his small failures, had been his inability to lure her into bed. Usually, his money and position, made him very desirable, but not to her. Grant had to be honest about it. Weighing an even 200 pounds, and only standing 5'8", didn't lend any assistance in the female department. Grant got his mind back on task, and dumped the woman from his mind. Steve came in, just as the secretary was walking out. Steve Maris wasted no time and got right to the point.

"Sir, he has completed the research, and as far as we can tell, it is going to be huge! The applications are more widespread than even Westlake thought, when he submitted his ideas for patent." Grant smiled and reached in, to get a cigar. He did not even offer his subordinate one. Maris was the kind of man Grant loved to use, and then discard. He was everything Grant wasn't .Tall, six foot, dark wavy hair, and penetrating blue eyes. Grant looked forward to the time he could put the man aside. He got back on topic and said "That is good news."

"Have you managed to contact your old buddy Brenner?" Steve pulled some paperwork out of his pocket and handed it to Grant.

"This is the contract information and he is flying here now to finalize everything directly with you as requested," Steve added.

"That is better news than I hoped for. Is he as good as you say he is?"

"Sir! He is better, but as I told you, it will be bloody if he is in charge. I don't think he ever ran an operation in the military, or with the CIA, that didn't end in a lot of dead bodies. The positive is, there are seldom any witnesses to his special operations!" Maris wondered what the CEO had in mind, but knew better than to ask. He had done a lot of (off the book) operations for the short, pudgy CEO over the years, and wasn't going to mess up a good thing over his curiosity.

"Steve! I need to know how this guy is going to affect you. Are you able to act as the liaison with him and deal with the outcome, if he needs to disappear?" Steve took a moment to let this question sink in, but before he could respond, the CEO said the magic words.

"Don't worry, the money is going to be incredible on this one, and it will be off the books, completely!"

"Sir, I have no problem at all, and am ready to do whatever you need."

"That is good, because I may need some special jobs done. Start by setting up a meeting with Brenner, anywhere but here. Then, I want you to set up a fund account, in a bogus name that you can monitor, but that Brenner can access from anywhere in the world."

"How much do you want in it" Steve asked?

"Since you can access about ten million from the security fund, without raising any notice, start there and I can add funds when needed, through the same fund." Grant knew that the plan gave him useful distance from the business. He had to hide the smile on his face from his subordinate.

Maris was thinking along similar lines as well. He knew this plan gave Grant separation from the entire business, in case things didn't work out. Maris realized, as soon as the action started, he would be on the hook for the entire thing. He resolved to insure his own escape plan. These thoughts coursed through his mind, but he had to respond. Grant started to feel the stress, waiting for a response, but when he was almost ready to push some more, he was rewarded by the right response from Maris, and was not disappointed.

"Okay, I can do it that way, but I expect you to supply cover from auditors and other company hacks!"

Grant could feel almost a sexual reaction to the answer. He took a deep breath and continued. “This project is worth so much money, that if it goes well, both of us can do what we want. Besides, you have enough information on me to ruin my future. Did you think I didn’t know you were keeping track of some of the off the book stuff?” Grant knew this was a critical time, and if Maris bought in, there would be no going back.

Maris didn’t hesitate this time, he just dove in with both feet. “I think it’s time for you to share some of the project plans with me.”

Grant knew he had his man. “The plan is to have Brenner snatch Westlake, and then suck him dry. I want total control of this technology. I may, or may not share it with PEDEI corp. I think that keeping it in company, will be the best choice, but, I am open to changes, if it later looks better to go it alone.”

Grant watched the expression on Maris’ face at his statement.

“Are you sure you want to meet with Brenner at all? I could do the entire meeting and he would never need to know you are involved.” Steve liked the idea of being in the driver’s seat.

Grant could almost feel the thoughts in Steve Maris’ head. “I need to meet the man before this begins. There is too much at stake, to not get involved and take a few risks myself on this one! I want you present though, to be able to evaluate the military aspects of Brenner’s plan. Steve Maris turned and left the office, with a smug, satisfied look on his face. He was sure the world had just opened before him. If he had bothered to turn around, he would have seen the same smug look on the CEO’s fat face.

Leah got ready to leave for lunch, as soon as the door to her boss’ office closed behind Maris. She got a funny feeling, any time she was around the guy. This job was the best-paying job she had ever had, but over the last few years, her comfort-zone continued to drop. Having the boss make a pass at her the first day, had not been a real surprise. Leah had come to expect that. Her disillusionment had started, when Mr. Bismarck had started involving the chief of security in a lot of quiet tasks, she was not allowed to be involved in. Before that, she had always been present when there was a conference of any type, to transcribe notes, or some other duty.

Bismarck had been a reasonably good boss, other than the one pass the first day. He was usually friendly and always had a good word for her. When Maris started showing up a lot, her relationship with Bismarck changed.

Maris was quite attractive, in a rugged way, but she had realized at the first meeting, that he was a slimy kind of man, and not to be trusted about anything. Her concerns had risen, when she happened to overhear some conversations between the two men, that involved a research scientist, Rob Westlake. Why that had caught her attention, was that she and Rob had been in a close relationship since they met years ago, on her uncle's fishing boat in Juneau, Alaska.

Rob was everything she had ever wanted in a man: tall (6'2"), with warm blue eyes and an open, quick smile for everyone. Even though he was already a college graduate and working on a Ph.D., he had been able to fit in with a fishing crew, or a bunch of eggheads at a university. Rob had been totally committed to his work, attentive to her, and last, but not least, great in bed. She was totally in love with him. They had kept the relationship quiet, but had begun planning to leave the company, as soon as possible.

Rob had purposely written some slanderous articles about PEDEI policies in a science journal (her idea), that led to him being asked to leave. Leah had decided, then and there, that she would find a way to even the score with Mr. Bismarck, her boss. He had been the one that had fired him. She had to prepare the paperwork herself. Over the next three years, she had built a small collection of office memos and other material, about under-the-table dealings and some dubious operations. She had some knowledge of a covert operation in Ethiopia that had gone very bad, and cost the Corporation a lot of money to hush up. The problem was, she wanted something that would affect Bismarck personally.

Leah could not help thinking about Rob on a daily basis. She had only seen him sporadically over the last few years, since he had moved to the West Coast, and she was at corporate headquarters in New York City. The separation had not dampened her love for Rob, or her resolve to get Bismarck. Rob was working alone now, but she knew that he was very close to completing his research. As soon as that happened, he wanted her to quit her job and come live with him.

Leah wanted to be able to hand him something that would give him leverage with PEDEI. So, that was the reason she was listening at the door of her boss She couldn't hear everything, but she did hear Rob's name several times Leah listened as long as she could, but decided to leave, prior to the end of the meeting.

She went out of the office and across the street to a sidewalk coffee shop. She got a cup and watched the building, feeling like a secret agent. After ten minutes, Maris came out and grabbed a cab. Leah was about ready to leave, when her boss exited the office as well. He looked a bit nervous and looked around, as if to see if he was being watched, then walked away. Now this was strange, since he never walked anywhere. He was easy to follow, with his distinctive clothing and size. He was a large man, not in height, but he was as wide as he was tall. Her mother would have called him "well-fed." Bismarck went three blocks and then entered a bar. Leah waited a few minutes and followed him in, acting as casual as she could. The bar was quite dark, but she saw him in the back in a secluded booth. She grabbed a seat, close to the entry, where she could see the booth, without being seen. Leah ordered a sandwich and waited to see what was going on.

Nearly an hour after entering, Leah was finished with her lunch and nursing a cup of coffee, when she saw Maris come into the bar with a stranger. The man was screaming military. He could have been wearing a uniform and not stood out any more than he already did. Leah tried not to stare and remembered to snap a photo with her phone, as they moved towards the back. She decided it was time to go, before her luck ran out. Maris made her nervous. A year earlier, he had made a blatant pass at her. He made her skin crawl every time he was around. By the time she returned to the office, she was back in control of her beating heart. Leah was not sure she was up to this cloak and dagger stuff!

Chapter Three - THE TRIGGER MAN

Brenner was very happy when he got off the plane in New York. The jobs had been few and far between, since his departure from the CIA and he knew his men would start looking elsewhere, if he didn't find a good one soon. The last little side war in Ethiopia, had been over for six months, so when an old acquaintance from West Point contacted him with a proposal, he didn't hesitate more than the requisite minute to accept the offer, and then jump on a plane. It didn't hurt when Steve Maris mentioned that he represented Petroleum Development and Exploration International. He knew the corporation was worldwide and had used covert operators in the past. He had been involved in a couple of CIA ops that had involved PEDEI and knew about one colossal failure in a third world takeover attempt. They should have deep pockets and shouldn't be worried about how things were done. This could be right up his alley. Brenner had been surprised at how difficult it had become to find work, now that he was not working for, or with, the CIA. Most open job offers, were not available to him, so he had to settle for the jobs no one wanted to be seen in the light of day when Brenner thought about it, that was what he preferred.

Maris had sent Brenner a tentative agreement, along with a very limited outline of the proposed operation and a first-class ticket. Based on the tentative info and a lot of prior knowledge of the targets operational field, he had sent his best operative to Anchorage, to begin the groundwork early. Her side of the op, required a little time to develop the contacts, and pick her fall guys. By sending her right away, he got her in position at least a month before his advanced team could arrive. If the job fell through, she could always tap the marks for expense money. She was quite good at that.

Maris was waiting for him, as he came off the boarding ramp and shook hands, before heading out "Brenner, I see you are still in as good a shape, as when we were at the Point." Maris flashed back to the time they were both new cadets. Brenner had been the stand-out among the plebes from the first day. He had everything going for him. He looked like an officer should: confident, and strong. Brenner had a take-charge personality, and was placed in leadership positions right away. He became the bench-mark for others.

Only later, did Maris and his classmates begin to recognize the not-so-great sides of the man's personality of course, looks were never the problem. Brenner had leading man looks: tall, dark, and handsome. Women flocked to him. Maris might have been bothered by the looks thing, except he did well with the ladies himself. Brenner's shortcomings became visible under the demanding training. He would always win encounters, whether it was a simple boxing match, or field maneuvers. The problem was, how he did it. He didn't care who he had to hurt, or leave on the field as a casualty. In training, it was only noticed by his fellow cadets. The instructors only seemed to see a hard-charging soldier. Maris new thought that, that changed when the man was on active duty. He had risen quickly through the ranks, but the body count in combat was always high, when Brenner was in charge. His way of winning, had finally gotten him tossed out of the military. The entire episode that let up to his dismissal was never made public, but Maris had heard through the grapevine, that Brenner had wasted an entire village to get one Taliban operative. Why the thing was hushed-up, never did surface.

Maris pulled his attention back to the moment in time, to not be noticed by Brenner. "Well Steve, in my line of work, an extra pound can make the difference between getting out and lying in a pool of my own blood!" The smile, as he said that, said more about the man He saw himself as invincible.

Maris chose to lighten the moment by pandering to the man's ego "The way I hear it, you tend to leave everyone-else in a pool of their Blood!" Brenner chuckled and added

"Isn't that the main idea I don't remember any class at the Point that said I had to bleed, only that I had to make the enemy bleed!"

Steve thought about this for a minute and then added "You're right, no one told us to die; just that we probably would, and to do it with style."

"Ya!" Brenner said, then continued. "I never did buy into too much of the old hurrah crap they threw at us. I just wanted to go out and kill people for my country." Steve raised his brows at this last statement. Brenner saw the look and responded. "Ok, so I was willing to settle for just killing people for me, if well paid; and isn't that the entire point of this meeting. If I remember correctly, you didn't jump up to support me, when the Army showed me the door," Brenner added.

Maris had to smile at that retort. “You’re right, let’s get down to business. I have a car and a meeting for you. This is going to be a real opportunity and you’re going to make a lot of money.”

Brenner smiled. “Now you’re talking my kind of game. Let’s get going, the sooner I am out of New York, the better. I would just as soon not let my old company know I’m in town.”

A few minutes later, they walked into a quiet bar, close to the corporate building. Grant had a booth in the back. Brenner and Maris joined him. “Mr. Bismarck, let me introduce you to LTC Robert Brenner.” Brenner put out his hand,

“Just call me Bob, sir. I have a suspicion we are not going to want to use full names any more than needed.”

Grant took the offered hand and smiled. “I like a man that cuts to the chase. You are right; first names are going to be fine. Steve has told me a lot about you, and I have done a little research myself. It seems that you always get the job done.

Well Grant,” Brenner purposely used his first name. There was no need to let the short, but powerful, fat-man think he was going to kowtow to him at every step. “I just need to know what you need, how much money is available, and some kind of time schedule.”

Bismarck paused before continuing. “Like I said Bob; I like direct. I need a man grabbed and held somewhere safe, where special knowledge can be extracted and verified. He will have to be kept alive for at least a month, and three would be better.”

Brenner was totally interested now! “I like direct too, so is this man someone famous, or what?”

Grant shook his head “Not famous, and he should be easy to grab, but there is one caveat. The world can’t know I have him and it would be better if he is thought to be dead.”

Brenner thought for a minute, or two. “I can see little real difficulty about this, so how about telling me the real deal any two bit crook could grab the guy off the street. So far, you are talking about a penny ante scam. I need more than that, or this is a waste of my time.”

Brenner started to get up, when Bismarck spoke. “Sit down. I didn’t bring you here for a little job. I am talking millions on this one.” Brenner sat down and reached for his drink.

“I think it’s time to get down to the real deal.” Grant got thoughtful, then added,

"Okay! Here's the deal; I need this man to disappear, so that the world knows he's gone. My thought is to take him, along with some more high profile people. It will be big news, but not focused on him."

"He is scheduled to speak at a fisheries conference, in six months from now in Juneau Alaska. Senator Warren is hosting the affair, and several international representatives and scientist will be there. If you could make them all disappear, that would fit the bill perfectly. How you choose to make this happen, is entirely up to you."

Brenner sat back and began doing some quick planning, but took time to wonder if he could somehow include a little personal business, while he was in Juneau "I can make this happen, but it is going to be expensive. I am thinking several million to just set it up. Do you have a place in mind, to hold the people after I grab them?" All Brenner could do was contemplate the amount of money he could make on this job.

Grant looked at Brenner, and knew this was the man. "PEDEI owns several mine properties in the area. One is on the back side of Chichagof Island. It has been abandoned and is only reachable by water, or air. We tried to do a little exploration several years ago, so the docks are in good repair, and there is power in the mine. We keep a watchman onsite, but no one else goes there. The dock is a deep-water moorage, so a large craft can get right up to the pier. Another is located on Admiralty Island. It is much closer to Juneau, but is in operation," Grant concluded.

"That sounds like a great start. How much are you willing to spend to make this happen? I have to tell you it is going to be costly with the short time frame."

Grant looked at Maris and nodded his head. Steve took out the pass book for the working account, and handed it to Brenner.

"This should get you started! Let me know, if and when, you need more." Brenner opened the pass book and used his best poker face, when he saw the balance was ten million.

"This will be a good start, but I am going to need a very fast boat, capable of carrying at least fifty people, safely off shore. I would prefer something that can top forty knots, though thirty-five would do. The boat needs to look like a local fishing boat, if possible. Also; a couple of helicopters, one four place, and the other needs to be larger, and should have the range to reach the mine with a good reserve, from Juneau. I mention this, because this equipment would wipe out the ten million alone!"

Grant smiled. "I expected some special requirements like this I have a boat available in Seattle, that will fit your needs, and the helicopters will be on board in two weeks. Do you have any preferences in the model, or make of choppers?"

Brenner thought for a minute "Yes! The larger helicopter needs to be the same model as the Coast Guard flies in Alaska." Grant looked at Maris.

"You know the choppers PEDEI keeps out on the coast, to ferry crews to oil rigs are the same as most Coast Guard helicopters."

Brenner smiled. "I figured it would be that easy. I will do the modifying of the chopper myself."

Maris looked at Brenner, then asked "How about weapons?"

Brenner looked smug. "I will acquire those, I like to be hands-on, when it comes to the things that keep me alive." Brenner figured that he had given them enough. "I think that will do for now. The only thing left to discuss is my fee, and my men's fee!"

Grant just looked at him for a moment, and said, "I will deposit twenty million in an account of your choice now, and another forty million, when the job is done. You can decide on the split with your men." Brenner was so excited, that he could barely contain himself. This was his big job. No more scrambling for dirty work in third world dumps. When this was done, so was he. He knew that he would lose most of his men, during, or after the operation, accidents happened. The split would favor him.

As soon as Brenner was on a plane out of New York, he relaxed and began planning. The difficult part, was how to make the world stop looking for the people. His prior research on the Juneau area, and the bribable public figures, was giving him a real leg up. He had done the initial research, when he found that Vladimir Choskey lived there. That was one page of unfinished business that still needed to be turned. He knew that he needed to focus on the operation, and not old laundry, but if he could do both, so much the better. Choskey went back in the 'kill later' folder in his mind. Once focused on the project, he was able to start getting the plan roughed out. This was going to be almost as spectacular as 911. Potentially more bystanders were going to die (no big deal). He was going to be rich! As he planned, he realized he would need at least one more large boat.

To make everyone stop looking, he was going to blow up the entire city of Juneau! Before that, the city would have to be totally isolated from the outside world. The good news was, that the city was only reachable by boat, or air. He would cut off air access and thought that water access could also be cut for several days.

Once Brenner was home in Seattle, he started making calls for his private army to assemble, then collected the charts for all of the waterways, in and around Juneau. He would have to make a run up there, as soon as he could crew the boat PEDEI was furnishing. Better yet, he would have a crew of his men take it to Sitka, and he could fly in there. The first order of business, was to select any special needs for equipment, and to recruit the people he needed. His ace in the hole, Sandra Brown, had worked with him on several jobs, while he was with the CIA. She could seduce anyone on demand, and shoot them, when the time came. She was the consummate professional, from her beautiful head, to her beautiful feet. She had returned from a little job in England, just in time for her departure to Anchorage.

She was already working on recruiting some inside help a local research company, had compiled data on Juneau, including everything available about local politics and politicians for him, a year earlier. Brenner knew that these were the easily-used people. Throw a little money, or booty (Sandra) at them, and they were yours. He was sure a couple of properly-placed stooges, could be found. The research company was also acquiring municipal planning plats, utilities maps, and as much information on the local police department, as possible.

Brenner had been slightly unhappy to have to send Sandra away just a day after getting back from Europe. Sandra and he, had barely gotten reacquainted, when he received the initial job offer. That had allowed him to make some early decisions. Even though he had no idea what the ultimate objective was, the man Maris, had implied it would be right up his alley and had given him a tentative outline of the objective. Brenner had been a bit surprised, when Grant had acted like Brenner knew nothing about the kidnapping plans. Apparently Maris didn't share everything with his boss. That was information that cloud be handy later.

He and Maris had been in the Army together, years before, and Maris knew the kind of work Brenner did. That knowledge had led to his decision to send Sandra off to Anchorage, two days after hearing about the job. Those two days had been spent in bed and planning.

Brenner paused in his planning, to reminisce about the turbid two days. The focus of the first day, had been on the political data for Juneau. He chuckled, as he remembered how excited she had become over the operation. He still remembered the entire conversation, since the best sex he had had in months, followed.

Sandra had immediately spoken out. "This Mayor is perfect. I bet I can wrap him up in a day."

I would be disappointed, if you took longer than that," Brenner paused. "I think, though, you may need more time. You are going to move in with the man." "I also think the chief of police can be a big help. When we put the cruise ship on the beach, to block the water access, I want all of the police occupied by the shipwreck, and not looking elsewhere."

"That should be no problem. When can I make my approach, and how long am I going to have to sleep with these two guys?"

Sandra was quite excited about this. She always enjoyed seducing men, or women in high places. It was more fun, when she got to take them out at the end. Remembering the two days, was almost as good as real sex. Brenner thought about the last detail he had put in motion at the same time. Brenner got his mind back in the present, and moved on with his planning.

Brenner began compiling a weapons list. The job was going to require every man he had. That meant he was going to need small arms for twenty-plus extras. Sandra would supply her own weapons, including her body. Some crew-served deck guns, for the boat, and demolitions, to include components for a large air-fuel bomb, would be the most difficult to get. Brenner decided that these would have to be acquired without CIA, FBI, NSA, Homeland Security, or any other agencies knowledge. The small arms and ammunition, could be more openly procured. The trick, was to hide the final location from them.

As soon as he started spending money on weapons, the CIA was going to start looking at him, so he decided that, instead of hiding and trying not to be seen, he would select several locations around the world, and make sure he was seen.

Let the dammed CIA try to figure out where he was planning to strike. This entire operation was going to be his way of showing the company, how stupid they had been, to stop using his special skills. Thinking about his old employer, also made him think about a lot of interesting contacts he had around the world. Brenner knew some people in Russia that would be very interested in this scientist guy. Maybe he could sell the information he was getting, to another source as well. (The only thing better than a big payday was a double payday.)

It took Brenner three days to finalize the basic plans. He then put together his timetable. The research had found that the Mayor was attending a conference in Anchorage, two months prior to the fisheries conference. That information had led to his decision to send Sandra up there when he did. All information pointed to a man that was always looking for action, when he was out of his wife's sight. Sandra had been there, to start her infiltration and seduction. Brenner decided that he would have his advanced team in Juneau, a month after her. That would give Sandra time to find the locations for the attack on the infrastructure of the city. The team could finalize the targets, then, prior to the attack, plant the needed bombs. The biggest difficulty, was taking out the airport.

The second priority job was to immediately get his man on board one of the cruise ships that were going to be docked in Juneau, at the time of the conference. He needed to become one of the maintenance crew members. That would give him access to the areas of the ship he would need. The op would be triggered by the departure time of that ship. Every other mishap, would key off the ship blocking the channel.

The surprising good news, was that the local National Guard unit, was on an extended deployment to Afghanistan, and would not be in town. That still left the Coast Guard. They had two cutters in the area, plus three search and rescue helicopters. One cutter would be out of town, but the second would have to be handled. That was what the large helicopter he requested, would do. Brenner decided that he would have most of his men move up to the mine site, as soon as possible, so they could stage out of there. The boat he was going to use for his city buster bomb, would act as transportation as much as possible, until the bomb had to be loaded. He would keep the super-fast boat a secret, for as long as he could.

Two weeks after his initial meeting with Grant and Maris, Brenner had taken delivery of the helicopters and the two boats. The fast boat was perfect. It was capable of forty-plus knots, and looked like an old displacement fishing boat, until it was up on plane with the hydrofoils deployed. The bomb boat, was a rich man's go-fast toy. It was thirty feet long and had twin, six-seventy-one turbo diesel engines. The boat could safely transport ten men and equipment. Brenner sent the hydrofoil and the bomb boat to Alaska, as soon as the men arrived and the supplies were loaded. They took enough food and other needed supplies, to support the entire operation. No extra trips to a town would be needed, except to make the run off the coast, to meet the ship bringing the weapons from Mexico. Brenner had been able, through his old CIA contacts, to get everything shipped the second day of planning. The ship was scheduled to arrive in Sitka in four weeks. Everything was going well.

Brenner sent another man, directly to Juneau, to find and meet the captain of the day cruiser, the conference people were going to use, to visit the fisheries research facility, outside of Juneau. It was great to have the advanced schedule for the conference. Sandra had gotten that for him, through a contact she had made in Anchorage. Brenner was totally confident in the overall plan, but recognized the many potential problems in the complex op. The good news was, the real job was the easy part. The cover-up was the complex portion. The actual kidnapping, would be complete before most of the tough stuff even started.

It was time to hit the road and start seeding the CIA with misinformation. Brenner planned on flying into six different countries, over the next few weeks. Each country was a potential site, for his kind of operation. The company wouldn't know what was coming. He would include Juneau in the confusion tour. Brenner had last traveled to Anchorage to meet with Sandra during her approach to the mayor. That had gone like clockwork. The man had been an easier target, than even he expected. Brenner finished his preliminary planning, and started the confusion tour. During the flights, Brenner had time to think about his personal business in Juneau (Choskey).

If he got real lucky, Choskey's partner-in-crime, Sergeant First Class Walters, would be around as well. That would be the icing on the cake for this op. The only question was, kill them first, or let them die with the rest of the city!

Chapter Four - JIM WALTERS

(Ten days to start.)

Jim was in his bunk, thinking about what had brought him to this place and time in his life. His bunk was the forward cabin on his fifty-five foot motor sailor, made by Chris Craft in 1965. He was currently berthed in the public marina, in Juneau, Alaska, a long ways from Wallace, Idaho, where he grew up. He couldn't help but flash back to his high school days. He had been a good student and a very successful athlete. He had been offered several scholarships in both football and basketball. His six-two frame, coupled with his get it done attitude, had led to a lot of success on the field, or court. His good looks, nothing that he ever dwelled on, had made him quite popular with the women throughout his life, (he once dated twins at the same time). He had been blessed with a strong face, often told that he was very handsome by female friends. He had blue eyes and dishpan-blond hair (already turning gray, by the way). Jim chuckled at that thought. He returned to his reminiscing about home.

Wallace is a mining town in northern Idaho, on the decline. Mining is nearly shut down by EPA edicts, and other environmental pressures. Currently, limited production is ongoing in three mines. The Lucky Friday mine in Mullan (The town to the east of Wallace) is the largest remaining operation and employs about one hundred miners. At one time, nearly five hundred were employed in the Lucky Friday mine. The Friday is operated by the Heckla Mining Company, based in Coeur d' Alene, Idaho. At one time, the company operated several mines in the silver valley.

When Jim was in school, Wallace was a waning boom town, just starting to feel the pressure from environmentalist and other government agencies. The town boasted fifteen bars, six gas stations, two grocery stores, and last but not least, four houses of ill-repute! Friday night in the fall, centered on the high school football games at Sather field. The highlight of the year, would be the game against rival, Kellogg. Kellogg was the next town west of Wallace, twelve miles down Interstate 90. This area was called the silver valley. For many years, the valley was the leading producer of silver in the world.

The normal transition from high school, for most Wallace graduates, ended in one of the mines. The pay was excellent and weekends were free. Jim chose a different option and enlisted in the Army. His early time in basic training, and then in infantry school, was a blur. Something to be endured, with hopes of things to come. The surprise for him, was how much he liked the Army, and especially the combat training. Infantry school was followed by airborne training and Ranger school. Jim excelled at all. He found himself back in the Pacific Northwest, stationed at Fort Lewis, outside of Seattle, Washington.

Since this was the post-Vietnam era, the Army was in flux. The draft was gone and a new core of professional soldiers, was established. Everyone was in the service by choice, and not conscripted. The training was challenging, and promotion was based on performance. Jim did well and prospered, having been deployed several times, to trouble spots in different parts of the world. Then, 9/11, changed everything.

After his first deployment to Iraq, Jim left the Rangers and moved into special operations. He became a very good sniper. Days and days in the desert, and then the mountains of Afghanistan, led to daydreaming about the times he had spent sailing and boating, with friends in the Seattle area. He used the down time, between missions, to learn coastal navigation and to research the perfect boat! Jim settled on the idea of the best of both worlds, a motor sailor. You could have the quiet solitude of sail power, or start up the engine and get someplace when you wanted, instead of when the wind would let you.

While in special ops, Jim got the opportunity to go through several more specialty schools and was scuba certified, halo certified, most interestingly, small boat certified. This last, was rare in the Army, but strange things could happen. All of this training was divided by several deployments back to the desert and mountains, of the war. Sooner or later, everyone reaches a point, where enough is enough. During his seventh deployment, something happened, that convinced him that it was time to move on.

After all the years in the army, Jim found himself standing on the shore, overlooking a marina in Monterey, California, staring at a boat named Satisfaction. As soon as Jim received his final discharge from the Army, he began searching for the boat of his dreams, the perfect motor sailor. While in Afghanistan, he had seen an article about obscure boats built by Chris Craft, a company famous for small runabouts and ski boats. In the late fifties and early sixties, they had built several motor sailors, in the fifty to seventy foot range. These boats were fiberglass-hulled and extremely over-built. Jim found several, but one in particular caught his interest. The particular boat of interest was fifty-five feet long and cutter-rigged. It had a center helm, with a large aft cabin. The boat was in need of TLC, but was in good order. The sail inventory was adequate for a motor sailor and included a spinnaker, which was rare on that type of boat.

Getting the boat ready to cruise, helped Jim relax and find balance in his life. After too many years under extreme stress, and watching too many friends and enemies die, Jim was ready for serious changes. He found that he could not totally leave his past behind, and found a safe hiding place, for several reminders of his past. He stored a highly-illegal MP4 assault rifle, an AK47 assault rifle (liberated from a tribesman in the desert), and last, but not least, his Barrett M107, 50 cal. sniper rifle He bought a 45 cal. Government and a 270 Weatherby Magnum, with a 3 x 9 power scope. These last weapons were brought on-board legally and stored in the open.

Jim spared no expense. Seven deployments in a combat zone had allowed him to accrue quite a lot of seed money (no wife). All of the navigation aids were modernized, to include integrated GPS, radar, and depth-finder equipment. The final preparation, was a major change in power. The boat had come with an eighteen-horse, Perkins diesel, capable of pushing the displacement hull at five to seven knots all day long, on a sip of fuel. The selling owner could not remember the last time he had purchased fuel! Jim chose to make an extreme upgrade in power, to a large Cummins diesel, capable of producing one hundred HP, on demand.

What he did not share with the marina that installed the engine for him, was the things he added after they were done. The special modifications included a larger, turbo-charging system and other electronic upgrades that allowed the engine to produce over three hundred horse power. This made his boat a real sleeper in performance under power, but still a capable sailor with the prop folded up.

During some early training in the Rangers, Jim had spent some time in Alaska doing winter mountain training. During his off-time, he explored the state and had, on a whim, taken a drive down from the interior to Skagway, and a ferry from there to Juneau. He loved the coastal waterway and found the people friendly, but very private. The real surprise, was how much Juneau reminded him of his hometown. Not surprising, since many of the same miners and companies built the two towns. Both were originally all about mining. Many of the early structures in Juneau, were incredibly similar to architecture in Wallace. This was the area that became his cruising target. As a bonus, he knew a person who lived in Juneau, who was a close friend from the past.

He loaded his boat with supplies, that included scuba gear and tools that would allow him to scratch a living out of any boat harbor along the coast, cleaning bottoms and doing mechanical repairs for other boat owners. One of his strengths, throughout his military training, had been his innate mechanical skills. He could make anything run. He had learned basic mechanics from his father, who worked as a diesel mechanic for the Heckla mining company. Several months after leaving Monterey, he arrived in Juneau.

This introspection brought him back to his bunk, floating in the boat basin. He had been here for five months and had established himself as an all-around good guy to know. He fit in well with the other live-aboard people, in that he expected the same level of solitude that they wanted. If asked, he was available to assist the other boaters, but only charged the commercial fishermen and weekend boaters for his services. He had enough available income to have standing with the local law, to be seen as a positive resident and not just a bum. He socialized with the locals, but remained private about his past. He had met several local women that occasionally spent some time on board, but none knew what he had stored below, or what kind of boat he had.

Jim realized it was time to stop dreaming and get to work. He had an appointment to help a local character, Bill Bates, remove the screw from his forty foot Stan Craft. Jim had met Bill in a local bar and had been drawn to him right off. Bill seemed to know everyone, and was friends with all. He especially seemed to know every available woman in the city and borough of Juneau. He had a different lady on his boat most evenings. Bill kept his boat two slips down from Jim's own boat, so the revolving women walked right past his own slip. Like any red-blooded male, Jim was a bit envious of Bill, but in a friendly way.

Jim walked over to Bill's boat, to make sure the work was still on. Jim knocked on the rail of the boat, The Smiling Drunk, Bill popped out of the hatch with a smile, and almost nothing else. "Bill? I thought we were going to pull that bent prop today," Jim said.

"Well heck yea! Just give me a minute to pull on some trunks and say goodbye to sweetie," Bill chuckled.

"I'll get my gear and be back in a couple of minutes." Jim turned and left, before finding out who, or what "sweetie" was. He went to his boat and put on his wetsuit. He didn't think he would be down long enough to need the dry suit. He grabbed the rest of his equipment and went to work. Two hours later, Bill helped him out of the water for the last time, and headed for shore, with the bent screw.

"Hey, I will settle up with you when I get back," Bill yelled, as he hurried towards the ramp.

Jim smiled and headed for his boat to change and get dry and warm up. The wetsuit had been a mistake and he wished he had taken the time for the drysuit. The prop was in bad shape, from hitting a sunken log, when Bill was returning from halibut fishing, two days before. He had to limp in, on his starboard prop. Bill had complained that he got a cramp, keeping the boat straight, on his way back to Juneau. Jim was not worried about payment, since he decided not to charge Bill anything. He valued Bill's friendship and especially his great contacts, and saw that as all the payment he needed. Bill was a real character. He knew everyone in town and probably throughout Alaska. He was on first name basis with the standing President and the first husband.

It was a real mystery why the women seemed so taken with him. He was average height, average looks, and was usually short on money. Rumor had it, that he was paying support for a couple of ex-wives. The only critical piece of knowledge about Bill that mattered to Jim, was his loyalty to a friend. Jim knew that if he needed to get somewhere quickly, Bill would fire up his Cessna and take him on a moment's notice. Jim had a lot of great friends from his military time, but none any better than Bill.

After changing, Jim headed for the marina parking lot. He had a hot date with a girl he had met at a local bar. Lorrie worked on one of the cruise ships that were currently tied up at the downtown pier. Jim was still getting used to the idea that a small town like Juneau, could nearly double in population, when the cruise ships were in town. He and Lorrie had dated several times since meeting, but this was the first date he planned on ending up in the bunk on his boat. She was a real knockout; five foot-seven with long red hair and the most amazing hazel eyes. Her legs went on forever. She was one of the most attractive women Jim had ever dated. He caught himself, before admitting that Lorrie was prettier than his one real love. Jim filed his thoughts about Andrea Warren away for another time. Concentration on the catch of the day, was in order.

Jim picked Lorrie up from the ship dock and they headed for the Baranof Hotel, for the best steak in town. "Lorrie, you get prettier every time I see you." Jim said with a smile that he was famous for.

"Well! You don't look too bad yourself," Lorrie jibed right back.

"Tell me again what you do on the big boat Lorrie," Jim asked.

"You know as well as I do, that it is a ship, smart-aleck, but to answer your question, I am the main singer, in the best lounge on the ship, and love my job," Lorrie said.

"Well, sometime you are going to have to sing some place, where I can hear you; but, I have to admit, I have other ideas for tonight, that don't include singing!" Jim smiled.

"I was hoping you didn't plan to just take me home to the ship after dinner. There is a guy on the crew that freaks me out, and he is onboard right now," Lorrie said.

"Well If I have my way I think you should get back to the ship about time to wake up in the morning."

"Tell me more about this creepy guy on the boat." Lorie raised herself up, and turned to look at Jim. "He just came on the ship a week ago, and is an engineer, but you would think he was captain, the way he acts, and of course, he thinks he is God's gift to women." Lorrie sneered. "I really don't know what it is about him that upsets me so much, but he is always showing up in the strangest places. Yesterday I was coming out of the lounge, and saw him coming out of a passenger's room. I thought for sure that would be the end of his employment, because he seemed to be arguing with the passenger! Usually that is the end of a crew member, but he is still onboard." Lorrie sighed.

"What was the argument about?" Jim asked.

"I didn't hear much, but it sounded like they were arguing about the bow thrusters and putting the ship on the beach!"

"That sounds serious. What did you do then?" asked Jim.

"You know, I got busy and totally forgot the incident, until you asked me that question. Maybe I should go tell my boss about it," Lorrie thoughtfully said.

"Well, let's not go off half-cocked. Maybe you just miss-heard him and let's not ruin the evening, before it gets started," Jim chuckled. That seemed to get the evening back on track, and Jim and Lorrie were headed for Jim's boat, soon after. The conversation was quickly forgotten.

In the morning, Jim was just waking up, with Lorrie still sleeping. A sudden movement of the boat, abruptly brought Jim out of his semi-sleep. Jim grabbed his favorite .45 Colt, kept handy, and headed for the deck. When he carefully raised the forward hatch, he quickly stowed the handgun, He had been boarded by the only person in town he knew from the past, Vladimir Choskey. Jim had met Vlad years ago, while still in a regular Ranger unit, and then became close friends, when they were both working in special ops.

Vlad was a CIA rep during a joint action in Afghanistan. Jim and Vlad became close, because he was the only CIA puke Jim felt he could trust. Vlad had been the only sane person, when the senior man, LTC Brenner, started executing prisoners. Brenner was a CIA guy, and didn't act like he answered to anyone. That action had been the final straw for Jim, and he soon left the armed forces for good. Jim and Vlad had spent months, setting up the op, that Brenner had come in to handle, even though Vlad and Jim had wanted to do the op with only the team Jim already had.

Brenner had shown up with the proper codes and orders, along with the worst-looking group of contractors (mercenaries) Jim had ever seen. This whole thing cemented Jim and Vladimir's relationship. They had to stick together to survive.

"Vlad, What the hell are you doing? I have a boat guest downstairs; I don't want to blow your cover here in Juneau, you know!" Jim said with a smile. Vladimir was the only good thing that had come out of that last operation in the mountains. It had taken both of them, working together, to get out alive and to bring Brenner up on charges.

"Well, I was in the area and thought I would stop by to see a friendly face. You will not believe who I saw today getting on an airplane headed for Anchorage." Jim was a bit disappointed at being interrupted, even by Vladimir, especially if all he had to talk about was some old acquaintance. Vlad saw the look on Jim's face and belatedly realized what he had said at first.

"Look I will get out of here and come back later, when you are alone. You will want to hear about this!" Vlad turned and walked away, but stopped and looked back at Jim. "Our old 'friend' was in town!" On that note, he left. That finally got Jim's undivided attention. He knew right away, who Vlad was talking about, but he could not, for the life of him, think what LTC Brenner (ret), could be doing in this corner of the world? No wars, no big money corporation to extort, or anything-else. Jim decided that he needed to get Lorrie off the boat ASAP. He had to know what was going on right now.

Jim woke Lorrie up, as soon as Vlad was gone. It was hard to refuse the unspoken request for some morning delight, but Jim knew this was a serious problem, and he had to know what was going on. He patted her beautiful bottom, and made a quick excuse why she had to go. Lorrie was not happy about this turn of events, but she was totally impressed by Jim and was willing to take his word, that it was important for him to get going. Jim called a cab for her, and kissed those gorgeous lips, and thought to himself "This had better be good, or I might have to kick Vlad's ass, and that would not be easy." He promised her a repeat, without the early morning wakeup, when her ship returned to port. As they walked to shore, Jim kissed her, and opened the door of the cab he had called, to take her back to the cruise ship.

Lorrie opened the window and leaned out. "I will be back in eight days, baring breakdowns, and I expect a warm welcome when I return." Jim smiled when she blew him a kiss.

He yelled out to her "Call me when you land."

"Don't worry I will," Lorrie teased. "Remember, I know where your boat is now, and it better be just you on board, when I get back!" Lorrie said as a parting shot.

As soon as he was back aboard his boat, Jim did the first thing that came to his mind. He checked weapons he had aboard, and reviewed in his mind, where he had stashed other goodies he might need in a hurry in the coming days! Working with the tools of his trade, got Jim's mind drifting back to the hills of Afghanistan.

When Brenner started shooting people, Vlad had gotten behind him and put a .45 to his temple, to get him to stop his men. The mercenaries outnumbered Jim and Vlad's team, so they used Brenner as a shield, to give them time to beat feet out of the area. It had taken two weeks to get back to a friendly outpost, and then, months of questions and investigation followed. The findings were totally against Brenner, but when Jim found out that he was going to walk (no press), he was done. He requested immediate separation and considering the information he could leak, he was out with an honorable discharge faster than he had come in years ago.

Jim didn't know whether to be angry, or thrilled that Brenner may find his way back into his sights, after all this time, in this place!

Chapter Five - LIEUTENANT COLONEL BRENNER

(One month prior.)

When Brenner sat down on the airplane, he didn't know whether to laugh, or be worried. He was sure that slime, Choskey, hadn't spotted him, but it had come as a total surprise, when Brenner spotted him. Brenner knew, through intelligence, that he was in the Juneau area, but didn't want to run into him, he just wanted to kill him! Brenner reviewed the sighting, but was sure the recognition was one-sided. Even if Choskey had seen him, that was part of the misdirection plan anyway! Having him in Juneau, only made this operation that much better. Now, if his buddy, the special ops soldier, that had aided Choskey in Afghanistan, was around as well, Brenner could clean the slate and get paid for it! Those were the two guys that had led to his fall from grace with the CIA.

This was not the first problem for Brenner. He remembered when he was a newly-minted officer, in good standing in the Army. He had started as a pilot on a Black Hawk helicopter. He loved flying, but when he found that he liked the action on the ground even better, he had gone into special operations. As his rank went up, he quickly realized that he was rare, in that he liked the blood of combat and had no remorse, when he killed. As a special ops commander, he had a knack for finding other soldiers like him that loved the combat. He was in charge of some operations in Somalia, that drew too much attention to himself, and he had been advised (back room, no record) to retire. He had weighed his options and made the move.

Before the ink was dry on his retirement papers, he was back in action, as a contractor for the CIA. They, unlike the Army, thought his overaggressive style, was just what was needed. He was making tons more money, and had better equipment. He recruited most of the soldiers that had worked for him in the past, and everything had been good, until Afghanistan. He was moving the operation along, when Choskey stuck a .45 in his left ear. He decided, then and there, he would kill Choskey and his friend. Who would have thought that the Russian immigrant would have a problem with wasting a few rag-head families?

After stopping the executions, Choskey and Walters had taken the special ops soldiers, and headed out. Brenner knew, if they got to a friendly outpost, he was in real trouble. His men chased the soldiers for a week in the mountains, and engaged in several short fire fights. Eventually the special ops soldiers got out. The investigation made his options slim. Just like the Army, the CIA wanted him gone and forgotten. The only thing that saved him from prosecution, was the people he could take down with him. This saved him from jail, but he was done with working for the United States in any form. Fortunately for Brenner, there were plenty of other governments and corporations that are not so choosy about his ways of getting things done.

This operation was going to be his final, 'get rich and quit' op. The process of creating all of the false trails for the CIA, had gone off perfectly, until He spotted Choskey in the line at the terminal, in Juneau. Brenner reviewed the plan and how things were going to date. Sandra had already infiltrated the target zone, even before he was sure of the job. He had sent her to Anchorage, the day after his initial contact with Steve Maris. Maris had mentioned the operation would be in the remote location, but staged out of Juneau. Brenner had decided that the merging of the job, and his hated enemy being located in the same town, in southeast Alaska, was a good omen.

Sandra was so adept at compromising dirty politicians and other minor authorities, it was just a natural. She had hooked the Mayor the first couple of days in Anchorage, and had infiltrated the man's life within days. She had moved into Juneau, with the assistance of the Mayor. She co-opted the corrupt police chief, a few days after arriving. Brenner had no doubt about her side of the op. His next move, was to get back to the mine site, as soon as he landed. It seemed a little crazy to fly to Seattle, just to turn around and fly back to Sitka. Brenner knew he needed to separate the two moves though. He would fly under a different name, and disguise when he returned to Alaska. He was done telegraphing his moves to the CIA.

Brenner continued review of his operation plan (military to the end). The idea was to kidnap a scientist, who had developed a leading-edge technology that the corporation needed to control. Brenner had to make this guy disappear, and make it so no one would even look for him.

The guy wasn't a very high profile man, but his technology was going to change the landscape of world energy. Brenner knew that several countries were already looking into him. The plan to grab a bunch of world dignitaries, including the senator from Alaska, who happened to be the daughter of the sitting U.S. President, was going to make the loss of this no-name scientist, a simple byline. Brenner had been given a huge budget to accomplish this, and no limits on how he did it. Only results mattered to these people.

Brenner smiled at the memory of finding out that Juneau would be the location. A more perfect spot couldn't be found. Juneau was isolated, but still important enough, to attract a lot of important people. Brenner had found that in the summer, the population swelled by thousands, when up to five cruise ships would be in port. The corporation owned some old mine properties in the area and when he had checked them out, he had found the perfect place to take the scientist, where he could be permanently controlled and used.

The advanced operation had gone in, with the cover of re-evaluating mining properties for re-opening. The one he was going to use, was deemed no good by the corporation, and focused on the ongoing operation on Admiralty Island. That gave cover for the real choice on Chichagof Island. The distance from Juneau, was quite far, but a fast boat, or helicopter, could get there in a reasonable time. Brenner had asked for a very fast boat, capable of transporting fifty men, at a speed of forty knots. The boat had to look like a regular fishing craft, found in the Gulf of Alaska. They had delivered a great boat, called the Northern Lights. It would go at a scary rate, when the hydrofoils were in the water.

Brenner reviewed all of his plan and equipment, for the hundredth time. This got him thinking about his last meeting with Sandra in Anchorage. She was perfect for this job. He had worked and slept with her, off and on, for several years, and he knew she was up to the task. She had started life as a high-priced hooker, in New York City, but had found that she needed more excitement in her life. Brenner had worked with her several times, when he was still with the CIA, as a decoy and an assassin. She had never failed to accomplish the mission and the post-mission sex and relaxation, had convinced both of them, that they made a great team.

Brenner trusted her more than any other, single person, even more than his special group of shooters.

Brenner relived the last time they were together in Anchorage, a month earlier. He had flown up, to be present, when she started her conquest of the Mayor from Juneau. When he landed, Sandra was waiting for him, and was as keyed up about the op, as he was. "Are you ready for this to get going?" asked Brenner.

"You bet, the sooner the better. I know this sleazy Mayor is already in town and I casually met him last night, in a hotel lounge. That guy is such a pussy-hound, that I could have taken him home last night," Sandra said with a smile.

"Remember that you are building a relationship, not just rolling him for his wallet," Brenner spat.

Sandra just smiled again and said "Don't worry, by tomorrow I will have him thinking about love and life together forever."

"I expect nothing less. Remember, he is our fall guy for this entire operation and we need him totally in your control," Brenner said with his own smile. "We need to get photos of you with him, in a compromising position, to send to his wife. They need to be slightly perverted. We want her gone from Juneau, in a spectacular way," Brenner reminded her.

"I have the perfect plan that should fit the bill, and hope to have them for you tonight. This is going to be fun," Sandra said, as she licked her lips in anticipation. The sex didn't thrill her, the idea of getting the pictures and ruining a man's life, was what excited her. Brenner and Sandra headed into the hotel room, to blow off a little steam before the operation went into high gear.

Brenner had to force himself back into the present. He needed to spend some time with Sandra pretty soon, or he would explode. He could not help but reflect on how good Sandra was in the sex department; a real pro. Brenner did wonder, if he would always survive, but what a way to go. He had spent quite a bit of time in preliminary planning, and moving all assets into place in Juneau. At this time, he had his shooters in Juneau, setting charges to take out power and other needed disruptions to life in Juneau. There were a total of fifteen separate bombs to build and set, and that didn't include the main attraction. A boat, this time an 'in your face rich man's toy' (fifty feet of luxury).

The boat, aptly named 'Explosion of Riches,' was already loaded with an air-fuel bomb, capable of leveling Juneau, and knocking down a bit of the surrounding mountains. The hull had been packed with plastic explosives, and the fuel bunkers were full. The boat had a large storage area, behind the engine room, and this area was full of fertilizer. The area had about three times as much as the bomb used years before in Oklahoma City, and that bomb had not included all of the plastic explosives. This would be sailed into the boat basin, when the time was right. Brenner's plan, called for a lot of people to die to hide the abduction of one. The initial plan had called for the capture of the scientist and the death of a boatload of important people, attending a fisheries conference, along with the primary target. Brenner had decided that the Senator, and all the other dignitaries, would be useful to control Westlake (the scientist).

This was Brenner's crowning glory operation. He had planned for every contingency, but there was still room for a lot to go wrong. Sandra was the real key, not to the op, but to the escape. She was giving them the keys to the city, and when there, she would rope in some other inside people, to make everything work. Brenner knew this was the last operation he would ever plan and execute, so it had to be great. The money was already the most he had ever made, and if things went well, another few million from the Russian government, would only sweeten the pot. What his men did not know, was that he planned for only Sandra and himself to walk away from this one. It was time to burn all bridges to the past, especially after this op.

Chapter Six - JIM

(Just two days to go.)

Jim could hardly contain himself, waiting for Vladimir to come back. He cleaned his .45 three times, to try and settle himself down. He had dreamed of getting a chance to take out Brenner ever since the mountain raid had gone so bad. The only thing that had kept him from killing him on the spot, had been Vlad's insistence, that getting out alive, would be a real good idea. Jim had realized that he would have been happy to die, as long as Brenner had gone with him. Jim didn't pull the trigger, because he was not good with getting his entire team killed along with him. He owed Vladimir his life and sanity. Jim was just thinking about stripping the pistol one more time, but instead went up on deck to wait, where he could see Vlad from a distance. The sun was shining, which in Juneau, was a good reason for celebration. Jim was struggling to keep from calling Vlad again, when he saw him start down the ramp from the road.

Vlad walked back down the dock and didn't hedge around. He could see the look in Jim's face. The look that said 'tell me now before I do something I will regret.' Vlad said. "Jim, I know you would like to be on a plane to Anchorage right now, but give me a chance to explain why that may not be a good idea." Jim sat down on the deck chair and said,

"Well I owe you a lot more than a little time, but I hope you are not going to try and tell me that that slime of a man deserves to continue living!" Jim retorted.

"No, I want him gone as much as you, and I probably know more reasons why that should have happened a long time ago. Do you think we could get below deck, where everyone can't see us?" Vlad asked. When they were ensconced in the aft cabin, with a cold one in hand, Vladimir began telling his story.

"You know that I still contract with the CIA, but what you don't know, is that I am working right now! I have been assigned a protection project here in Juneau," Vlad stated.

"Well, I knew you were up to something, when I saw you all decked out in a business suit last week, and totally concentrating on other things. You did not even see me," Jim added. Vlad knew Jim didn't really believe what he was saying.

"I saw you alright. I was gathering information and you would be surprised at how most people will not recognize me dressed that way. I knew that you would, because you know my other characters from the past." Jim flashed back to old times in different places.

"I guess I do! I still remember the first time I met you, when I thought you were with the Taliban." Jim had a vivid picture in his mind of the scruffy, bearded Afghan terrorist, as he said it. Vlad had blended in perfectly. His average height of 5'9" with dark hair and dark eyes, fit the area like a glove. There was nothing to separate him from the natives. Later, Jim saw him blend into crowds in other countries just as well. "Come on Vlad, quit beating around the bush and tell me why I shouldn't get on a plane and go take Brenner out right now!" Jim replied.

Vlad recognized the intense mood Jim was presenting. He would put a round in Brenner's head, in an instant. "Well, I would take it as a personal favor, since I would like to at least be present, when the scum takes one in the left ear, preferably from your fifty Barrett, I know you have hidden someplace on your boat!" Vlad surprised Jim with that!

"I didn't know you knew I had that still," Jim said softly. Vlad smiled and said "I knew you would never be far from that particular item, until Brenner was gone from this world." Jim let out his held breath. He was afraid intelligence had told Vlad, and that would mean that too many people knew he had not left government service, without a few special bonuses.

"What else do you have on hand?" Vlad ask Jim.

"Well, I might have a liberated AK 47, and some other stuff, but let me keep a few secrets, until a need arises. Be assured, I am ready for almost anything; now stop beating around the bush and explain what's going on," Jim said with a small grin.

Vlad told Jim about his assignment. "I'm tasked with protecting a scientist that is coming into town next month for the fisheries conference, scheduled with the United States, Japan, and Russia, talking about sustainability for the first time, when something might be worked out. This guy I am protecting, has developed some new technology that will protect the fishery, while allowing oil drilling in sensitive areas, never before safe to work. This new tech is hot stuff and the idea of sharing it with Japan and Russia, is the hook to get them to the table about controlling fish harvests, and finally getting Japan to stop killing whales."

"Jim, this is a big deal, and I can't let our feeling towards Brenner interfere," Vlad wound down.

"Well, I can wait a while, I guess, as long as in the end, I get the shot," Jim said with emotion.

"You can count on that," Vlad said "But first, let's make sure this conference goes without a hitch."

Jim relaxed, which Vlad read as cursory agreement. Vlad waited for his next question.

"Explain to me how Brenner is hooked up in this, and why he needs to stay alive for now," ask Jim.

"Well, intelligence knows he has been recruiting his old team of mercenaries, and a lot of black market weaponry has disappeared off the market. This conference is about the only thing going on, that could interest someone enough to pay the kind of money to get Brenner interested. This would have to be a seven figure project, I would think," Vlad threw out.

"I still don't see why a well-placed bullet would not work just as well, and eliminate the problem," Jim argued.

"It might, but no one knows for sure, what his operation is, and his personal hit squad, completely dropped off the map two weeks ago," Vlad was a bit embarrassed to say.

"You mean, with all of the assets of the CIA, FBI, Homeland Security, NSA, and, and... You have lost track of a bunch of known mercenaries, armed and known to shoot first, last, and repeatedly, to drop out of sight?" Jim was astounded.

"Well... Yes," Vlad said. "Even in these times, people can still go off-grid with enough money and help from inside sources," Vlad added.

"Now you have lost me," Jim said. "Are you telling me that Brenner has help on this, from inside government sources?" Jim was astounded, that after everything Brenner had done, anyone would still choose to work with the animal.

"Well, no one is proud of this, but yes, someone is working with him from the inside."

"We know he has received intelligence updates, about a bunch of world meetings and gatherings of important people, throughout the world. That is why this conference is not the only possible target;

In fact it is not the highest priority at this time. Brenner has been spotted in three other places in the last few weeks. I do not know what he could be planning, or if everything is already in place. That is why a fifty to the left ear would not work at this time Jim," Vlad added and hoped it was enough.

Jim sat silently for several minutes to digest this information and then he got thoughtful. "Vlad, are you trying to recruit me for this witch hunt?" Vlad looked a bit uncomfortable, before continuing.

"I would never ask you to come back to government service, without a real good reason, but don't you think this is it? Before you answer that, I need to tell you that you are more linked to this than you know." Vlad seemed to pause for effect, before continuing. "Andrea Warren is on the list to attend the fisheries conference as well." Vlad dropped that like a bomb.

Jim was silenced by this. Andrea was a state senator for Alaska, the daughter of the sitting, first female President of the United States, and last but not least, a very close friend and confidant of Jim's. He had met Andrea several years before, when he was on leave, and wandering around Alaska, looking for some place to come, when he was done with war. She had been doing a little wandering herself, before she buckled down to the family business (politics).

Jim had been drawn to her on first sight. She was almost as tall as him at 5'10".She was attractive, with her black hair, dark eyes, and athletic physique. But the thing that had drawn him to her, was the incredible level of confidence, oozing out of her body. He recognized the inherent power in her personality, before he knew who she was, and more importantly, who her mother was. Jim had happened to be on the ferry, the same time as Andrea, and had spent a great time in Skagway and Juneau, sightseeing with her. Riding the crazy railroad to the Chilkoot Pass, had proven to be the best time for Jim, since high school.

Jim and Andrea had become close friends over the ensuing years. Jim would love to move the relationship to a more permanent kind, and if he was being honest with himself, she was a major reason that had brought him to Alaska. The bug was her career choice. Every decision she made, was weighed and measured by political expediency. Did a choice help, or hinder her options? A long-term, open relationship with him, was deemed a problem. Andrea had made it quite clear that she felt strongly about Jim, but would not risk her political life. She had insisted that they each move on, with no strings, and no commitments.

Jim had agreed (any relationship, was better than none) and they still saw each other on occasion, being careful not to damage her political career, or reflect on her mother's.

Jim had met the President one time, and felt happy to escape unscathed. She was one very smart woman, who could read you like a book. He was in her presences about two seconds, before she told him what would happen, if he ever hurt, or disappointed her daughter. She then proceeded to tell Jim everything she knew about him, including his grade school love affair, that didn't last out the year. The President knew everything about him. Obviously Andrea had mentioned his name before they met. Jim did move on and had several relationships, like Lorrie, casual, close but no hint of permanence. He still hoped Andrea would come to her senses and get out of the political world.

"Ok, now you have my total attention! Why is she going to be there, and what other surprises are you holding back? Knowing up front, I don't leave this area, until this is done, and don't expect me to cow tow to Washington, on this one. If I need to take out Brenner, to save Andrea, he is gone, end of story!" Jim had to take a calming breath after that.

Vlad jumped in. "I would expect nothing less, but remember, this is about more than your love life, and you need to maintain operational security."

"This means you cannot mention this to Andrea at this time. This comes from the top, by the way," Vlad said, very nervous that he may have pushed Jim too hard this time. He needed Jim on this op, not a loose-cannon loner. Jim took a few minutes to digest everything Vlad had said. Andrea was, without a doubt, the most important person in Jim's life. Even though he saw and liked other women, she was the one he could imagine spending his life with; if she would ever get out of politics, that is. "Ok Vlad, I'm in, but I am working with you, not for the government

Vlad didn't hesitate. This had gone much better than he had expected. "I am good with that." He knew that this was one step closer to getting Jim back into the fold, back into government service, where his special talents would be best employed.

Jim was the best sniper Vlad had ever worked with, and beyond that, his skills as a soldier, were exceeded by his operational awareness, far better than most line soldiers. As an NCO in the service, he had planned and executed, several ops with little assistance from any commissioned officers. He had never been aware that he had worked directly under Vlad and the CIA on more occasions than he thought. He was a valuable asset, on loan to the civilian world, as far as the CIA was concerned.

Vladimir began working on his plan, as soon as he was away from Jim. He started, by reviewing his assets on site. They were not what a normal CIA operator might consider assets, but Vlad was not your run of the mill CIA operator. He knew a lot of characters in the Juneau area, and knew he could use them for eyes and ears. The mercenaries had to be active, if this was Brenner's target, so the first thing was going to be getting the 'Army' of eyes looking for them. Vlad got to his place in town and started calling in favors. He contacted every character he knew in town that could move around without comment from anyone and would recognize strange men, out of place, or acting in an abnormal way. Ling Cod and GoGo Joe were the first two men that Vlad thought about.

Both were local characters who knew everyone and everything that was going on. Ling Cod lived in Juneau his entire life and worked as an electrician and plumber for the city. If anything was going on, he knew about it. The jackass Mayor, Norman Treadwell, tried to fire him ever since he bought the election, but no one knew the city water system and sewage as well as Ling Cod.

GoGo Joe was a drunk, who was on the streets all of the time. Most people took him for a bum, who was past any ability to think. Vlad remembered a story Jim told him about meeting GoGo for the first time. GoGo was bumming drinks from anyone who would let him approach. Jim had noticed GoGo had, what looked like, a screen-door spring, tied to his shoe, and the other end hooked on his belt (rope). Jim bought him a drink and asked him what the spring was for.

GoGo just looked at him and said "I have a bad knee that doesn't like to bend when I start to lift my foot to walk. The spring helps the knee get started. Works like a charm!"

Jim and Vlad had gotten a good laugh out of this encounter. After a lot of thought, they decided that GoGo could teach a lot of smart people a thing, or two, about making things work. Both of these guys would do anything for a friend.

Vlad began looking for GoGo and Ling Cod, while thinking what he would tell them. He knew he was not ready to tell all, but he would tell them enough to allow them to start looking for the men he was sure Brenner had out there somewhere. Another good one to recruit, would be Bill Bates. He drove a tour bus, when he wasn't flying a charter, or fishing in his boat. The only worry about Bill, was the possibility that a pissed-off husband had shot him. He was quite notorious with the local free-minded wives. These three guys would know, or be able to find out, about any strange group of men, in, or around Juneau.

Thinking about Ling Cod, made Vlad wonder where the honorable Mayor was right now. His location could be critical. He was a total loss, as any kind of help, but he could cause serious issues for Jim and himself. Vlad finally got Ling Cod on the phone. "Hey Ling Cod, how they hanging?"

"Hey Vlad, I haven't seen you around for a while, what's up?" Ling Cod talked like he had a sandwich in his mouth.

"Not much, I just got back in town. Ling, I need a favor, could you stop by my place?"

"Sure Vlad, no problem. The great Mayor, is so tied up with his new squeeze, no one is on my ass right now. How about in a couple of hours? I have to run down some pump problems first. Two of the cities primary, potable water pumps quit this morning," Ling Cod paused. "You know, as long as I have been doing this job, I never had two pumps fail at the same time!" Vlad instantly filed the information under, 'may be important.'

"That is strange for sure, Ling. If you need any help, give me a call." Vlad nearly hung up, but then continued. "Actually, this may be related to what I was calling you about. I need to have you keep your eyes and ears open, to anything going on, that is out of the ordinary and this could be one."

"Vlad that is not the only strange thing right now. A couple of days ago, I was out at Auke Bay, working on a water main, when I saw a bunch of strange-looking tourists getting off of a ferry. The strange thing was, the guy that met them. He was ex-military, or I don't know a thing," Ling Cod added.

"Can you describe him better?" Vlad asked. Ling took a minute to gather his thoughts and memories.

"He was about six feet tall, with white hair, but the dead giveaway, was the way these other guys responded to him. I thought they were going to come to attention and salute him." Vlad knew he had to get Ling Cod to look at a photo he had of Brenner! This was the break he needed, to start getting some support here from the lower forty-eight!

Vlad hung up with Ling Cod, and went to find GoGo. He didn't carry a phone, so he would have to find him on the street. While driving down to the city docks, where GoGo could usually be found, Vlad tried to get Bill on the phone, but only got his answering machine. Vlad left a simple message for Bill to contact him as soon as possible. Vlad worried about Bill getting in real trouble one of these days, with his propensity to find his way into the wrong beds, with the most interesting women in town. He knew that Bill was carrying on an affair with two, or three different women at this time, not counting his ex-wife.

Eventually Vlad found GoGo, and was able to explain what he wanted, and what to look for. He made sure GoGo had enough cash to get some lunch. He left GoGo on the cruise ship pier, where he had finally found him, caging tourists for lunch money. Vlad headed back to his home. He was just lucky Juneau was small.

As soon as he got in the house, he headed to the basement that had a secret door. This door gave him access to the Buford and Jenkins mine shaft (called the BJ by the locals). The BJ mine was one of the things that convinced him to move to Juneau years ago. His uncle had been one of the last watchmen, before the mine was shut down permanently. He had told Vlad stories about the mine, and how the operation had missed the best vein of gold. His uncle had found the vein, just before he was sent home for the last time.

The first thing Vlad had done, when he got to Juneau, years ago, was to locate several of the old portals to the mine, and then got inside. He had been exploring the mine ever since. Several years ago, he had started doing some mining on his own. He actually found enough gold to start carefully buying up all of the stock still available, then using some of his money from his CIA work, managed to become the sole owner of the entire property.

Not even the CIA knew about this, and he planned on keeping it that way. Deciding to tell Jim about the mine, was a big move for him, and he was still not totally comfortable with the choice. Vlad moved through the mine at a brisk walk. He knew every rock and turn in the tunnel. He did have some electric lighting in the mine, but since the power was technically stolen off the grid, he tried to only use it, when he had no choice.

The destination was an underground structure he had repaired in the mine. The structure was originally what the miners called a dog house. This was a place to leave lunches and tools. The small underground structure usually had lighting and some amenities for the workers. His great-uncle had told him stories about how the crew would hide in the dog house, until just before a shifter (boss) would come around on his rounds. Just before he was due to arrive, the workers would scramble to the stope they were working on, and work like crazy, until he got to them. Those were the days-pay workers (minimal hourly wages), not the contract miners, called Jipo's. Now this was where Vlad stashed his weapons and ammo, along with communications gear, and other interesting equipment. No one in town knew about Vlad's life, outside of Juneau. Most thought he was some kind of ex-Russian gangster, or something like that. He always made sure he was ready to buy a round, or help someone down on his luck, and had managed to have a lot of close friends in the area, without ever having to tell his true story.

Vladimir had been born in Sitka, only three days after his parents arrived in country. They had immigrated to Alaska, to escape persecution by the Soviet government. The government of the United States, had granted his father and mother humanitarian asylum. Vlad's father had been an officer in the Soviet Army, when the troubles started in Afghanistan. His father had been assigned there, prior to the trouble, and had fallen in love with the daughter of a local head man. When the shooting started, his father had smuggled his mother out. When he was wounded, he was sent back to Moscow to recuperate. Vlad senior, had done well in the war and was able to use this, bought with blood, prestige to marry, and start his family. As the war continued for way too long, he knew that his prestige was about worn out and decided it was time to go. He had family in Sitka, Alaska, and decided that was the place to go.

Vlad's great-grandfather had been raised in Sitka, when it was the Russian capital. His great-grandfather had chosen to return to Alaska, when it was sold to the United States. The man's brother and sister had chosen to stay. When Vlad's parents moved back to Sitka, everyone just acted like they had been there all along. Vlad loved Sitka, and never missed what he had never seen in Russia. His father and mother, both dove into American life with gusto.

Vladimir had grown up exposed to both cultures. The Russian population in Sitka insured he learned to speak English, Russian, and the native dialect of his Afghan mother. He learned how to sound Russian, or American, depending on the situation. By the time he graduated from high school, he was as American as apple pie. He graduated with honors, and a full-ride scholarship to any University of his choice. Since his best asset was his ability to speak several languages, he chose to study languages and international studies, at Georgetown University. He planned on going in the armed forces, as soon as he finished his degree, but was recruited by the CIA, before he could enlist. He started out as a Far East analyst, but was quickly moved to operations, when his command of several Afghan dialects was discovered. He rose quickly in the company, and was running covert operations before Desert Storm.

After 911, he was quickly moved into Afghanistan, where his contacts were just what the company needed. This was when he came into contact with Jim and LTC. Brenner, for the first time. Jim quickly became a person of interest, because of his abilities and trustworthiness. Brenner, on the other hand, became someone to be wary of. Vlad had made several negative reports about Brenner, before the incident that had nearly gotten them all killed. Vlad had to go in and clean up several dirty jobs left behind by Brenner and his mercenaries. He used up a lot of friendships and contacts to smooth over angry tribesmen that Brenner had used, or abused.

Well, enough on the history lesson, Vlad knew he had to get down to the now stuff. He quickly made a visual inventory of his available ammo and weapons. He knew he had a couple of boxes of armor-piercing rounds for Jim's .50 cal., but could not remember if he had anything for the AK.

After ensuring everything was where it was supposed to be (he did have a case of ammo that would fit an AK), Vlad headed for the surface. As he walked out, he remembered that Ling Cod had answered his question about the Mayor, without being asked. It was good that the Mayor was totally distracted, even though he was in town. That left one less thing to worry about. The other real local worry was the Chief of Police. He was a piece of work for sure. Vlad was sure he was a dirty cop at the best, and probably a total crook. The thing that he was worried about, was that these two public servants would be ripe for Brenner to recruit, as pawns in his little operation.

Chapter Seven - THE MAYOR! NORMAN TREADWELL

(Thirty-four days to start.)

Norman had been in anchorage for two days, with four more to go, before he had to go back to Juneau, and face his family. The best part of being the Mayor, was lots of chances to get out of town on city money. Norman hadn't missed a conference, or seminar in the two years he had been in the job. The only way he got elected, was with his family name, and his father strong-arming the Democratic Party.

He had managed to get elected one time before, to the city council (no one else ran). His father had stepped in, when the mayor job came open, and set it up for him, but said that this was it, no more help.

Sitting in this boring sustainability seminar, was giving him plenty of time to review his boring life. Norman was fifty-five years old, and ready to retire at the end of his term as mayor. Married to the same woman for thirty-five years, and still not in love, Norman could only daydream about the women he saw around him. Just once in his life, he would have liked to score big, with a beauty of his dreams. There was a prime example in the room, moving around, taking press photos for the seminar. Norman smiled big, when the camera was pointing his way (please the public). Norman lost interest, and went back to his real life, a wife and three adult leaches, that lived at home and did nothing, but spend his money. He didn't like her any better than she liked him. As the seminar continued, Norman decided it was time to hit the bar (maybe today was the day of his dreams).

Norman decided to eat first, to allow more time for drinking. He had dinner in the Captain Cook Hotel, then went into the bar for drinks. All the tables were full, so he sat at the bar, ordered his drink and sat there alone, watching a ball game, on the bar TV. All of a sudden, the most beautiful women Norman had ever seen, asked him

"May I sit down?" "Uh-huh, please...

"Yes, sit down beautiful lady," Norman said.

"Thank you kind sir, I will."

Norman asked "What would you like to drink?"

"Oh just a little white wine please."

Norman signaled to the bartender, "White wine for the lady."

He could not believe his good fortune, though she looked quite familiar. "Have we met somewhere before?" he asked.

"Well, in a roundabout way. I saw you at the convention today. I take the video for the mayor's convention," she stated. "That's probably where you saw me," she added.

"Well, let me introduce myself: Norman Treadwell at your service. And you are?" he managed to get out.

"Sue Lang (offering her beautiful hand). Very pleased to meet you Norman," she finished.

"Sue, have you had a chance to see much of Anchorage?" Norman asked, in a 'hope you haven't' way.

"No, I just got into town yesterday," Sue said.

"Well, I would be glad to show you around tomorrow, as I have a free day, and the rest of the conference is not that important to me," Norman added.

"I have three more days before going back to Juneau, and I would love to spend it with you," Norman gushed.

"That would be great, as I would like to see more of the area, and take some pictures," she said in a demure way. "I hope you don't think I am being too forward," Sue added. Norman just smiled, afraid to say anything that might jinx the whole thing. This is the best conference he had ever been to. Sue and Norman agreed to meet in the lobby, bright and early the next day.

Norman went all-out, showing Sue all around Anchorage, then Knik arm, and on out to Wasilla and Palmer. He was soon, so at ease with Sue, that he told her about his bitch of a wife, his three worthless kids, and how badly they treated him. "Sue, I have spent my entire life in Juneau, and when I retire, I will get about half what I should, for all the time I have put in," Norman whined.

Sue gave the man a little hug. "Maybe something better will come along, you never know. I feel so bad for you, and the way they are treating you at home. I don't know you that well, but I think you are a wonderful man and I would be proud to be with you." Sue said this with an (in your pants smile). Norman swelled up, hearing that, and dreamed about how great it would be to have this woman in his life, full-time.

"I sure wish you were in Juneau. I would have someone to talk to, and spend time with," Norman said, with a ('please say yes' look on his face).

"Well Norman, I have a confession to make, I did not just run into you in the bar last night."

"You see, I have a job offer in Juneau, but didn't know if I wanted to take it, or not. It is a good job, and the money is better than what I make now, but it could be a lot better. I saw you, and knowing that you were the Mayor of Juneau, I wanted to meet you and talk about Juneau." Sue felt her gag reflex working overtime, as she spewed out this crap. "I am a little embarrassed. When I saw you, I felt like a school girl again. You are so handsome," Sue managed to continue the flattery.

Norman let strange thoughts run through his mind. He said to himself "If I can just find a way to get rid of that skank of a wife, I could be with this woman on a permanent basis." He got back to the moment and said "I think Juneau is the perfect place for you right now, and I think I can arrange a much better job in the city government." Norman was pulling out all of the stops on this selling job. This led to the hotel and a night of incredible sex. Norman did some things he didn't even know what to call, and Sue was the best woman Norman could even imagine being with. The next day, Norman was on cloud-nine and lost all interest in the convention; not that he was interested in the first place.

Sue spent every waking moment, for the remaining three days, with him. He lost total awareness of his surroundings, and Sue had to remind him, when it was time to go. At the airport, Sue kissed him savagely, in public, but Norman was beyond caring. "Norman, I will finish up my business in Anchorage, and be in Juneau in a couple of days, so find a place for me to stay! I am more excited than senior prom," she said. Sue, again had to fight her impulse to throw-up with these words, but she knew he was hooked deep and would do anything she asked, in the future.

The Letter

(Thirty days to the start.)

When Norman landed in Juneau, he picked up his car and headed home. During the short drive home, all he could think about was "How can I get the old bag to go visit the parents, or friends for the next fifty years?" Pulling into the carport, he was surprised that her car was gone, but the real surprise came when he walked in the house! It was completely empty. Everything was gone, the wife, the kids and all the furniture. He walked through the house and entered the bathroom. On the toilet was a letter. Norman's first impulse was to flush it, but he read it instead.

"Dear asshole, I left this letter on the toilet because when I get done with you, the toilet will be your last resting place. You worm, did you think you could go to Anchorage and take up with that little slut and not have to pay for it (WRONG AS USUAL).

The children and I have gone to New York, to daddy's house. He told me 35 years ago that you were a worthless bum, but you had that Harvard degree and the Treadwell name. You said I could be anything that I wanted to be just come to Juneau. The only good thing you ever did is knock me up three times and give me these beautiful children that you could care less about. Norman-- I stopped by the bank on the way out of town: I left you ten bucks in the account so it would stay open and you could look at it. I also sold all our stocks, maxed out every credit card including the Alaska Airlines card. As soon as daddy's lawyers get done with you that forty foot grand banks boat you love so well is GONE. This big house you had to have because you are mayor is GONE. My only hope, Norman, is that you die soon and I can collect that million dollar life insurance. With any luck that little chippy will give you something that will help you along. Norman I would wish you a happy life but I would rather see you dead! Enjoy the next couple of months because the rest of your life will be hell. I have the deviant pictures of your debauchery and the lawyers are going to clean you out."

Norman was a bit surprised and for the first time, he thought things were working out better than his long-time wish that she had died in child birth.

The Mayor's day

(Thirty days to start.)

The first thing Norman did, was call his office and have an aid go to the local Fred Myer store and pick up a bed and two chairs. That was all he needed, and the good thing was, he would write it off as office furniture and let the citizens pay for it. Could life get any better? A long drink later, Norman started planning his new life with Sue! He spent the night in blissful dreaming about his future, without the ex and the snots.

The next morning, he stopped at the office to check in and announce that he had hired a new publicist, and would be picking her up at the airport. He had his private secretary set up an office, and had her order business cards and a nameplate for the desk. He wanted Sue to walk into a real surprise. He headed for the airport an hour early, just because he couldn't wait any longer. Watching Sue walk off the airplane was the most exciting thing in Norman's life. He felt like a little schoolboy, to the point that he had an erection.

When Sue reached out her hand to shake his, he grabbed her and gave a hug.

"Norman! What if someone tells your wife about this?" I could care less, she is gone and so are the three brats from hell. I don't know how, but somehow she found out about us in Anchorage and cleaned out the house, bank accounts, and anything else she could take, to the lower forty-eight with her."

Norman quickly hugged her again. "This is like a gift from heaven. You're here and she is gone. You can live with me and just wait till you see your new office. You are officially the new publicist for the City of Juneau!" "

"Wow! You do move fast. I had no idea this could all happen in such a short time," Sue purred at Norman.

Once in the car, Sue managed to get Norman excited all over again, when she started stroking his leg. "Do we need to go to the office first?" She asked with a smile. Norman almost lost control right there.

"No, I think you need to get moved into the house first. It is a bit empty, but new furniture is on the way. Right now, we have a couple of chairs and a new bed."

"It sounds like a full house to me," Sandra almost laughed out loud. She was sure it was not out of character though, so who cared.

Sandra managed to get multiple rises out of the dipshit over the next few hours. Norman was so taken with her, that she was sure he would be ready when it was time to take the relationship to the next level (crime).

The next day, Norman introduced her to the office, and got her settled in. Sue met everyone but the Chief of Police, over the next week. For some reason, Norman seemed to purposely keep the Chief of Police from coming in contact with her. Sue even did a little actual work, by appearing in front of the Chamber of Commerce and proposing some new tourism advertising. She did finally manage to meet the Chief of Police, when Norman was out of town for a two day conference in Anchorage. He had wanted to take her, but she managed to convince him it would be unprofessional and damage her relationship with the staff. Sandra used the time to meet the Chief. She then laid the groundwork for a covert tryst with the man. He ended up being as much of a pussy-hound as the mayor, but in contrast, was quite good in bed. A month later, Sandra's little covert operation was running like clockwork. She was playing both the Mayor and the Chief like the patsies they were.

When Sandra and Brenner had been together in Anchorage, they had set a tentative date to meet again, just prior to the conference date. Sandra had to have Norman prepped and ready. The morning before the proposed meeting with Brenner, she mentioned to Norman that she would need to make a two day trip to Anchorage.

"Listen Sue, I don't understand why you have to go for two days. Couldn't you fly up in the morning and be back on the late evening flight?" Sue licked her lips and kissed Normans erection. "You can stand to miss me for a night. I may have exciting news for you when I get back. I have a friend that may have a plan to make a lot of money, and I know you are as broke as I am. The kind of lifestyle you and I like, takes a lot, so suck it up and let's have some fun right now." Norman immediately dove in for more. He had not had this kind of sex for years. Okay, he had never had this kind of sex. Sue was better than any prostitute, or escort he had ever paid for, and his wife wasn't a pimple on Sue's ass, on her best day.

Sandra was basking in the glow of her one-night with Brenner, a real man in bed, on the short flight back to Juneau. The night had been short, but he had to finish his confusion tour for the CIA, and get back to Seattle. The meeting with the client had gone exceptionally well, and the operation was officially on target. She mentally began preparing for the next few days with the dipshit and Nate, the Chief of Police. She was totally sure Norman was in the bag, but was worried about Nate. He was a lot more in tune with reality, than she liked. She had prepped him for the official first meeting to come, on her return. He would act indifferent towards her and not excited about having to work with her.

Sue ran into Norman's arms when she came off the ramp. "Oh baby have I missed you or what!" She kissed him and managed to rub his crotch with her knee. Norman looked like a kid in a candy store.

"How did the trip go baby?"

Sandra took a deep breath and put her game face on. "I have some very exciting news for you. The meeting went perfect and I think our worries are over. Get me to a bed, I can hardly keep from stripping right here." Norman would do anything she asked of him.

On the short drive to the house, she managed to totally confuse him with a simple hand job. The guy was putty in her experienced hands, literally. "Norman, baby, I have a bit of news myself. Remember I mentioned that I had a line on a way to make some real money. Well your ship is about to come in. How would you like a million dollars, or more?" Norman nearly ran off the road when he heard that. Money was the only thing more interesting than getting Sue naked and in bed.

"Who do I have to kill?"

"What would you say if I gave you a name" Sue asked, but laughed to ease the tension that permeated the air inside the car? Sue left the conversation there, because Norman had pulled up to the house.

An hour later, with Norman totally sated and looking half-dead, she leaned over and stroked his chest and slowly moved down his torso.

"Now stop that!" Norman sighed. "Give me a chance to recover and then we can have at it again."

"Norman, about the money conversation, how would you like to do this all of the time, anywhere in the world, instead of in no-where Juneau?"

"I would do almost anything, as long as jail didn't come with it!" he sighed.

"Look Norman, I can't guarantee we will have no problems, you know that risks are what lead to great success!"

"Sue, you tell me what I have to do, and I will tell you what I'm willing to do." Norman was in a whirlwind of emotions. He would do anything to keep this woman in his bed, including shooting someone!

"Norman, you have to do nothing and that will be enough. I think you will be able to claim total deniability. I will need to get one more person on our side. I think we need the Chief of Police?"

Sue knew that this was the critical question. If the dipshit answered, then he was in.

"Look, you could buy our Chief for a couple of bucks, so no problem." Norman knew from personal experience, how crooked Nate Holland was. "I hired the guy, so maybe things could be set up, so if anything does need a fall-guy, he could be it!"

"Norman, you are a genius." Sue nearly gagged when she said that. "Look Norman, just get me close to this Chief and I will rope him in."

"Just don't be wandering out of my bed," Norman looked a bit worried, as he said that.

"You don't need to worry. Anything I do with this guy, will be an act. Now that I have the best stud in the world, who is about to be rich, I might add. I have no need of any other man in my life." Sandra again had to withhold her emotions, when she spouted out all of this crap for the idiot. It was a good thing she liked sex so much, she could even enjoy this simple turd. Brenner was going to owe her big time for this one. After another round of sex, and learning new depraved things to do in bed, Norman and Sue headed for the office. Norman decided that it was time to have the Chief of Police in, to meet the new publicist and to decide how he was going to fund her budget.

Chapter Nine - The Chief

Nate Holland had been the Chief of Police in Juneau, for over three years. He had planned on this being his final law enforcement job, when he had gotten the Mayor to hire him. He had been working for the Anchorage Police Department (well, for himself), when one of his hookers had gotten into bed with Treadwell. Nate had been sure his big break had finally happened. Treadwell had been in Anchorage for a Democratic Party meeting Nate had thought he was a real up and comer (instead of the dead-end he was). With the incriminating photos and statements from the under-aged hooker, Nate had Treadwell right where he wanted. Norman had to give him the Police Chiefs job. The plan was to use the job to move up in the party and take over as Mayor when Treadwell moved on. The surprise came for Nate, when he got to Juneau and realized how inept Treadwell was. There were no coattails to ride to better places. Nate changed his plans and found Dana.

Dana was part of the local political scene, and in public office herself. She was attractive and available. Nate moved right in on her, and in the biggest mistake of his career, married her. It hadn't taken long for him to realize his mistake. Juneau was just too small and such an enclosed environment. Everyone seemed to know everything about everyone. He had done well enough with his little side-jobs (protection for local crooks) to retire quite comfortably.

Nate knew that time was running out on his ability to keep his extra income under the table and had started the wheels turning for his retirement. One issue he still had to deal with, was his crazy wife. She needed to be out of his life as soon as possible. He knew she was cheating on him, every time his back was turned. His plan was to catch her with someone in the sack. Nate didn't want to share his nest egg with anyone, especially Dana. If he could catch her with that slob Bill Bates, it would be even better. He knew she was poking him on a regular basis, but he must be taking her somewhere out of town. Nate knew Bill had a plane and a boat, so he had been waiting for a slip, when they stayed in town and used the boat.

He had a local bum called GoGo Joe to watch and tell him when he saw them go aboard, but so far no results. GoGo had proven reliable in the past, but something didn't seem right lately.

Bates had tried to get Nate fired last year, and had forced him to spend a bunch of his hidden funds to get a couple of people out of town quickly. That alone was good enough reason to take the guy out.

Nate was busy planning his exodus from public life, when he got a call from the Mayor's office.

"Sir, this is Alice (the Mayors secretary), the Mayor would like you to come over as soon as you can."

"Alice, tell the mayor to..." Nate paused and decided it was too early to tell the scumbag how he felt about him. "Sorry Alice, I lost my thought. Tell him I will be right over. Any idea what he wants? If I need any records, I can save time and bring them with me!"

"No, I don't think you will need anything. He wants you to meet the new publicist he has hired."

What she didn't say, was more telling to Nate than what she said. It was apparent that Alice didn't like the new hire. Nate was totally intrigued by this. He was sure the little thing he had going on the side with Sue, the publicist was secret. He hung up and grabbed his hat and gun. "I am headed over to the Mayor's office, so don't expect me back soon. You know how the old windbag gets!" He shouted to anyone who might care, as he left. "I'll be on my cell, not the radio," he added.

He reviewed his last afternoon session with Sue, on the way over to city hall. He had been disappointed when it didn't end in bed. He and Sue had been spending long lunches for a week, so not getting laid was a surprise. She had spent the time instead laying out a plan for this approaching meeting. Nate knew what was expected and he also knew that a lot was going on that Sue was not telling him. He recognized a professional, when he slept with her. He pulled up in front of city hall and used his personal space (in front of a hydrant). No one would dare complain about his car.

Norman stood up as the Chief walked in the office unannounced. Norman still got slightly nervous when he was around the guy. He couldn't get the hotel scene out of his mind when Nate had caught him with the hooker in Anchorage, a few years ago.

"Well, that was fast Nate. Thanks for coming over." Nate had to work to not stare at Sue, and give himself away.

"Nate, I would like you to meet the new Publicist, Sue Brown. I met her in Anchorage and spent some time discussing the challenges of running a remote outpost like Juneau. She has spent the last month getting her feet on the ground here in Juneau and is ready to discuss a proposal for your department. I hope you can find time to give her a tour of the police department and get to know her better."

Norman had to rub his hands on his pants to dry the palms, he was so nervous about this first step into the world of crime. Nate walked over to her and held his breath as she stood to shake his hand. "Chief, I am so glad to meet you. I think we are going to be spending a lot of time together over the next few months and I hope we can be friends." Sue's smile could have melted the Mendenhall glacier.

"Well Sue, I can guarantee that we will be great friends, and I look forward to working closely with you." Nate had to hold his breath at that comment; fighting to suppress thoughts about the last tour he had taken her on (the tour around a bed).

"Norman, I can make some time right now to familiarize Sue with the department and take her on a tour." All Nate could do was hope.

"Nate, I think you must have read my mind." Norman really hated sending his girl off with this shithead.

Sue smiled at both men and added "Chief, I would be honored to have you show me your department, and I also have time right now. Maybe we could start over lunch?"

Norman felt lost, as he watched Sue walk out with her hand on Nate's arm. "This is going to be real hard," was all that went through his mind for the next few minutes.

Nate and Sue took a quick cruise around the downtown area, before stopping at the Baranof hotel for lunch. Nate pulled in front of a fire hydrant and parked.

"Don't you worry about giving people the wrong idea?" Sue asked.

"I don't much care what folks think about me, I do a good job and crime is way down right now!"

Sue finally stopped the game and turned into Nate's arms. "Okay, we can drop the act. The great thing is, we can meet now with the idiot totally aware of it. " Sue smiled when she said this.

Nate reached between her legs and rubbed her, the way she liked. She nearly purred, as he stoked her.

"Nate we are out in the open and even though we don't care about Norman finding out, we still need to be a little discrete, don't you think?"

"Look Sue, the boat is just a couple of blocks from here and no one will dare bother us." Nate started the car and pulled into traffic. There had to be at least two cars on the road right now. That was rush hour in downtown Juneau. During the short drive, he thought about his luck. Sue was the best lay of his life and he had never suffered any long layoffs in the sex department. He had always been good with the women all the way back to his high school football days, and hadn't slowed down when he got married. That had just changed the way he ended relationships. It always worked to give them an 'I'm married' line. Juneau was so small he had to be a little more careful than if he was still in Anchorage, he had to curtail a lot; but, he still managed to get out of town often and he always had access to the boat.

Sue was so excited about the afternoon and how easy the Chief and Mayor were to manipulate. She totally enjoyed making both men's days. Screwing them was fun, because she knew she would get to kill them later. "Now that was the way to a great thrill." Nate dropped her back at the city hall, in time for her to drive home with Norman. He could hardly contain himself with excitement. "Tell me how the meeting went."

"I will have the Chief ready to do just what we want, very soon." Sue smiled as she thought about what she already had him doing.

"I would really like it if you would tell me what we are doing." Norman looked a little perplexed. Any time he was away from her, he tended to start thinking about the words she said and not so much of the bedroom stuff.

"Norman, don't worry I will tell you everything, as soon as I can, but right now, all I want to tell you is what I am going to do the minute we walk through the door." She reached over and gave his dick a squeeze. That washed every thought from Normans mind. Sue took a deep breath and thought to herself "Shit, I can't let this goof be alone at all, or he may actually have a thought that I don't want him too. This is going to be harder than I thought."

Chief Holland sat outside the Mayor's house for a few minutes, after they had gone in. "I knew something was going on," he thought to himself. Nate could always tell when he was being conned and the woman had been too good and too ready for the entire thing to be simple sex.

She was after something and Nate was more excited about that, than he was about the sex. He could smell money, just when he needed a break. He was sure he was going to be able to leave town with a lot more than his original plan had allowed. If he had had any real indication, he would have jumped ship right then! The problem was, that he might smell a con, but had no idea what he had just walked into. Holland drove away, with a big smile on his face. "Now if GoGo would come through with some good Intel on Dana, and that slime Bill Bates," he thought to himself. "Life would be perfect."

Chapter Ten - BILL'S PROBLEM

At the same time, down on the docks, William (Bill) Bates was wondering almost the same thing. He couldn't decide what to do, so he headed for Jim's boat. Jim always seemed to have an idea of how to fix problems on a boat, or the more personal kind. Bill needed some big help right now. As Bill got close to Jim's slip, he saw Jim heading away, so he yelled out, "Hey Jim, I got to talk to you." Jim was not surprised to see Bill striding down the dock towards the boat.

"What's up Bill? You got women troubles, or boat troubles?" Jim knew that with Bill it would be one of those.

"Well Jim, I have really bad split-tail problems. You see, it's not my fault that women find me so-o-o irresistible."

"Bill, it's not the fact that you're hornier than a four-peckered penguin is it?" Jim laughed. "So, what seems to be the problem Bill?"

"Well, I have been flying Nate Holland's wife, Dana, out to my cabin on the Taku River. It started out to be moose hunting trips, but she wasn't hunting moose, she was hunting me. You know me, I have a real weakness for lonely women. Besides she is so damn nice!"

Jim was a bit stunned but asked "Bill, please tell me that you are not messing with Nate Holland's wife, who happens to be the Chief of Police?"

"Yeah Jim, that's what I'm telling you."

"Shit Bill, that's bad, but you can get out of this. Just stay out of the way, until she moves on, then the next guy gets the blame, when they get caught."

Bill looked even more sheepish as he said "Jim that would work, except it gets worse. About a month ago, I took Julie Abbott out Halibut fishing, but the fishing was slow. With no plan in mind, one thing led to another and the next thing I know, we're in the rack and she can't get enough of me. I guess its karma, or whatever they call it these days," Bill concluded.

"Damn Bill!" Jim was astounded. "Don't tell me that this is Jack Abbott's wife, who just happens to be the Director of Public Works."

"Jim that's what I am telling you, but that ain't all, it gets even worse. I just found out that Dana and Julie are best friends, like sisters almost. They compared notes and found out that I have been balling both of them at the same time."

"Bill, you are the most lame-brained, pussy-whipped prick, I have ever met. All my years in combat, I never met a woman chaser that could compete with you, bar-none. You couldn't have picked a worse couple of men to mess with right now, with everything going on. I would throw you to the wolves, if I didn't like you so much." Jim shook his head before going on. "Besides, I've had some female troubles of my own, on occasion. I just wish you had picked a better time for this."

Bill smiled at Jim's comments. "Yeah, I know I screwed up, but damn, they are incredible."

"Okay Bill, here is what we are going to do." Jim was thinking on the fly. "I am going to take your boat down to Taku Harbor and moor it there. You are going to pick me up in your plane and take me back to town, then fly back to your cabin on the Taku River and stay there for a while." Bill looked a bit concerned at having to leave town.

"Well, how long do you think I will need to stay? I can get pretty bored all by myself and I really want to help you and Vlad with whatever you have going on. I know it is more than just finding some strange tourists. I have never seen Vlad so keyed up in all of the years that I've known him."

Jim wasted no time, and began casting off Bill's boat. He turned to him, before going aboard. "Don't worry Bill, I have a strong hunch you are going to be involved up to your overactive pecker before this is all done. You stay at the cabin, until Vlad, or I call you. Make sure you monitor the radio, and no guests," Jim added.

The 'get Bill out of town' mission took the next few hours, but Jim finally got back to his own boat and watched Bill take off, headed for his cabin about 10:00 p.m. Good thing it was light enough for a water takeoff and landing, till almost midnight this time of year. Jim dove back into planning his next move against Brenner. Every time he thought about the man, he seemed to flash back to the time in Afghanistan, that he had him in his sights. Vlad had to talk him out of shooting him and only stopping the vehicle with a round from the .50. The damn gun was heavy to pack around the mountains, but nothing could stop a thin-skinned vehicle, as quickly and permanently. Of course it would nearly take a man's head off at a mile. Vlad had convinced him that living, and not ending up in jail, was a real good idea, and not killing Brenner was the only way to ensure that.

After spending too much time thinking about what he wanted to do to Brenner, Jim began thinking as a soldier. Not knowing for sure that Juneau was Brenner's target, didn't help the planning, but Jim decided to assume it was. If the plan included the city docks where the tour boats were tied up, Jim knew he would have to find some very good over-watch positions that would allow him a good view of the docks, ships, and the downtown area. He remembered that Vlad mentioned his access to the old BJ mine workings. He knew there were old portals on the hillside, facing the water, they could be perfect for his positions. The next thing he had to do, was get in them and find out.

Chapter Eleven - The Mercenaries

(One week to go.)

Jason had been in Juneau, for over three weeks, and most of his team came to town a week ago. The last three came in on ferry Columbia that very day. He already had the plan for the Coast Guard in place and had already taken out the auxiliary water pumps. When he had found out that the two pumps were broken periodically anyway, he had decided that sabotaging them, would probably go unnoticed, as an attack. This was the first time he and Brenner had ever run an operation in the United States, and it was exciting, to say the least. Everyone spoke the same language, but you did have to follow a lot more rules. Much easier to just shoot a few people, to get what you wanted. His biggest challenge, was taking out the airport at a specific time. That was his main concern right now. The good news was Sandra.

Sandra was so ensconced in local government already, that you would think she had lived here for years, instead of a month. Jason had to spend a minute, or two, thinking about the great tools she had at her command. Who would have expected her to have the Chief of Police doing scud-work? He craved a little time with her, but was not willing to mess with Brenner's main squeeze. "Mind out of the gutter..." (And she was the gutter). Jason had started setting his plan for the airport explosion in place, a week ago. Sandra had given him the name of an electrician (Jack Worzel). The man was a gambler, and not a good one. He had made sure there would be a game in the man's favorite hangout and all of the other players would be working to clean him out. That would give Crown the leverage he needed, to use the man. The best part was, the Chief of Police was willing to take the guy out, when the job was done. Jason couldn't imagine a better plan.

(Two days prior to the start.)

In a hotel room, not far from the Mayors home, a group of men were gathered. Jason Crown was going over the operations plan, for the last time. Every site had been visited and no one had even had a sniff of trouble. Jason had to chuckle, when he thought about how easy it had been to fix all of the bridges in town, to blow at the same time as the airport bombing. He had worried about getting the bombs in place, until Sandra had hooked the Police Chief. He had supplied two patrol cars, to manage traffic, while Jason and his 'state inspection' team surveyed every bridge. The team had driven around in a utility truck, with state plates, and done everything in the daylight.

Each bridge cut off a primary access route around town. The Mendenhall Bridge cut the loop road and the highway was cut in two places. The bridge leading to the police station and the Lemon Creek prison, would make any response difficult. In total, six bridges around the city were ready to blow, including the Douglas-Juneau Bridge. That was a massive concrete bridge that had taken the better part of a day to set. There had been no problem with the two dumbass policemen controlling traffic.

Jason quickly reviewed the remaining bomb sites, with each man. "You each know your primary targets and the time frame. I expect every bomb to be in place no later than 0500, Thursday morning. Make sure to double-check each set. There will be no going back after tomorrow. Everyone be at the rally point by 0700, Thursday and no contact prior to that. We have to be ready to follow the Northern Blast, when the delegates go on the day cruise. Are there any last minute questions?"

Jason made eye contact with each soldier as he spoke. All he saw were confident looks back. "This operation is going to be a breeze," Jason thought. He added "Don't get overconfident," more to himself, than the rest of his men. He spent a little time reviewing the over-watch position on Blueberry Hill, with the men that would be hidden there. "Make sure that starting Thursday, all of you are in position. Remember, after the airport explodes, no one is moving in this town including you."

Jason had the bombs all set to explode with the same radio signal that would set off the airport. The confusion would be incredible. The big bridge to Douglas Island, would have been nice to blow at the time of the cruise ship grounding, but he had decided to wait. The Douglas Island Bridge, would block the major waterways for anything larger than a small speed boat. No one in town would doubt the seriousness of the ransom, after all of the bombs went off. This would create the most confusion possible. All response vehicles, would be stopped from getting to the airport, or anywhere else around town. There wasn't going to be any way, other than a row boat, to move around, when the dust settled.

The only real difficult portion of the exercise, was going to be dealing with the Coast Guard and the airport bombing. The good news, as far as Jason was concerned, was that the Coast Guard was not his problem to worry about. Brenner had some inside help for that operation. Of course Brenner always seemed to have all of his bases covered, with the exception of the one time in Afghanistan!

Jason had to be honest though; he hadn't seen that coming either. Jason took a quick glance around the room. Everyone here had been with him and Brenner, chasing the Russian and the Special Forces guys, around the mountains. Everyone was completely linked to Brenner and the lifestyle he provided. Jason had been with Brenner longer than any of these other guys. He had actually been with the Colonel, when he was active duty. Brenner had always seemed to come up smelling like a rose, and Jason got to do what he loved, kill people. He mentally shook himself and got back on task.

After everyone was gone, Jason reviewed the entire plan in his mind, then called Brenner, to tell him how things were going. He had made contact with Sandra and the dead-drop was working perfectly. She had given him the name of the air traffic controller he would use for the timing of the explosion. He spent enough time with the man, to be sure he understood the exact time to 'signal' him. The guy had no idea he was blowing up an airplane and a large portion of the city. He just thought he was sending a radio signal to Jason, to confirm a good landing. He still had to find a way to get the airport set to explode on demand. It was the critical part of the operation. It had to go off right when the government investigation team was landing.

Brenner knew, that as soon as the day cruiser, with the President's daughter on board, blew up, a team of NTSB and FBI would be on the way.

Jason was amazed by how well Sandra had set up the Chief of Police. He had seen her driving with him that day. Everything was going well. Jason had already met with the Coast Guard guy and the cruise ship was docked, right where it was expected to be. The entire op was going almost too good. He couldn't remember a plan working right to script, like this before. The only surprise was, spotting a familiar face down on the docks yesterday. He had had to hold himself in check, to keep from taking a shot on the spot. Walters had been talking to a guy and seemed distracted at the time, a good thing.

Jason knew Walters didn't get distracted easily. He also knew that Walters would shoot him on site, and favored using his damned .50 Barrett. The only target that would take priority, would be Brenner himself. Brenner and Jason had tried for several days to run Walters and the Russian down in the mountains, but somehow they always slipped away. Jason had to run for his life, when Brenner had been tossed out of country by the CIA, all easily blamed on the do-gooder, Walters. Maybe he would finally get the shot at the ex-army sniper during this op.

He subconsciously rubbed the spot on his leg where a bullet from Walters .50 had grazed him. He wished it had been a miss, but, Walters had hit what he was aiming at, the engine block of the Humvee. His leg just happened to be in the way. That had been the last time they had gotten close (if you called a mile and half close) to the Russian and Walters. Losing the Humvee, had been the last straw. They couldn't catch back up, before the special ops team made it to a friendly base. This operation was shaping up to fix a lot of unfinished business. The Russian and Walters were here, and one way, or another, would not walk away from this one. Jason was sure of that!

Brenner

Brenner was as happy as was possible. The call had come in from Jason. The op was officially under way. The best news was, that not only was the Russian in the target zone, but so was the scum sniper, Walters. Brenner was totally confident that Jason would follow the plan to a tee. He had found Jason when he was still on active duty. Jason had been in some trouble and under investigation for a possible war crime. Brenner had been appointed as the investigating officer, and had covered up some critical evidence, to get the man off. Jason would do anything he asked him to. Brenner was going to regret losing him, but that was the cost of doing business, and besides, there were always sociopaths available, if you knew where to look.

Brenner had spoken to his man (Steven) on-board the Cruise Ship, and verified the time for departure from Juneau, on Thursday. That was the trigger for every other action to commence. The Day Cruiser was going to be out of Auke Bay, before the ship ran aground, and would be in his hands, prior to anyone onboard, finding out what was going on. The best news was, that the President's daughter, The Senator, was definitely onboard. Now, that was a real distraction from the primary mission. The world would assume she was the target. There was enough anger over the first female President, to point to all kinds of terror groups, interested in getting to her. The two secret service officers with the Senator, would be a possible problem, but Brenner was sure Jason and his team could handle them. Everything was a go.

After arriving at the mine, Brenner reviewed every detail of the operation. His crew had taken the Fish Killer (forty foot hydrofoil) out, met the cargo hauler out of Mexico, and transferred all of his weapons, ammo, and explosives to the mine site. The boat supplied by PEDEI, had been the perfect choice. It looked just like a local fishing vessel, as long as it was moving under fifteen knots, but with the hydrofoils extended, could easily reach over forty knots. The other craft, was also at the mine. It was a forty foot, off-shore racing boat, all pimped out. It could travel almost as fast as the Fish Killer, but burned fuel like no tomorrow. That limited the range.

Brenner had sent the off-shore race boat, to Juneau several times already, carrying men and supplies. The last trip, had ferried in the explosives, as soon as it had arrived, so his men could set all of the bridges and other target bombs. The boat would return to Juneau tonight, loaded with the air-fuel bomb. The boat had been in and out of Juneau, several times now, so it would draw less attention. This time, it would stay. The boat had to be tied up in Juneau, prior to the grounding of the cruise ship. Time would remain critical for the remainder of the operation.

Brenner expected Jason to have all the targets ready, within the next few hours. All of the bridges had been rigged in daylight, with the assistance of the local law enforcement. That had to be a new twist in terrorism. Brenner had to pat himself on the back. This was going so well. Now, the wait for contact from Sandra, was all he had to do, other than meeting the Northern Blast in St. James Bay, for the kidnapping. Brenner spent several hours loading the bomb boat, and double-checked each detonation device. He had set a remote detonator, controlled by cell phone, but also, a timed device, that could be used, if something happened to him, or the primary detonator. Brenner had known all along that the bomb was going off, no matter what happened. This was the final cover for the kidnapping. It would be hard to worry about a few dead people, when a whole city was in rubble. Just the cruise ships alone, had thousands of people, and most of the city would be gone. Brenner got quite excited, thinking about the devastation. This was going to be good.

Chapter Twelve - THE MAYORS DILEMMA

Norman woke, with Sue next to him in bed. He ran his hand down her back, and marveled at how smooth her skin was, and how perfect her body was. He had accomplished things in bed, over the last month, he had only dreamed about. Multiple orgasms, more positions than he knew about, and oral sex he had always had to pay for in the past. He got a hard-on just thinking about the last go-around.

Sue stretched and turned to him "Listen stud, I need a little break here. Food would be good; besides we both need to be in the office, first thing this morning. I have a meeting with the Chief, and you need to release the letter I gave you."

Norman took a deep breath. "I guess this is the put-up, or shut-up time, isn't it?"

"Listen stud, this kind of life we have been talking about, takes some real money, and the last time I looked, your account is empty, the bank gave you a month to move out of this house, and this bed is the only real piece of furniture in this empty place!" Sue stroked the man's body and his ego, before continuing "This plan I have been working on, will make us both wealthy and we can live where we want."

Norman sighed, then stiffened his back. "I am ready; it just is going to be a struggle to sell-out someone, even slime like Nate Holland."

Sue shook her head and said "Just remember how he got his job." Sue punched him in the shoulder and turned away. Norman touched her back and bent down to kiss her neck.

"Oh, I don't have any trouble with him as the fall guy, but I do worry about any records he may have, of the problem in Anchorage."

Sue rolled back into him and started rubbing between his legs; always the best way to stop any real thoughts in his pea-sized brain (the only thing smaller than his penis).

"I promise, I will get anything he has on you, just tell the news media about the bomb threat to the city, and the cruise boats first thing this morning. You can play it down as an idle threat, but get it out there. That should get the police department running around like chickens, with their heads cut off. I told you last night, that the men I am involved with, will plant the bombs in the utilities and set them off when I tell them."

"The city (you) will have to come through with the money and the evidence linking the great Nate Holland will be found."

Sue had to fight her desire to tell the man how she really felt about him, but managed to go on. "You just have to act like the strong Mayor, and stay in the office, even when you release the second threat to the city buildings and the Governor's mansion. Everyone will think you're a real manly hero." Sandra had to turn away, to hide the look of total contempt that washed over her face when she said that. She was so ready to be done with this sorry excuse for a man. He had surprised her with his stamina, but there were always more men in the pond.

Sandra got out of bed, and after a shower, quickly dressed. She left for the meeting with Nate. This was going to cost her some more time in the sack, to insure he was going to do what she wanted. He still didn't know what was going to happen over the next few days, but she felt confident he would be willing. When she saw him the second time, after returning from her meeting with Brenner, she was surprised to find out he was way ahead of the Mayor, and knew she was trying to play him . The real surprise came, when she found out he was more than willing to get involved, as long as the money was good, and he got to take out the Mayor, on the way out of town. He had come up with the name of a state worker at the airport that had some gambling issues, that she had passed on to Jason Crown. He had also arranged for a float plane, to transport the explosives to the airport.

Sandra was really surprised, when she discovered how good the sex with him had become, when they both knew it was a game. Jumping from bed to bed (or car seat), was a real turn-on for her. Nate was working out even better than Brenner had ever hoped. He had supplied all of the evidence against the Mayor, about the under-aged prostitute, he had been caught with in Anchorage. He even had photos of the man in bed with the teen. When this was found, along with the plans for the extortion, and locations of all of the bomb sites in his home, there should be no more questions of who did what.

When Jason Crown had contacted her, about arranging a float plane, for use when the airport was taken out, she had used Nate again. He supplied a plane and pilot, who asked no questions, and would never meet her or Brenner. Sandra almost hit a passing car when she started laughing uncontrollably. This was real fun!

She had taken longer to get Norman on board with her plan, but now, he was committed, and there was no stopping the momentum of this operation. The conference people would be taken tomorrow, and the cruise ship would go on the beach, a day later. She made a stop downtown, to leave a note to Jason in the pre-arranged drop. Everything was going to start in the morning.

She put on her war face (a smile), and walked into Nate's office a few minutes later. "Hey baby, how they hanging?"

Nate looked up and smiled, but just said "Cut the shit, no one is around. Is everything ready?" He paused for a moment, then continued. "I can't believe you got the gutless wonder, to actually go along with this!" Sandra almost laughed out loud at that.

"Don't under-estimate me. Men usually do what I want them to do." Sandra smiled and walked over and gave him a kiss and a quick tit rub.

Nate took advantage and said "Okay, let's get out of here. I have everything ready to dump on the prick, and then, I am going to have to make sure all of my officers are in the right places, when the bombs start going off, the day after tomorrow." He planned on insuring as many as possible, of his men, went down with the ship.

They walked out of the office and stopped talking, until getting in his patrol car. Nate turned to Sue (he still didn't know her real name). "Remember! Don't try to get too cute with me baby, I have been doing this kind of stuff for a long time, and I would have no trouble putting a bullet between those perfect tits, if I have too." Sue looked at him and trotted out her (oh I am scared) expression.

"Nate, give me some credit, I know who is in charge here. Just remember, I hold all of the cards with the mercenaries." Nate got a thoughtful look on his face. "Maybe now would be a good time to explain how you set this all up?" Sue looked thoughtful.

"I think we need to get through the next two days first. The bombs are going to change everything around here. I need to know you can keep any inquiry away from the boat in the harbor!"

Nate hesitated, but knew he had no way out. He had to continue with the plan. “That is no problem,” Nate smiled. ”I have the harbormaster, right where I want him. I set him up with a stripper in Anchorage, last month, and have the photos to prove it. He will do exactly what I say.”

Sue turned and kissed him. “You know, it is a real pleasure to work with such a well-prepared man.” The surprise was, that she only stated the truth. She wasn’t going to enjoy killing Nate, as much as she thought she would. She’d still do it without a second thought, but she did wonder, who else this guy had the goods on, in this town?

The Electrician

(A week prior to start.)

Jack Worzel was just waking up. Last night had been one of his more successful in quite a while. He had walked away, the big winner at the poker table. The two thousand dollars in his pocket, was feeling so good. Every gamble, seemed to work out last night. It was the proof he needed, to know he was on a real winning-streak. He had taken down the best players in town, plus a couple of Anchorage men, that were in town. Too bad the Police Chief hadn’t been there last night. Jack had lost a lot of money to that slime ball over the last year. On occasion, he knew he had a problem with gambling, but so what. He was stable in his state job, and had no other commitments. Living alone, had several positive attributes. The biggest was, that there was no one to complain about his gambling. Unfortunately, he had to go to work today.

Jack got ready and headed for the airport. He couldn’t help but gloat about his night. Wait until his buddies at work heard. Okay, so they weren’t buddies, just coworkers, who he hated. Still, it was going to be fun, flashing his huge money role. Jack always cruised at work. He did just enough work to get by, and always paid his union dues (couldn’t be fired). He never made waves, and he never confronted anyone. The other workers had always given him a bad time, when they heard about a big loss at the card tables, but who was smiling now? He could hardly wait to get back to the tables tonight. He had heard that a big game was planned.

The entire day dragged by. He had to change several taxi lights and had to go in the service tunnel that carried utilities to the float plane basin. That was always the worst job. He had a bit of claustrophobia in the narrow tunnel. Ground water was always dripping, and it rumbled, when an aircraft went over. The euphoria over the big win, carried him through the day.

Jack had a surly disposition on a good day, and just totally withdrew from any interaction, on bad days. He had been this way his entire life. He probably got it from his father. Too bad he had never met the man.

He had grown up in the Anchorage orphanage. It was a bit of an improvement on juvie hall, where he spent a lot of his time as a teenager. Just like now, he had skimmed through that time, not making friends, and just getting by. He had been dumped on the doorstep of the orphanage, soon after his birth. No name, no family, and nowhere to go. He watched other kids get adopted, but he was a bit on the ugly side, and had a disposition when young, that turned prospective parents off.

He had spent time in a couple of foster homes, but that never lasted long. The saving moment for Jack, had been when he had been assigned a summer job, working with an old groundskeeper at the orphanage. This old guy, was his kind of man. He didn't take shit from anyone, and pretty much did what he wanted. As the summer went along, he filled young Jack, with all kinds of sage knowledge, about life and women. The man's philosophy evolved around getting a state job, and riding it for all it was worth. Jack had decided right there, that he would do this himself.

Jack's only redeeming trait, was in the classroom. Schoolwork was easy. He could have done real well, but that would have taken work. Instead, he did okay, and never took a book home. After graduation, he had gotten into a local trade school. After an internship, he was ready for his license in electrical work. He applied for every state and municipal opening in the state of Alaska. That had brought him to Juneau.

He felt like he had it made, when he had worked long enough to lock in his retirement. He could do almost anything he wanted, and never get fired. He was a classic lifer with the state. He would never be promoted, but since he did his job and didn't complain too much, he went under the radar, most of the time. Life was good for Jack.

On the drive home, Jack stopped at Fred Meyer, to pick up his bottle of booze. He favored Jack Daniels, but in reality it didn't much matter what he drank. This was his only vise, along with gambling. He did grab a couple of TV dinners, to get him by for the next couple of days. He pulled into his driveway and was surprised to see a light on, in his living room. He grabbed the .25 auto from under his seat, and went in. The door was unlocked, but then it was always unlocked. He moved towards the living room, it was empty.

He chuckled to himself and realized there was nothing in his house worth stealing. He headed for the small kitchen, to get a glass and poured himself the first of several shots of Jack.

He was on his third glass of Jack Daniels, when his TV dinner was ready. He finished the dinner and washed it down with one more tumbler of the good stuff. He grabbed his pistol and money role, and headed for the local bar, where the big game was starting. He was ready to ride this lucky streak for all he could. If it went as well as last night, he should go home with five figures. Wouldn't that be something? Maybe it was time for a new car, or a long weekend in Anchorage, with a sweet prostitute he knew. When he arrived, the game was under way. He could hardly contain his excitement. The table was covered in money. Jack took the last open seat and pulled out his stack. No chips in this game; it was cash only. The game was seven card stud (no trendy Texas holdem' here). Jack ordered a drink and settled in for the night.

The first hour of the game, saw Jack up five thousand dollars. He was riding his luck like crazy. He bluffed and won, and always seemed to have the hand, when someone called him. Jack was so high on adrenalin that he could have flown without an airplane. The second hour saw him start to give some winnings back, but like most typical gamblers, he just started taking more risks, instead of less.

By hour four, he had lost everything and had borrowed a thousand from the house. He continued to drink and lose, until that was gone as well. The rest of the night turned into a blur. He just remembered a lot of drinking and gambling. The drive home was more by luck, than skill. Fortunately, he saw no police, and didn't hit anything. He made it to his chair, and was a bit disappointed to find he had drunk most of his bottle, before he left. He fell asleep, wondering what had happened.

The morning brought a huge headache, and nothing to chase it with. He was mumbling to himself, when his front door opened and a man walked in. The man had a familiar face from the night before. He remembered the man was called Jason. "What the fuck are you doing walking into my house?" Jack fumbled for the pistol, still in his pocket. He nearly got it out, when the man reached over and twisted it out of his grasp. "Now Jack, is that any way to treat the man you owe a lot of money too?"

Jason Crown smiled, then sat down on the only other chair in the room. He calmly field-stripped the pistol, and threw the pieces on the coffee table, on top of the TV dinner remains. Jack was having a lot of difficulty holding his head up. The pain was pretty bad. "Look I don't know what you are talking about and I have to be at work real soon, so get the hell out of my house."

Jason decided it was time to get to the point, but first he pulled out a small bottle of Jack Daniels and threw it over to Jack. "Take a shot of that, I need you to listen a bit." Jack opened the small half-fifth and drank a good portion, right down. He felt better, almost right away. He took a deep breath and looked at Jason.

"Why do I owe you money?" Jason pulled out an IOU, for six thousand dollars.

"Well Jack, you made a fatal mistake last night. You drank way too much, and didn't know when to stop. You borrowed from the club, until they wouldn't give you any more, then I loaned you the six."

Jack stared at the IOU and did some fast thinking. He had gotten in trouble with his gambling before, but never like this. "Look I will pay it back, but it will take a while."

Jason smiled at Jack. "I don't have a while, so I am going to make you a heck of a deal." He took the IOU and tore it up, right in front of Jack. He then pulled out the biggest stack of money he had ever seen at one time. "This is one hundred-thousand dollars. How would you like to earn this, and another hundred?" Jack could hardly breathe, as he stared at the stack of money on his table.

"What's the gimmick? Who do I have to kill?" Jason knew this was going to be easy.

"Jack you don't have to kill anyone, just do a couple of favors for me at the airport." Jack got a real sinking feeling in the pit of his stomach, but he saw no other choices. He sat and listened to the man.

"Tomorrow, a yellow Beaver will land in the float basin at 5:00 p.m. I want you to meet the plane in your airport truck and pick up several boxes of fish."

Jack thought for a minute then "You telling me that that sanctimonious prick, Bill Bates is involved?" Jason was surprised by that.

"I don't know any Bill Bates. These boxes are very important, so take good care of them." Jack was as relaxed as he had been all morning.

"I don't care what is in the boxes, but why are they worth so much money?" Jason stood up, walked over to Jack, grabbed the front of his shirt and slapped him across the face twice. Jack fell back, as he felt his nose start bleeding.

"Hey what did I do?" Jason calmly sat back down.

"That was a lesson in proper etiquette. When I ask you a question, you answer. When I tell you to respond, you do. Other than that, keep your mouth shut and your ears open. There is more. I understand that there are three service tunnels that run under the runway and taxiway at the airport. Is that correct?" Jack was having trouble focusing. He had never been hit so hard in his life, and it had been a slap.

"Yes, that's true. I have access to them, to check lighting and electrical lines."

Jason smiled at the quick answer. It was always enlightening, when a worm knew his place. "That's good. I want one box set at each end of the tunnels, and two set in the middle of the center tunnel. Just make sure no one will move those boxes. Is that a problem?" Jack could hardly believe his fortune. "I can do that, no problem at all. I am the only guy who goes in the tunnels most of the time, and all kinds of stuff is down there. I can hide the boxes so only I would know they were there."

Jason was sure he had his man. The dipshit hadn't even asked what was in the boxes. "Well, that is good news. I want you to know, you will be watched, so don't get any funny ideas. I will leave you ten thousand now, and the rest when the job is done." He peeled off the ten thousand, and put the rest back in his case. "You should know, that the Chief of Police will be watching you for me. Don't spend any money for a week. Do your job and stay sober until the boxes are in place. Oh, by the way, the alternative is the Chief just shoots you. The Chief especially liked that idea by the way!"

Jason stood and walked out, without another word. Jack had almost relaxed, when he heard another person come into his home. It was Nate, the Chief of Police. Jack had played cards with him on several occasions and was sure that he was dirty. Now he knew for sure. Nate walked up to him and pushed him back into the chair. "Listen scumbag, I want to be clear on this. You spend a dime of the money and I will feed you to the fish! Do what the man wants and you make a shit-pot more money than you are worth Mess it up and there is no place safe." With that, he turned and walked out. Jack was so afraid that someone else would walk in, that he didn't move until an hour later finally he settled down enough to count the money that had been left. The funny thing was, that he would have done the job for the six thousand he owed the man!

The next day, Jack felt a lot better and richer. He got to work a little early. This raised a few red flags, but he put it down to his clock being set wrong. He spent the morning, replacing bulbs in a bunch of taxi lights and checking the runway approach lights.

By five, everyone, but a couple of night crew, were gone for the day. Jack was waiting, when the plane came in on final. It looked just like Bill Batas's new Beaver. That was great. Maybe he could use that against the man in the future. Jack took a quick look around the basin and saw no one. His only thought was how easy this was going to be, and how he would spend the money. When he walked out on the float, the man that got out, was not Bill. That was a bit disappointing, but you can't have everything. "You know, this looks like a guy's plane I know here in town."

The man smiled and just shrugged. "Listen, I don't know a thing about anything. I just got paid to fly these boxes of fish here. He opened the large door of the plane, and started handing out large fish boxes (they looked just like the boxes used to ship fish on Alaska Air Lines). Jack took each and humped them up to his truck. He helped push off the plane, and watched it taxi out to the end of the basin. It was back in the air and on its way, before he was back in his truck, headed for the other side of the runway.

It took Jack two hours to get the boxes into the tunnels and placed where he had been told. He was pretty sure what was in the boxes, but finally looked to make sure. He didn't recognize C4 plastic, but he had seen enough movies to recognize a timing device, or maybe it was a remote detonator? The bottom line, he didn't care what it was. He made sure he left no fingerprints on the boxes, and covered them with other junk he found. Even he wouldn't notice the difference in the tunnels. He finished, and headed back to the maintenance shop, to clock out.

As he drove home, he thought "How cool is that! I am going to get overtime blowing up the runway!" The good mood vanished, when he saw the police cruiser following him from the airport. He went straight home, without stopping for his regular bottle. He was surprised when he found a bottle on his table, when he went in. He never gave a moment of thought to where the bottle came from. He just spent the night drinking and thinking of how he would spend his money. "Maybe I will buy that prostitute," was his last thought before falling asleep. The police cruiser pulled away from the house, soon after Jack had gone in. Jason turned to Nate the chief of police. "Have you ever met a stupider man in your life?" Nate thought for a minute before responding. "Probably, but I wouldn't bet on it!" They drove away. They had good photos of Jack and the pilot unloading the boxes. The photos would implicate both Jack and Bill, with the explosions. He had Jack offloading the boxes and he had good shots of them being carried down into the tunnels. Nate would include them with the other stuff he planned on leaving with the good mayor. He was pleased that none of the shots showed the pilot real well. The size and build could easily be Bill Bates. This was better than getting to shoot him. He would go to jail, and Nate would be living the high life with Sue.

Nate dropped Jason off at the Baranof Hotel, and returned to the dipshit's house. When he walked in, he was not surprised to find Jack snoring away in the chair. The bottle he had left earlier, was nearly empty on the floor. He turned out all of the lights and found the pistol Jason had reassembled. He put on gloves and forced Jack's hand around the gun. It was no problem to pull the trigger with it against the man's temple. He let gravity take the gun to the floor.

He quickly checked the scene, to insure there were no voids in the blood spatter and that he left no telltale tracks. Jack was not dead since the gun was a shitty .25 auto. He wouldn't live out the night, and there wasn't a chance in hell, anyone was going to check on him. Nate left and waited several minutes in his car, before leaving the area. The man lived in one of the poorest sections in Juneau, and it wasn't uncommon to hear shots in the night. He listened for an hour, to make sure no one called it in, then headed back to the hotel. He had an appointment with Sue, before putting her on an airplane in the morning. "This had to be worth a good screw, maybe two." Nate was a happy man.

After the Chief dropped him off, Jason finished his update to Brenner, and made the call, using the special code. It was almost scary, how easy it had been to get that idiot to do the job. Ten thousand was a drop in the bucket, and left him a lot, for the rest of the possible problem areas.

The airport had been the most challenging to figure out. The trick, would be triggering the explosions at the proper time. His man in the tower, would do the trick. The man would be able to see any approaching aircraft, be able to monitor all movement on the airport, and know exactly when the aircraft was on approach. Jason had timed several airliners, to insure the explosion would do the job. He had selected a timing spot that the aircraft overflew on final, to the center of the runway. Brenner had worried about this part, but it was going to be a piece of cake. He spent the rest of the day, preparing for the arrival of his team that would do the kidnapping. He got rooms, rental cars, and supplies to keep them for three days. He would meet them, coming off the ferry, and get the ball rolling. He was as ready as he could be. The crazy thing was, that Sandra had gotten the Chief to take out the electrician and the Mayor. He usually had to tie up all of the loose strings himself.

Chapter Thirteen - The Chief Makes Some Moves

Nate couldn't remember being quite so happy before. He was playing this bitch, like a fine machine. When she had asked about arranging a float plane for the operation at the airport, Nate decided to kill two birds with one stone. He had a friend in Anchorage, with a Beaver that had been used by the same company that had owned the plane that Bill Banes now owned. They were both painted exactly the same. He had found a photo of his wife and Bill standing on the float; with the N numbers of the plane easily seen. He had his friend alter his numbers to match. If anyone saw the plane, and linked it to the airport attack, Bill would be implicated. GoGo Joe had not come up with anything for him, but this would work out even better. People were so sure no one ever changed N numbers on planes. Just the thought of Bill Bates in jail, while he sat somewhere sipping cold drinks on a beautiful beach, was fantastic. The only thing that would be better, is if he could take out his slimy wife at the same time. Nate could hope that she was in one of the public buildings, when one of the bombs went off! Nate headed out, to start getting his police department ready to do the wrong thing, when the excitement started. This had turned into the craziest few weeks of his life. The good news was, that his new life started soon.

Sue, Sandra? (Hell, she was having trouble remembering her name on this one) left the Chief, and headed back to her office. She decided to leave the phone message for Brenner, just before leaving Juneau. At lunch time, she went back to Norman's house, and gave him a quick ego boost that left him starry eyed. After he left to go to city hall, she cleaned out any signs of her ever being in the house. She took the time to wipe everything with bleach, where any residue could be found. The sheets they had been using, went into a bag that she could drop off somewhere else. She had done the same thing to the office, before leaving. The last thing she did, was to put on a wig, glasses, and some very conservative clothing. Looking in the mirror, she thought she looked a lot like a school teacher. Wasn't that a joke?

Nate pulled up outside, in his private car and she quickly walked out. She got in, without saying a thing. "Well if I didn't know better, I would say a pretty school teacher just got in my car!"

Sue smiled and said "Don't worry, its only makeup. I am the same bitch that can make you scream for more." She smiled as she said this.

Nate pulled away from the curb, and headed towards the airport. "I sure hope you are at the top of the gondola, the night after the state and municipal buildings, along with the Governor's Mansion explode. I would hate to get there and not find you baby. I am left hanging out, if I don't have a way out of town!"

Sandra got back in-character and said "I will be there with a helicopter. We will be out of the area and on our way. You just make sure you have a case full of money and a passport in a different name." Nate patted his top pocket.

"Don't worry about me. As soon as I pop Norman, and plant the evidence, I am ready to go. I just hope the bomb you have set, does a complete job on the station." Sue patted his cheek and gave him a long kiss.

"There will not be enough left of anyone in the building to identify, except forensic DNA."

Nate got thoughtful for a minute, then asked. "Explain to me one more time, how this ransom is going to be so easy?"

Sue smiled and reminded him, "Look, you are going to be the designated bag man, and the Mayor will hand the money to you. The authorities will assume the drop is only aimed at drawing out the terrorists. You make the bag switch, and do the fake drop, as the note will specify. Norman will convince the Governor that paying the price, is much better than losing the Governors' Mansion and every other state-owned building in town. The first payment, is just an installment to hold off the explosions. They will come through with ten million, but not the billion we ask for. Ten million, split two ways, is a lot of cash. All of the mercenaries, along with the Mayor, will be more than enough fall guys. Sue gave him a hug. "Just make sure you do a good job with the suicide."

Nate looked at her. "That's a piece of cake, this isn't TV you know! Every case doesn't get solved by one hair. I have arranged a suicide before and had no problems."

Nate watched her walk into the terminal, before he pulled away. The last few weeks were a blur. When he demanded to be let into the operation, or he would blow it up, Sue had finally chosen to let him know what she had planned. He was surprised by the size of her plan, but thrilled by the payoff. He rolled the entire plan around in his mind, as he drove back down town. The best part of this whole thing, was that he got to take out the sleazy Mayor, and blame the whole thing on him.

Too bad he had to plant a lot of money on him, but what was ten thousand dollars compared to the millions he and Sue were going to share? The money to plant had been a minor problem, not getting it, but having to use his stash for it. He still was not willing to admit that Sue had used him more than he would have liked. He went to his office and waited for the Mayor to call the press, and release the ransom note, along with the first list of targets. This was so neat. He didn't have to set any bombs himself, or even get shot at. In a few days, he would meet Sue, and fly out of this rat-hole, for the last time.

Sandra (finally her own name for good), was relaxing, as the flight to Sitka started the descent. She was feeling quite smug. Everything had gone better than planned. Nate would kill Norman, and then she would take care of him. The material Nate had on people, had made the job of setting everything up, easier than she had hoped. As she came up the ramp, Brenner was smiling at her from the visitor's area. She walked out of the boarding area and he grabbed her around the waist.

"I hope you took time to clean the stink of those two guys off, before you got on the plane!"

Sue looked at him and said, "What's the problem? You send me to do a job, then question how it got done." She knew this was just foreplay.

Brenner couldn't hold himself back any longer and laughed. "I just can't believe you got this Chief of Police to do the killing for us! Are you sure he will go through with it?"

She smiled and thought back to the conversation. "I had to fight to make him promise to make it look like a suicide. If he had his way, he would have chopped him into little pieces and fed the fish."

Sandra put back her head and took a deep breath. "It is so good to be done with my part. Killing Nate will not be easy. I have to admit, he ended up being very helpful and we could have used him again, but all good things must end."

Brenner got a startled look on his face. "You sure you didn't fall for this one?"

"No! He was pretty good in the sack, but why settle for a good sheep, when I already sleep with the wolf?" She gave him a squeeze. Sex after an op like this, was always great with Brenner, and this would be no different. She looked totally satisfied.

Brenner drove right down to the docks, and quickly got Sandra onboard. "Everything is going well!" he added. "The mine on Chichagof is perfect. I think we could hold the guy for a year, without being discovered. The security man is on the payroll, and has started baiting the local brown bears to stay around the mine entrance. No one is going to come snooping around."

Sandra was a bit taken back, by the image of a big bear hanging around.

Finally she asked "That's good news, but how is he doing that?"

Brenner smiled and said "Wait until you see. The animals are crazy hungry and will eat any meat you throw them. I think I will have one of the diplomats from the conference fed to them, to make a point about escape!"

Sandra caught her breath. "I hope you don't plan on using the Senator? She could be useful to us in case of any problems!"

Brenner did a little thinking. "No, I think one of her secret service guards will do nicely." I understand she is quite loyal to her hired help, so that should do better than her." They went below to make use of the time, to run around to the mine. It was quite a long run, but would not be boring to them.

Later, Brenner sat drinking some coffee, as the Fish Killer continued towards the mine. The five hour run, gave him time to prepare the ransom notes and his next report to PEDEI corp. He wrote out what he planned on telling Maris, and then used his satellite phone. By using a simple, pre-arranged code, the time frame for the action was relayed, and more money was requested. Brenner planned on getting as much out of the company as possible.

The best news, was the arrangement he had made with the Russians. They wanted the technology and didn't much care how they got it. They would have some men with the fisheries conference people that would be taken with the rest. Brenner's man knew who they were and would insure they were not injured (permanently). The key, would be to convince the other delegates, that the Russians were as much involved as hostages, as the rest. What the Russians didn't know, was that Brenner planned on double crossing them all anyway. "With great risk, came great rewards." Brenner wondered where he remembered that from.

PEDEI Corp

Steve Maris was in a staff meeting when the coded message came in from Brenner. No big surprise, he wanted more funds made available for the completion of the mission. The good news was that the mission was starting. The scientist (Westlake) would be in Brenner's hands in a day or two. Maris put in a call, to schedule a sit-down with Bismarck, for the afternoon. It was time for Bismarck to put himself in a very public place, with a lot of important people around. He should never need an alibi, but better to have one and not need it. Maris was sure that Brenner would have the initial report findings from Westlake, soon after the abduction. Maris made some other private calls, to set in motion his own stop-gap plan for himself. Thinking about meeting with Grant, always reminded him how he had failed to tap Grant's beautiful secretary. Maris was not used to failing, when he set his mind on a woman.

The woman in question, was just getting ready to leave the office for lunch, when the call from Maris, to set up an appointment to see her boss came in. Leah couldn't believe how fast her heart began beating. After the first attempt at the spy game, Maris had stayed away from this office, which was quite different, compared to the months before, when he was in and out quite often. She was just as prepared, and very anxious to take risks for her lover. Rob had called her a few nights ago. He had been very excited, and given her his itinerary for the conference in Juneau. He had told her to start planning the wedding. After telling the world about his discovery, he wanted her to quit the job for Bismarck, and move out west with him. Leah didn't want to quit, until she had evidence that would sink Bismarck, and protect Rob. Just thinking about him, made her crazy excited.

While the boss was out to lunch, Leah placed a high-quality recording device in a planter, in his office. It was right on the desk, and should, according to the man who sold it to her, record any conversation within the room. She was working away, when Grant came back from lunch. "I hope you don't mind, but I would like to run out and get a quick sandwich. You have an appointment with the head of security at one-thirty, but nothing for the rest of the day."

She was sure he was going to see her heart pounding through her dress.

“No, that’s fine. I am sorry you had to wait until I got back.”

Leah smiled and excused herself to go to lunch. Bismarck stopped, as she was ready to leave.

“Listen Leah, you have been working quite hard lately, and since it is already past one, go ahead and take the rest of the day off.”

Leah was surprised, to say the least, but quickly agreed, and grabbed her purse and left. Her heart didn’t stop pounding for two blocks. She was sure the meeting would be interesting, since he sent her out of the office so seldom. Too bad she hadn’t had the recorder going for the last private meeting. Leah spent the afternoon shopping for a wedding dress, and fantasizing about her future life with Rob. She hoped the conference went well.

Chapter Fourteen - THE EXCURSION

(The operation begins.)

"Ladies and gentleman welcome aboard the excursion boat Northern Blast. This is the Northern Pacific Fisheries Conference cruise." The representative from the Conference got things going. "The first order of business is to introduce your tour guide for the day, Andrea Warren. Senator Warren is the senior senator from the great state of Alaska."

Andrea stepped up to the mike. "Hello everyone; I know some of you already and I hope, by the end of this trip to the research station, to know all of you. I would first like to welcome everyone to Alaska and say I am very excited about this conference. Finding a way to bridge our differences to improve the fisheries, is going to benefit the world. So let's get started!" The boat pulled away from the dock as she spoke.

"We are sailing out of Auke Bay. This is the ferry terminal for the area and has constant traffic." The group of dignitaries were a little surprised to find out that the Senator planned on actually acting as a tour guide. Andrea continued "The island, dead ahead, is Coughlin, as you can see we must go to the left, which is out of our way, but the waterway to the right side of the island is only thirteen feet deep. We must go around to the left. As we go around Coughlin Island, if you look to the left, you will see Spoon Island. The big island behind Spoon Island is Douglas Island, where the town of Douglas stands. It is attached to the mainland by a bridge leading to downtown Juneau. Douglas is no longer a separate town, but part of Juneau. The big mountain, off to your left, is our ski area, which we are proud to say, has produced Olympic medal winners."

Andrea kept this dialog up throughout the trip, mentioning Portland Island, Tee Harbor, and Shelter Island, as they came into view. She managed to inject enough historical facts and some folklore, to keep everyone interested. After about thirty minutes, the boat turned towards shore. "We are now going to dock at the fish lab. There will be guides to take each of you through the lab and answer any questions you might have. I hope to speak with each of you, when we are back aboard. There will be a nice lunch served during the trip back to Juneau. Please have a great time."

Just minutes after the Northern Blast had cast off for the cruise, her sister ship, the Alaska Queen, also moved out of Auke Bay. Jason Crown was at the helm; His men had met him as planned, at 3:00 a.m. At the docks, Jason had met with the captain on the Northern Blast a couple of days ago, to get the keys and schedule for the two boats. He had already traveled the route to St. James Bay, before taking his team into Juneau. He knew how to get there and how long it would take. Brenner was supposed to be on location in the Fish Killer, to take off the remaining demo and bring him two more men. He had left four men in town, to insure the bombs went off on time and to take care of the remaining Coast Guard men. This was the riskiest part of the whole plan, as far as Jason was concerned. He knew that at least two of the Russians were security, and two secret service men were with the Alaskan Senator. Must be nice, to be the President's daughter. Jason had his men check equipment, as they moved towards St. James Bay.

Sure enough, as he pulled into the inlet to the bay, the forty foot Fish Killer, was already there. Brenner met him, when he pulled alongside. "Good job Jason, You are punctual, as usual. Did you have any trouble taking the boat?"

Jason was a bit offended by the question, but buried his feeling before responding. "I could have gotten the job done without the keys and security codes, but with them, I might as well have been taking my own boat!"

Jason smiled and shook Brenner's hand. "Has Sandra called in yet? I got the note from her in the drop this morning." Jason added. "She said everything was on schedule."

Brenner hesitated, then said "No, but I expect her call soon. I will head out to Sitka, as soon as the call comes." Brenner thought for a minute, then added "I sent the bomb boat this morning, with the air-fuel bomb. I want that in Juneau, before the cruise ship goes aground tonight." Brenner was quite concerned, since this was the critical part of the timing. The boat had to be in place soon. The transfer was quickly completed, and the Fish Killer cast off. Jason got his men below decks, and started rehearsing the plan again. He knew that the security personnel, made the operation quite dangerous if all didn't go as planned. The wait was on.

The Kidnapping

"Welcome back aboard! I hope that you enjoyed the lab tour. I have just learned that we are going to extend our cruise. Our host wants to sail out past Shelter Island to beautiful Saint James bay. The captain of our little ship plans on serving lunch in the sheltered waters of the bay." Andrea was slightly confused by the note she had just read to the group. This was a total surprise and not totally welcomed. She grabbed her security detail and headed for the Bridge. "Captain, I think an explanation is in order!" The senator was in full command voice.

"Senator I am sorry about this change but we are having a bit of difficulty with the boat and the decision has been made to shift everyone to our sister boat, the Alaska Breeze. This will work out well as she is a larger boat and more room is available for the luncheon."

The captain was fighting to control his fear. This was the critical part of his involvement in the operation and the next moments could affect his life. Andrea looked daggers at the man, but finally decided to go with the flow. "I just wish I had been informed prior to the note being placed in my hand." Andrea was still angry.

The Captain looked miserable and did get the attention of Andrea's security detail. They both moved close to the man and waited for any sign from Andrea.

The Captain quickly added, "I apologize for that, but my office had told me to be discrete and to not get anyone worried. The boat is not in any danger, but you know how some people can get!" Andrea looked at the faces of her security people. She could tell that they understood, but didn't like this any more than she did.

"Ok! We will continue, but no more surprises captain." Andrea turned without another word and headed back to the conference group. The change in itinerary disturbed her more than she wanted to exhibit, so she kept to herself for the remainder of the short trip to the bay.

The Alaska Breeze was already anchored in the bay, when the tour motored in. The crew of the Northern Blast took little time to raft up to the Breeze. The security people did a quick sweep of the new boat, before anyone went on board, so Andrea was comfortable with the change. The transfer went off without a hitch.

The promised lunch was ready when everyone was on board. Andrea began working the crowd, as soon as eating seemed to taper off. The crew was serving drinks and everyone seemed happy.

The conference representative, Paul Swank, escorted Andrea around the crowd. "Senator, I would like you to meet Peter Ivanovo of Russia." Andrea took the offered hand and was glad she was in America, where a kiss was not mandatory. "It is nice to see you again Peter." Andrea was not real sincere in the greeting. The last time they had met in Moscow, he had made a rude pass at her. Paul continued with the introductions. "This is Suzuki Kazuki and Mrs. Kazuki representing Japan." Andrea smiled and gave each of them a small hug.

"I was looking forward to seeing both of you again. I hope I can show you as good a time as you did me last year, when I was in your beautiful country. Welcome to Alaska."

Swank hurried her on to the next delegate. "And from Norway, I would like you to meet Mr. Aksel Borresend." Andrea had no problem showing sincerity towards him.

"I was looking forward to meeting you, welcome to Alaska Mr. Borresend." He extended his hand towards Andrea. She shook his hand energetically.

Mr. Borresend looked a bit surprised by the greeting. "I have no idea why you would even have heard my name Senator." Andrea just smiled.

"Don't downgrade yourself. Anyone involved in the sustainability of the fisheries, must know you and your cutting edge fish-farming operation." Andrea smiled again, before moving on. Sometimes she was surprised, when other people didn't expect her to do her homework. She had not been surprised by a guest at a state, or federal party, for a long time. She had learned that from her famous mother.

Again, Swank cut short her time. "Senator Warren, let me present the Australian Minister for Fisheries and the sister of the Prime Minister, Amarina Copper!" Amarina stepped around the man and took Andrea's hand, with both of hers.

"It is so nice to see you again Andrea. I saw your mother in Washington D.C., last week and she told me to say hello when I got here. So hello, and hope your trip to Australia is still planned for next month." Andrea finally didn't have to play the politician.

"It certainly is. I cannot wait to see your beautiful country again. You always treat me so well, when I am there."

Andrea could only hope for the end of the group, or the sudden death of the contentious Swank. She barely had time for a quick drink of her juice, before she was again drug away by the pushy host. "Senator Warren, this is the head of fisheries from the Philippines, Mr. Pablo Antoine."

"Very nice to meet you, Mr. Antoine. I hear that you are doing some great stuff with your bottom fisheries. I want to sit down with you and pick your brain before the conference comes to an end." Andrea was pulled away before even finishing her thoughts this time. Swank seemed to be on a timed race, to get to each delegate.

"And from Great Britain, Miss Amelia Lawson," Paul Swank continued with his unending introductions, in a slightly pushy way.

"Welcome, Miss Lawson. I understand that you are the head of marketing fish products for all of Britain," Andrea said (with no teleprompter in sight).

"Why yes I am, and I am so happy to be here in Alaska, to actually see where so much of our fish comes from."

Andrea had no instant comeback for that. "I think you may have finally stumped me. I am embarrassed to admit, that I don't know what percentage of your fish consumption comes from our fisheries." Andrea smiled and gave a little laugh, to remove any negative emotion from the statement. Miss Lawson also smiled "I would have to say that we get quite a large amount from your waters. Our own fishery is in a sad state at this time. Hopefully, this conference can lead to some major changes for the better."

Andrea would have liked to spend more time with this woman, but again, Paul had one more introduction. "Senator, I am proud to introduce our star attraction at the conference, and our keynote speaker, Robert Westlake!" Andrea took the offered hand and liked what she saw.

"I am pleased to meet you Mr. Westlake." Rob shook the offered hand.

"Please call me Rob, Senator."

"Well, only if you call me Andrea! I have been around long enough to not need my ego fed daily; besides, when I hear Senator Warren, I still look for my mother. She was a senator a lot longer than she has been the President. Tell me a little about yourself, Rob.

I know that you are a fish biologist and a chemist. I don't know much about your current affiliation though. Are you with any university, or in private research?"

Andrea was a bit puzzled by the look from Rob Westlake. He actually appeared to be uncomfortable about his place of employment.

"I have always been in the private sector. I never could really enjoy teaching. My love has always been research. Presently I am working for myself, though I worked for a large corporation for five years. I found that my interests and ethics became less in line with corporate policy, the longer I was with them."

Andrea found herself staring, and had to mentally shake herself. She could tell there was a lot more to his story than she was likely to get from one handshake.

Andrea finished her juice, before continuing the discussion. "I hope you are doing well, and since you are presenting some new discovery here, I guess that goes without saying." Rob was no poker player. The brightening look on his face told all.

"Andrea, I have to tell you that Alaska has always been near and dear to me, and my research all started right here in these waters, with a simple fish called a Fibrous Flounder."

Andrea was a bit surprised, she had never heard of a fish named that. "I have lived here my entire life and that is a new one on me!"

Rob chuckled and just said "Well I better end this discussion, or you will not want to attend my presentation tomorrow. I don't want to be accused of monopolizing your valuable time." Rob stepped away, headed for the bar. He was surprised to feel an instant attraction, or friendship towards the Senator. That was not something he had expected.

Andrea continued working the crowd, and was glad the conference buffoon, had finally left her side. Her secret service man, Bobby Blackburn, was close behind her, but did not inject anything, unless she asked him a direct question. She was just beginning to wonder when the captain would start the trip back to Juneau, when two strange things happened. One of the serving crew, moved up behind Bobby, and stuck a gun in his back. "If you want the Senator to live, don't move. There are several guns pointed at you right now. That goes for you too Senator!" The man was so ready, she wanted to tell Bobby to stand down, but she was too late. Bobby made a fatal mistake and went for his gun, after he pushed her away. There was one shot, followed by several more further away. Bobby dropped. The eyes of the gunman never left her.

"Senator, this is your last warning, no more games." She looked at the man and knew she was in real trouble. Andrea told the man she would do what he wanted, but first she would help her security man. She went to her knees, to check out his wound. Andrea was trying to stop the bleeding in Bobby's thigh, when her other secret service man, Jamie, was drug into the room and dumped at her feet. The man who had shot Bobby smiled and said. "I guess that should cover everyone," and walked away.

Andrea took a quick look around, and was not surprised to see the two Russians she had not been introduced to, down on the deck as well. She had decided, soon after they boarded, that they were security types. The man who shot Bobby, walked up to the front of the room and picked up the mike. "Alright everyone, remain calm. No one will be hurt unless you fight the inevitable. We are going on an unscheduled boat ride. Every crewmember on this tub is with me, so don't even try to get close. They will shoot you without question, if they feel at all threatened. If everyone cooperates, this could be your highlight story for your grandkids, or maybe not!" He left it at that, and walked out of the room.

Andrea had never been so afraid before in her life. All she could think of was Jim. She didn't know anyone that could help her here, but he was still living in the Juneau area. He would know how to deal with this. She was sure he had been involved in every kind of crazy operation, when he was in Afghanistan. He hadn't spoken much about his time there, but the mental scars screamed at her when they were together.

All she could think about, was what she was never going to be able to tell him. A year ago, he had proposed marriage, or any other long-term relationship she would agree to. She had turned him down. Andrea still had big aspirations for her career, and feared that a husband who was an ex-sniper / special-ops man, could be exploited by her enemies. She knew he had been involved with several CIA ops while serving, and that really scared her. She could only imagine what some opponent might dig up. She had seen enough classified reports, to know a lot of the missions were not always run according to the rules of war. Recently, she had started rethinking her choice and had planned on seeing him after the conference, to see if he was willing to let her reconsider. Andrea realized that she may have waited too long.

"Well obviously, I don't have the knack for timing, like mom," she thought to herself. "Now what am I going to do?" Andrea looked around at a lot of scared people. They all looked shell-shocked, to say the least. Surprisingly, when she looked at Robert Westlake, the scientist, he looked almost calm. Andrea stood and asked out loud. "Is there anyone here, with any medical training?"

No one jumped right up, but Westlake walked over to her. "I know a lot of first aid. Let me look." He quickly examined the wound and helped Andrea rig a pressure bandage, to stop the bleeding. Bobby was unconscious, but breathing regularly. "I think he got lucky, I don't think any arteries, or bones have been hit. Your other man is unconscious and probably has a concussion. Sorry that I can't do more."

He started to move away but Andréa stopped him. "Doctor Maybe you could explain why you don't seem too surprised by all of this?"

He looked at her and gave a little chuckle. "Well, I guess I am not surprised, because this is probably about me." He turned and went back to check up on the other injured men. One of the Russian security guards was up, but the other was still on the floor, but conscious.

Andrea spent the rest of the trip by Bobby and Jamie. The bleeding finally stopped, and Jamie woke up with a bad headache. Peter Ivanovo came over, after his two men were on their feet, and inquired about her men.

"Well, it could be a lot worse," Andrea managed a small smile." It would be nice to know what was going on."

Peter looked around the room. "I think we are going to learn only what these men want us to. Don't you think this must be about you? Not any one of these delegates is as important as you, after all!"

Andrea shook her head. "Well if they think my mother will change her stance on dealing with terrorists, they have another think coming."

Peter looked at her and clasped his hands. “That may not be the best thing to let them know.”

Andrea got on her feet and said “Don’t worry, I already know that! I will not tell them anything.”

Chapter Fifteen - The Mine (In Captivity)

After about an hour, the same man, who was obviously in charge of the gunmen, came back into the room.

"Alright you people listen up, I am only going to say this once. You have been kidnapped and your lives depend on you being good little boys and girls." He waited for a minute before continuing. "Where you are being taken, has no way out. I think that your fine Alaskan Senator will tell you this, when she sees where you are going. If any of you try to be heroes you will be shot on the spot! We don't want to kill any of you. Don't get the idea that we care, one way, or the other, we don't. You behave and we let you all go home alive."

Andrea recognized bullshit, when she heard it. She was just a backwoods Senator, but she had seen and heard her fair share of bullshit. The men had made no effort to conceal their identity and they had to know that shooting a federal officer was bad news, if they were caught. There was no way any of them were leaving alive, unless they did it themselves, or got help from outside. Where is Jim, when I really need him? Andrea thought to herself. I need Jim more than I ever thought I would. If I get out of this, Jim is going to be mine, and to hell with politics.

Andrea calmed down and checked Bobby again. The wound had reopened when he had tried to sit up, during the little speech.

"I guess I am not doing well on the job today, sorry Senator." Bobby had difficulty getting even that much out, between the stabs of pain. Andrea just smiled and kept pressure on the wound.

"We get out of this and you defiantly get a down-tic on your record."

Bobby chuckled. "Yeah, I've noticed what a miserable person you are, and real tough too!" Andrea smiled again.

"Okay. No bad report. If you don't take it easy, you are going to ruin my record." Jamie entered the conversation.

"What record would that be?

"Well I have never lost a gunshot patient before," Andrea said with a little smile. Of course Bobby is my first! Right now I had better keep these people calm, and start seeing where we are going and what we are up against."

Andrea began tour guide duty to calm everyone. " I know we are in Icy Strait and that we just passed Pleasant Island and Point Adolphus, so that means that we are about to pass by Lemesurier Island." One hour later Andrea picked up the tour.

"There is Indian Island, which means that we are about to go through South Indian Pass. We are headed out into the Gulf of Alaska, not good."

Peter looked surprised by that statement. "Why is that a problem?" Andrea thought about any reason not to tell him and then shrugged her shoulders.

"That means we could be headed almost anywhere. This boat has a pretty good range. The further we get from Juneau, the harder it is going to be for anyone to find us."

Peter Ivanovo looked at her and said "Andrea, you have to remember who your mother is. I don't think they are going to stop looking any time soon!" Peter stopped at that, and turned back to his people.

When the boat got out into the Gulf of Alaska, they turned south. Andrea could tell they had just passed Yakobi Island, and that they were on the back side of Chichagof Island. She recognized that when they were passing Lisianski Strait. "I think that we are going into one of the bays on Chichagof Island." Andrea moved closer to a port hole, to watch the progress along the shore so she could see. She couldn't help but think about the time she spent on this island, with her father and his good friend Bill Bates. She had hunted bear and deer here many times. Andrea tried to keep everyone informed, while checking periodically on Bobby's wound. She finally got the bleeding from Bobby's leg controlled, and was able to tie off the bandage. Andrea stepped back from her chosen duties and found her mind wandering. Bobby had been the first agent assigned to her, when her mother had been nominated as the candidate for the Republican Party. Now that, had been a real surprise to a lot of party hacks.

When everyone had found a place on the deck, or in a chair to get comfortable, Andrea was able to relax as well. She had finally drifted into a fitful sleep, when the boat began slowing and obviously preparing to dock. She quickly checked on the others. Bobby and Jamie both were sleeping and most others as well. She noticed that both Russian security men were up, and watching things. It was still dark, but beginning to brighten.

"Do you know where we are?" Andrea glanced to see who had asked. It was the Russian who had been injured in the takeover.

"I can't tell for sure, but it looks a lot like the deep-water dock at the old mine works on Chichagof Island." When the boat pulled up to the pier, Andrea knew she was right.

Andrea watched out the porthole and tried to gather as much information as she could. The deck lights were all on and some other lights on the dock, as well. Though it was light enough now, to not be needed. The gunmen returned and hustled everyone out on the deck. The same spokesman again gave the orders.

"I want everyone to move off the boat and up the dock." Andrea and Peter Ivanovo got Bobby up, and helped him onto the pier. Peter was taken by surprise, when he saw movement on the ground. "Andrea, what the heck, what are those animals?" Andrea could see what he was talking about.

"Oh shit! Those are Alaska Brown Bears. No one is walking out of here; you can't outrun one of them, let alone a dozen."

Andrea was nearly numb, seeing the bears like that. She remembered walking up on a fresh bear kill years ago, with Bill. He had looked closely, and then recommended they move to a new location. The kill had been nearly cut in half and appeared to be one swipe from the bear. The sight of all the bears had brought the memory back in amazing clarity. "They must be baiting them, to keep so many here on the beach!"

Jason (head kidnapper), walked up beside Andrea and Peter. "I see you recognize our special friends. Have you ever seen a bear eat a human?" He said no more, but walked over to a large gunman. "Okay, demo time." Andrea was shocked by the crazed look on the man's face.

The large man and one other, handed their guns to Jason, and walked towards Andrea. She couldn't remember ever being this afraid before. "Keep your hands off me!" The big guy didn't even respond. He just gave her a shove, and grabbed Bobby's arm. The other man pushed Peter away, and grabbed the other arm. With no thought, or hesitation, they threw Bobby off the dock. It was low tide, so it was quite a drop. Andrea could hardly believe what had happened, as the bears converged on him. The largest bear knocked

Bobby down, with one powerful blow. Andrea knew he was probably dead at that point (hopefully). She and the others watched in horror, as the man was torn apart by the large bear. The bear tore off a leg and moved away, to let the rest of the hoard finish dinner. Andrea knew she would remember the big bear. He had very distinct markings, and they were etched in her mind.

Jason faced the stunned captives. "He was going to die anyway, so we just helped him along." Jason actually laughed, as he said that.

"You disgusting animal!" Andrea screamed and went after the guy. A gunman was ready to shoot her, when Peter Ivanovo got between them.

"Do you really want to shoot the daughter of the President of the United States?" The guard lowered his gun.

"I don't care who the bitch is, you better calm her down, or she goes over the side next!" With the help of the others, Peter got Andrea calmed down and they all moved into the mine.

Andrea got to thinking about the entire incident, during the long hike into the mine. "Why did the gunman stop, when Peter interceded?" was the thought that she kept coming back to. It almost seemed like he was willing to take direction from the Russian. She lost track of how far they traveled, but estimated that it had to be at least a mile. Jamie, her one remaining secret service man, continued to look worse during the hike. Finally, they arrived at what appeared to be a side room. They were all shoved in, and the door closed and locked, from outside. Andrea took a quick look at everyone and noticed that the scientist, Rob Westlake was not with them any longer. "Did anyone see what happened to Westlake?"

Amarina Copper, the representative from Australia, spoke out. "He was helping me walk, but when we passed a side tunnel, a guard grabbed him, and pushed me on. That was the last I saw of him."

Andrea realized the woman was limping badly. "What happened to your leg?" Amarina looked down at her offending ankle.

"I tripped and turned it badly, when we were forced up the steep ramp from the boat. If Rob hadn't helped me, I suppose I would have been fed to the bears." Amarina nearly cried at that.

Andrea gave her a hug and then turned to everyone. "Listen, I don't know what is going on, but I do know that we have to stay together and help each other, to remain in control. I guess that since they separated out Rob, he may have been the reason for the abduction from the start. Why don't we all lie down and try to get comfortable? Who knows what will happen next. Almost like her words triggered it, the lights went out. Through the door, they heard a voice.

"On the table, in the middle of the room, is a jerry can of water and some food. Take care; there may not be any more supplies until this is over!" Andrea could hear him walking away. She finally slid to the floor, too scared to say anything. Jim! I need you now, was her last thought as she fell asleep.

The group of victims, was almost used to the silence and solitude of the dark room, when they heard voices outside and had to cover their eyes, when the light came on. The single, hundred-watt bulb, seemed as bright as the sun, after days of no light. Andrea got to her feet, as soon as two men entered, with weapons at the ready. The good news was the new jerry can of water and some bags of food, they dropped on the table, in the center of the room.

The man in charge, looked around the room and pointed at Amelia Lawson, the British representative. "Get on your feet bitch, you're coming with us." The gunman had a strange gleam in his eyes, when he said that.

Andrea stepped in front of the man and said "Take me instead; I am a much better hostage, if that is what you need."

The man in charge just shoved her down. "I wish I could take you and beat some of the arrogance out of you, but the boss says no."

Amelia got to her feet, and the gunman, who had carried the food and water, grabbed her arm and dragged her towards the entrance. She had not taken two steps in a couple of days, and her legs were not working well. Amelia stepped on an uneven spot on the tunnel floor and her right ankle folded. Amelia fell to the floor screaming. The gunman started to drag her to her feet, but stopped when he could tell the ankle was broken. He just pushed her back into the room and quickly grabbed Amarina. He pulled her to her feet and pushed her out the door.

The man holding the weapon chuckled, when he said “Bitch, you have no idea how lucky you are, to have broken your leg. It beats the hell out of feeding the bears.” On that note, he turned and closed the door as he left. The light went out and everything went dark again. Andrea carefully crawled over to Amelia, and did what she could for her ankle.

The strange part of the entire incident, was the lack of any response from the others in the room. Andrea worried that the people would get so despondent, that they would just shut down and die. May times people survived being adrift after a sinking, to just give up and die, hours before being rescued. She started trying to cheer them up, any way she could.

Chapter Seventeen - WEIRD WILLY

(Day of the kidnapping.)

Weird Willy was doing a little maintenance on his sixty-foot fishing boat. He was moored in Auke Bay. Willy had watched the departure of the Senator and all of the visiting dignitaries with the fisheries conference. Being a fisherman, he was quite interested in what the politicians were going to screw up this time. Seeing the pretty Senator had reminded Willy of his recent conversation with Jim. He had asked Willy to keep his eyes and ears open, for anything strange going on. Willy was doing just that, when he had gotten a call from his fishing buddy. Jerry Burns was in real trouble and needed some help. He was out at St. James Bay, hiding from his ex-wife, the police, and a bunch of money-grubbing lawyers. He was behind on his alimony, and his ex was going to take his boat, if she could get her hands on it.

Jerry was planning on staying out, till he had enough fish to cover the back alimony, but had lost his hydraulics. This meant he could not pull his long-line. No long-line, no fish. He knew that if he came into port, the boat would be seized, so he had called Willy. The plan was to take him a replacement seal and some hydraulic fluid, to get him back fishing. Willy was going to motor out to Boat Harbor, and then hike the parts over the hill to Jerry in St. James Bay. That way, no one could connect the two, if someone happened to see them together. Besides, Willy liked feeling involved with some cloak and dagger stuff.

Willy got under way and headed out. His engine was running a little hot again and he remembered that he needed to get Jim to clean out his through hull fitting, for his cool water intake. He had been putting this off for quite a while, but nothing new about that. He was always putting off needed maintenance. Willy's preventive maintenance plan (as Jim called it) was 'when it don't work, change it. Thinking about Jim reminded him about the conversation again. Jim had mentioned seeing a very fast fifty-foot boat, a few weeks ago and Willy had done some detective work and found out about it. He had forgotten to tell Jim that, when they spoke two days ago. "Well, always another day."

It took an hour to run into Boat Harbor (time to replace those injectors) the engine just was not running well, but it got you there. Willy moored as close to shore and the trailhead that led to St. James bay as he could get. Jerry was going to owe him a lot of favors for this one.

The hike was more difficult, packing a five gallon jug of hydraulic fluid, but he made it. When he crested the hill and could look down into St. James, he was surprised to see the Alaska Breeze moored in the bay. The real surprise was that the boat that Jim had asked him about was rafted up to it. The boat looked like a well-maintained fishing vessel, but something was different about the boat, below the water line. Willy could see the boat real well from his vantage point, and he knew that it was no regular fishing boat sitting down there.

Jerry was not in the bay yet, so Willy decided to take a break and watch what was going on. He could help Jim and Jerry today, without getting off his ass. About fifteen minutes after sitting down, he saw a bunch of movement on the two boats. Men seemed to come out of nowhere and quickly cast off lines. The strange boat got under way, then seemed to accelerate at a very high speed. The hull seemed to begin slowly rising out of the water, much further than just getting up on step.

Willy wished he had brought his binoculars with him. The last he saw of the boat, he estimated it had to be going forty knots, if it was moving at all. That was one fast boat. He was also surprised at how many men had been on board. He had seen at least seven men. The one in command, was easy to spot, even from a distance. He had been white-haired and very much in command.

As Willy continued to observe the Alaska Breeze, he was again surprised to see the Northern Blast motor into the Bay. This was the excursion boat that he had watched leaving Auke Bay in the morning with the fisheries people aboard. The two boats rafted up and soon he could see all of the folks on the Blast, transfer over to the Breeze. Both boats were operated by the same tour company, so maybe the Blast was having some issues? As soon as everyone was transferred, the Blast headed out of St. James.

It wasn't long, until it appeared that a party was going on down there. He could hear soft background music and a lot of garbled conversation. This was going to be a long wait. He knew Jerry would not come in until the other boat had sailed.

Willy was beginning to get hungry and thinking about hiking back to his boat, when he heard a shot. He could see several men moving on the upper decks of the Breeze. They all appeared to be carrying weapons of some sort. There was quite a lot of shouting and then some more gun-fire. Soon after the action ended, the Alaska Breeze got under way. Willy could see none of the passengers, and only a couple of the gunmen on deck. As soon as they were out of sight, Willy took the parts down to the spot he knew Jerry would look, and left them, with a note explaining that he had to beat feet back to Juneau. Willy knew Jim would want to hear about this. He was very close friends with the Senator, and besides the boat he had asked questions about, was involved.

Willy made good time on the return trip, but when he tried to start the boat, he got nothing. Willy realized he had left his electronics on all day and his batteries were flat. He worked and tried everything he could think of, but was unable to start the thing. When he tried the auxiliary battery, it was just as dead. He tried his hand-held radio and was not surprised to find it dead as the engine. His electrical problems had finally got the best of him. Next time, he decided he better listen to Jim, when he recommended replacing a part. The only plan he could think of, was to hike back over the hill and wait for his buddy to show up.

Willy grabbed some easily-carried supplies, a tarp, and some water he had in bottles, and headed out. When he got back over, he settled down for an unknown wait. Jerry finally motored in, about three in the morning. Willy was half-asleep, but he heard the boat and turned on his flashlight. Jerry dropped anchor and paddled over in his skiff. "Hey Willy I didn't expect you to be waiting." Jerry threw him a beer, as he pulled up on shore. Willy caught the beer and thought, "At least his priorities are right."

"Jerry, I don't have time to explain, but I have real trouble and my boat won't start. I need you to run around to the other side and give me a jump. Every battery on my boat is dead as a door nail."

Jerry thought for a minute. "Look Willy, I still don't want to get you linked to me, so what say I pull out my extra, and you and I hump it to your boat? It will be faster.

"Sure, that will work, but give me your best. I don't think my electrical system is charging at all."

It took about an hour and six beers, to make the trip with the heavy battery, but it was finally installed. Jerry headed back and Willy headed for home.

As he got close to the entrance to Auke Bay, he was surprised to see Coast Guard boats and police boats, all over the place. The entrance waterway was totally blocked with debris and some smoke was still rising from several places throughout the bay. He couldn't even get close enough to find out what happened. Tee Harbor looked like his best choice for temporary moorage. He gave Jim a call on the VHF radio. "Jim, this is Willy, I just tried to come into Auke Bay and something weird has happened. I need you to meet me in Tee Harbor ASAP."

Jim would appreciate his military lingo. "I have some information for you that can't wait, over."

"Look I am tied up right now, give me an idea of what is going on, over." Jim was mystified.

"No, I need to tell you face-to-face, and nothing is more important than this. I will tell you that it involves that boat you asked me about the other day, and a certain Senator! But no more on this radio, out."

Jim wasn't sure he could deal with this distraction. He had been listening to his radio, waiting for any word from Vlad, or Willy when he had heard the explosion in Auke Bay. He had left the dock just about a half-hour before, and was just setting sail, when the explosion came. Jim had his radio tuned to a local station and was not surprised to hear that there had been an explosion in Auke Bay, just a few minutes before, but was shocked when he heard them say that it had been the Northern Blast that had blown up.

The announcer went on to say there appeared to be no survivors, but that no names of crew, or passengers were being released at this time. Jim had not felt so empty since losing a close friend in combat.

He had turned around, but was turned away as soon as he got close to the bay. He decided that Tee Harbor, would be his closest safe berth. He hitched a ride to town, as soon as he was tied up.

He had been trying to get clarification on who was aboard the Northern Blast, but the police and Coast Guard would not give out any information. He had even tried to call the White House, with no results. Andrea had given him a special number a year ago, that should have gotten him past the mass of red tape, but not now.

The news media was not getting any more information than him and he had not been able to reach Vladimir either. After considering everything, he decided to deal with the thing he could control right now. He left a note for Vladimir and headed out. He grabbed his .45, made sure it was loaded, then quickly cast off, and got the engine going. When he was safely away, and the engine wasn't stone-cold, he gave the boat full-throttle. He had never before displayed the full speed capabilities, but Willy was not an alarmist. If he said it was important, it was important. Jim was quite certain it would all end up tying together with Brenner, Andrea, and the threat Vladimir was working on

Willy was standing on the dock, as Jim steered in. "Hey Jim, I didn't know your boat could go that fast!"

"Willy I don't have time for questions right now, what do you have for me?" "The wreck in Auke Bay, was the Northern Blast, and Andrea was aboard that boat!"

"No Jim, she wasn't. That's what I need to tell you!"

Willy was talking fast. He could see that Jim was in no mood to gab. "I was in St. James Bay, waiting to meet up with Jerry, when I saw some strange things happen, and one was the passengers from the Northern Blast were moved on to the Alaska Queen."

"Okay Willy, you have my attention now."

Jim was so keyed up, he struggled to absorb what the man was saying. After a couple of minutes, the facts sunk in. Jim felt a great weight, lifted off his shoulders. Now he began thinking like a soldier again. "Willy, take your time and tell me the entire story right from the start! Don't leave out a thing!" After he had heard the entire tale, he made some quick decisions. Jim had Willy head out to sea, to try and locate the two boats in question, while he headed back to town.

Jim decided to leave his boat at DuPont Point, as that seemed to give him better access to open water, when he knew where to head.

He took the skiff and headed for Juneau. The skiff was faster anyway.

When he came in towards the dock, Vlad was waiting for him. “Jim, I don’t know where to start. I should have let you tell Andrea about the threat. If you want to shoot me, here I am!”

“Well, the good news is, I don’t need to shoot you; I need the bullet for Brenner.”

Vlad was taken aback by this; Jim was way too calm. He had to have heard about the explosion. “Jim did you hear about the...” He got no farther. “Vlad! She wasn’t on board! No one was; well at least any of the passengers.”

“Weird Willy saw them transferred to another boat, out in St. James Bay, yesterday.”

Vlad could feel the extreme tension drain from his body. “Wow! That is good news, but where are they now?” Vlad was doing a little quick analysis, as he spoke.

Jim answered, “I don’t know where they are, but I am sure they are being held by that slime Brenner, and rest assured, I know what I am going to do about it.”

Jim got angrier as he talked. It was time to end Brenner permanently.

Vladimir thought hard, before he spoke. “There is more going on, than even I had any idea about. We need to figure out what Brenner’s endgame is, and what his target is. I can’t believe this was about disrupting a fisheries conference, and I don’t think Andrea was the target either. It would have been much easier to take her out, than to blow up an entire boat and twenty people.”

Jim saw where Vlad was going and said. “You think it has something to do with this scientist, and his discovery, don’t you? What haven’t you told me about this guy? I know you too well, you never give everything you know to anyone, even me.”

Vlad grimaced, but decided to come clean. “I have not been entirely up-front with you, but Robert Westlake is probably the most important person alive today. His new technology is going to change the oil industry, and possibly other mining like my gold mining, here in Juneau.”

Vlad started the tale “I found out about his research several years ago, through the CIA. They were watching him and the corporation he was working for. He quit that company and moved into private research." Vlad paused, and then continued. "I have always been interested in finding a better way to extract gold from low-yield ore and his chemical process, seemed to be a possible way to achieve that."

"I have been getting gold out of the BJ for years, by finding hidden pockets the original operators had missed, but those are depleted now. The remaining ore, is very low-yield and requires the use of large quantities of mercury, or other caustic chemicals to separate the gold. You can guess how environmentally unsound that process is. I will not do it. I am not some environmental wacko, but I have my limits." Vlad took a deep breath. He had never told anyone before, about the extent of his mining operation, or how much he had extracted.

"Jim, I am going to tell you something no one knows! I have become quite wealthy over the last several years. I broke into a rich vein of gold a few years ago, and just before the last deployment to Afghanistan, I cashed in. At the crazy gold prices now, I banked about twenty million dollars, in a Swiss account. You could get me in a lot of trouble with the IRS, if you wanted to. I paid my taxes, but not exactly everything, was properly reported. It helps to be involved with the CIA, when you need to move a little cash around the world."

"Vlad, that is all great for you, but how does this change what is going on now?" Jim was a little angry that Vlad seemed to be going down these strange trails.

"The reason I brought this up, is that I invested a big portion of that money in Westlake's research!"

"About five years ago, when he left the Petroleum Exploration and Development Corporation International (PEDEI), he needed funds to continue his research. I invested, because of the possible ties for gold mining. Westlake doesn't know me from Adam, but I sure know him. He is a real good man, in a world of sharks. He has no idea how many people and governments know about his findings. I told you that some Russians are in the group with Andrea; well two of them are ex-KGB operatives, here supposedly, to protect the science representative from the government. In reality, they are here to gain control of the research, and our government is just as interested. So this whole thing, is all about this guy and his research!"

Jim was a bit stunned by the revelation. “What the hell is it anyway?” Jim couldn’t imagine what could trigger this thing.

The Alaska Queen

The numbness was difficult to shake off, as Jim woke the day after he found out Andrea was not blown up on the Alaska Breeze. He had hardly slept, trying to think of a way to find her. Vlad had discussed it with Weird Willy, and was sure as Jim himself, that the boat had headed out towards the main channel. That meant a million inlets and coves, on a dozen different islands could be the hiding place or worse. The boat could have kept going. The good news was, that the range of the day excursion boat, would not allow an extended cruise, without fuel and supplies.

Vlad was at home, contacting his CIA sources, but not giving up the Intel that the people were alive. The last thing Jim, or Vlad wanted, was the federal government, especially the President, mucking up the water. Jim had no doubt, that Brenner would kill the hostages, if he felt any pressure what-so-ever, from outside. He had to think his operation was going perfect. The most important thing to do now, was to continue collecting information, and to find Brenner's men in Juneau. That was the only way to get a lead on Andrea's location.

Jim puttered around the boat, and checked his weapons about six times, before finally deciding to do something, before he went crazy. Throughout his life, from childhood in Wallace, to the Afghan mountains, he always thought better in a high place. He grabbed a powerful spotting scope, a day pack with water, and a couple of sandwiches, and headed for shore. Jim only took his trusted .45, since he was not planning on shooting anyone right away. He drove to the trailhead that took him to the top of Blueberry Hill, on Douglas Island. He grabbed his stuff and headed up the hill. By the time he reached the top (military crest), the sun was rising, and it was going to be a rare sunny day in Southeast Alaska. Jim set up his scope and swept the waterfront and Gastineau Channel. The view gave him an unobstructed view of Juneau, and the docks where the tour ships tie up. There were four of the crazy, floating hotels in port. That equated to an additional 12,000 people walking the streets of Juneau. "A good time to stay out of the downtown area," he thought to himself.

Jim swept the ships with his scope. He was able to read the name of the Alaska Queen. Lorrie popped into his mind. He had spoken to her last night, just long enough to explain that something had come up, and that he could not see her again, before she sailed. Almost on cue, he could see deck crewmen prepare to cast off. Not too long ago, that would have required a couple of large tugs to move the ship out into the channel, but now, with navigation aids and powerful bow thrusters, the ships could do it themselves. There were no large tugboats in Juneau any more, with the exception of a couple of converted tugs that someone lived on.

Jim continued to watch the ship and scanned the mountainside above Juneau. He could see several of the old mine portals, that were part of the BJ. What a surprise to find out that Vladimir controlled the mine legally. He had known him for such a long time and still was not sure he knew him at all. Jim let his mind wander, as he had always done. He remembered being on a high point, thinking about life, from childhood on. As a sniper, he was rare, in that he loved the time spent waiting for a target, or counting vehicles. This pleasure started when he was young. He would climb the hills around Wallace, and spend hours watching life go on below him. He would do the same as now; counting the mine portals he could see, and wonder what the little people were thinking and doing. It always made him feel safe and special, to be up high like this.

Movement at dockside, brought his wandering mind back to the present. The Alaska Queen was pulling away from the dock. Jim realized that he should have called Lorrie at least one more time, to break off the relationship. He could not see her now that he was mentally committed to Andrea, at least until she was safe. He had checked with her, to see how the altercation with the crewmember was proceeding. He hadn't been able to speak to Joe, the piano man, but had received a note, mentioning the run-in he had with the same crewmember. Well, that would have to wait until the next trip to Juneau. Jim watched the cruise ship make the turn into the channel and begin coming up to speed. It was a bit awe-inspiring, to watch the huge ship move. Being so high up, tended to confuse the eye and the mind's ability to grasp the size, until you saw men on the deck. Then, the size was in your face. It didn't take long for the ship to make good time, out of the Juneau docking facility.

Jim returned his attention to the mine portals above Juneau. They would make good observation points, for someone trying to monitor the streets and docks. That was a good thing to know. He needed to speak to Vlad, about how to gain quick access to those portals. If he could move into them, from underground, he would be totally invisible to outside activity. Jim thought to himself, "I wonder how extensive the tunnels are, and what kind of shape they are in."

He was thinking in tactical terms, like he was planning an assault on downtown Juneau. "Maybe that wasn't too far-fetched," he thought. Brenner had more planned, than had happened so far, because it didn't make sense yet. As much as Jim hated Brenner, he never saw him do something, that didn't make some kind of convoluted sense. Even when he had his men start shooting innocent civilians in Afghanistan, there was simple sense, in gaining informants and eliminating support for the terrorists. Not to be confused with any kind of ethical, or moral sense though!

Jim's focus was pulled back to the ship. He had caught a funny movement, out of the corner of his eye. The ship was veering towards the old mine tailings dump, of the Treadwell Mine on Douglas Island. He focused the scope on the ship and could tell that the bow thrusters were pushing the ship toward the shore. Everything seemed to happen in slow motion from his vantage point. The bow turned, until it impacted on the mine tailings leading down to the water. The good news was, that the bank was quite soft, relatively speaking, with no large rocks capable of penetrating the hull. The bad news came, as Jim could see that the main screws continued to drive the ship aground. It was several minutes before the turbulence behind the ship subsided. It had taken the crew an overly long time to react to the grounding. Just to make things worse, the ships stern continued to moving towards the opposite shore. Jim couldn't hear anything from this distance, but had no doubt that the stern was just as grounded as the bow. The ship was listing towards the starboard side, at a fairly steep angle. The memory of the overheard conversation Lorrie had mentioned, had a lot more meaning now. Jim was as certain as he could be. Brenner had struck again. He took some quick photos of the portals and the ship, and headed back down the hill.

As Jim made his way down, off Blue Berry Hill, he did some thinking. There is no way the ship was getting out of this fix, without an ocean tug, or maybe two. This was even if the bow thrusters were working correctly. Jim knew he needed to find out where the nearest tugs were. He headed for Vlad's house, as soon as he made it to his rig. Vlad could get the information on tugs and other possible assistance for the Alaska Queen. Things had to be quite chaotic on board, with the shipload of tourists. Jim was thankful, that getting them off and to shore, would be someone else's problem. But, the real issue, was that the ship had the only deep-water access into Juneau blocked, just when Auke Bay was blocked by the boat that had exploded in the harbor. That could be cleared quickly, but the fire from the ship, had destroyed the docking facilities for the Alaska ferry system. Juneau was as cut off from the outside, as possible. He knew that the communications and the airport, had to be targets of Brenner as well. It just made sense. Finding out how to access those BJ mine portals, had just become a priority. Jim felt the old adrenalin rush through his body, as these thoughts formed. This was war on his home turf. He knew this time, either he died or, hopefully, Brenner died, along with all of his psychotic crew.

Chapter Eighteen - ABOARD THE ALASKA QUEEN

Joe (Piano Man) Spanos, had just left his room and headed for the lounge, for his first shift, when the ship made a sudden, hard turn. That was crazy, since the ship never made any hard movements. Joe had been on cruise ships for years and never experienced this kind of turn. He hurried on deck, to see what was up. Almost before he had started moving, the motion of the ship changed. It felt like it had gone aground, but Joe had not heard any loud noises at all. The strangest part, was that Joe could tell that the main engines were still running. The engine noise continued for several minutes, but finally, just as he got up on deck, the engines went silent.

Joe was startled to see land in front, and when he turned towards the stern, he realized that the land was right there as well. In all of his years aboard cruise ships, he had finally gone aground. Joe was trying to decide what to do, when finally, alarms started going off and the crew was scrambling everywhere. He moved to his assigned station, for emergencies. Since he was just entertainment, he did not have an assigned emergency post, but went to find the head of his department.

The ship did list to starboard quite badly, but nothing seemed in imminent danger. Joe finally found the head purser, and was directed to assist with the safe movement of passengers. Very little information was made available to the crew, or passengers, as to what had happened to the ship. The Captain announced that the ship was safe, but on the ground. All passengers would be taken off, until the ship could be refloated. The good news was, that only a few passengers had been injured and everyone was being taken care of. Most passengers were safe and not in danger. Twenty minutes after running aground, the Captain urged all passengers to return to their rooms, until plans were made for transfer to shore. Joe, along with the rest of the entertainment staff, was given lists of passengers and room numbers, to assist the purser in orderly movement off the ship. Joe ended up working with Lorrie. They went to each room and insured that all the people were present and safe. Joe and Lorrie explained the plan and what they knew so far, about the schedule for departure. It was several hours before Joe was told to move his passengers up to disembark.

Not surprisingly, one female passenger had to use the restroom, just when everyone was ready. Joe took the eleven other passengers, and left Lorrie with the lone female, to follow.

After Joe got his eleven off the ship, onto a shore-bound shuttle boat, he went looking for Lorrie. He found the missing female passenger first.

"Where is Lorrie, the crew member that was with you?" Joe was a bit surprised.

"She pointed me towards you, then left. She saw someone that she said she needed to watch." The passenger looked a little abandoned. Joe led her to the shuttle boat, then went looking for Lorrie. All he could think of, was that she was looking for the crew member, whom she had the run in with. He moved in the direction the passenger had last seen her.

Joe was about to give up, when he reached the port rail. He glanced down and saw Lorrie struggling with the engineer Steven. He was the same guy who had threatened him earlier. He yelled, but got no results. Steven was holding her, as a fast boat approached the ship. Joe didn't know what to do, but headed for the closest stair case down. He was several decks higher than the two, but he arrived at the ramp, just in time to watch a fast launch leave the ship. The surprise was, that it was not headed to shore, but out Gastineau Channel. Joe hurried back to the starboard side of the ship. He needed to get ashore and find Jim Walters. Lorrie had placed a lot of trust in the man. Hopefully, he would know what to do.

Lorrie didn't know what to do, scream, or cry, so she did both.

The engineer just laughed at her. "Scream all you want bitch, no one here cares. You're mine now, and you will do what I want. The only way off this boat is with me, so get used to it." He smirked at her, and lewdly ran his hand down the front of her body. Lorrie went rigid with fear. He acted not sexually, but more like he was stroking a piece of livestock. Steven grabbed her by the hair and drug her below. He pushed her into a compartment. Lorrie heard the door lock behind him. "Don't worry sweet meat, I will be back soon," was his parting shot. Lorrie curled up in a ball in a corner and cried, till no more tears remained.

Steven chuckled and moved back on deck. He went to the helm to get an update.

"Steven! I think you have lost your mind. No one but you, was supposed to come off that ship! Brenner is going to cut your balls off and feed them to you, and then feed you to the bears."

Steven looked at the man at the helm. "When I want your opinion on anything jerkoff, I will cut it out with a knife." He was playing with his knife, as he said this. The knife was his favorite weapon. He missed Afghanistan, since he had been able to get away with almost anything, in that backward world. His favorite thing was to rape a woman and knife her, as he came. This thought excited him, because that was his plan for the bitch below decks. He wanted to shove the knife in and feel her life leave, just not too fast. He wanted her to last a long time. He would show her what happens to a woman, who doesn't know her place. At least in Afghanistan, the women knew better.

The helmsman turned back to steering the boat. He was well aware of what this crazy man was capable of. Again, he wondered why he hadn't stopped working for Brenner a long time ago. "Too late now to change anything," he thought to himself. Better to let Brenner deal with Steven, when they got to the mine. The trip was going to take a good five hours. Too bad he hadn't been allowed to use the Hydrofoil for this trip. It would have been much faster. Even the off-shore play toy, would have been faster, but since it now had a huge bomb on board, that wouldn't be a good choice. He thought about the fact that he was now going to be a bigger killer of Americans than McVey was; since he planted the boat with the bomb. Not a comforting thought.

Steven was on deck, when they finally pulled up to the dock at the mine. No other boat was present, and the helicopter was also gone. Just as well he though, I can explain things to Brenner later, when I have the time to take care of the bitch. Steven was quite happy. As soon as the boat was tied up, Steven grabbed the Lorrie, and moved her up into the mine. Lorrie had gotten her emotions under control. She had already lost all hope, and was resigned to death. Steven had spent quite a lot of time with her, during the boat ride. The surprising thing had been, that he had spent most of the time telling her what he was going to do, instead of doing the things he was threatening. She had finally decided that this was worse. She had no doubt that he would get to the real bad stuff.

The first thing he had done, was to strip her and then held her down with his knife, as he described how it felt to slide the knife into the body of his lover. He even described how good the orgasm was, each time he did it. Lorrie again, had been surprised that he had left her on the floor naked, but not damaged. His parting comment had been. "Enjoy your remaining moments on this earth, bitch." As they moved off the boat, towards what looked like a concrete cave, Lorrie saw several large bears on the beach. They seemed to be fighting over some carcasses. One of them appeared to be human. Steven grabbed her arm and pushed her towards the edge of the dock.

"Hey baby, this is where I will drop the remains, when I am done with you."

Lorrie could only fight back the tears that she knew would only make this crazy guy happy. After allowing, or forcing her to watch the bears for a minute, he grabbed her hair again and drug her towards the mine tunnel. At the entry, there were several more men waiting for them. Steven gave her a shove towards the waiting men.

"Hey dick-heads! Take her down with the rest of the visitors. Just remember she's mine!"

Everett, one of the men at the entry, looked at Steven. "First off, I am not your bitch, so take her down yourself and secondly, what the hell is she doing here?"

Steven looked like he was about to explode. "Listen Everett, it is none of your business why she's here, and you will personally take her down, or you will never leave this island alive!" He had his knife in one hand and a .45 semi-auto in the other. Both were pointed at the man. Things were tense, but finally Everett grabbed the woman and turned to the tunnel.

As he left, he commented. "This is not over Steven; I think Brenner will have something to say, when he gets here. He should be back from Sitka, this evening any time. Better work on your story." One other mercenary went down the tunnel with Everett and the new captive.

Everett let Lorrie walk unassisted, until the tunnel grew dark, as they moved further into the mine. "I don't know what you did to get Steven's interest, but I have to tell you, it will not end well for you." He didn't sound like it would matter, one way or the other, too him.

Lorrie realized that the slight hope she had, when the altercation began, was gone. She was still on her own. "Where are we anyway?" she asked. Everett considered, before he answered.

"Since you will never leave the island, we are on Chichagof Island. About eighty miles out of Sitka, Alaska, whatever good that will do you." Light levels were getting quite low, when Lorrie saw more light ahead of them. There was a room off the side of the tunnel that had light coming through to them. Everett stopped her at the door and the other guy grabbed her arm. Everett entered the room and came out with mine helmets and lights, for himself and his partner. They quickly donned them, and then pushed her ahead of them. "Let's get going. It is a long walk."

Lorrie felt a little like they were walking down to hell.

The walkway had a significant slope, going down the tunnel. Lorrie had a hard time keeping up, but managed. She tried several times, to get the men to talk, but got no results. Nothing more was said, even between the two men, until they had been hiking for almost a half-hour more.

Finally Everett spoke. "I sure wish we had some kind of tram, or a four-wheeler, to move up and down this drift."

The other guy chuckled. "Should have thought of that before you pissed off psycho-man."

"Ya! You have a point there. I just hope Brenner finally does something about him. He was a real problem on the last Afghanistan operation, when he continuously had to have his way with every female he found."

"That sick fuck was never happy with simply raping, or killing them, he had to take hours to do it. Brenner finally had to sneak him out of theater, or he would have been put before a tribunal. Just don't ever let him get too close with that knife of his. He would cut his own mother's throat! Of course that's assuming he hasn't already done that." Everett stopped before another door that was locked. "Well this is the end of the line bitch." He opened the door and switched on a light. "Everyone, move away from the door," he shouted. He then stuck his assault rifle into the room first. "I have a new guest for your entertainment." The other man pushed Lorrie in and slammed the door after her. The lights went out immediately after.

Andrea spoke out. "Just stay still for a minute, until we are all in our places, then we can talk you to a safe corner. My name is Andrea Warren. The rest of the people here are all from the fisheries conference that was just starting in Juneau. What is your name and how did you get here?"

Lorrie stayed with her back against the door, took a deep breath and spoke. "You know that everyone thinks you're all dead!"

Andrea was stunned to hear that. "Why do they think that?"

Lorrie continued, "Well, the day you were taken, the boat you left Juneau on, blew up coming into Auke Bay, all on board were killed. It was a huge explosion that broke windows all the way to downtown Juneau." Lorrie stopped for a moment, then continued. "I would love to continue this discussion, but I am about to fall down. This has not been a good day so far for me!"

Andrea actually laughed at that. "As you can imagine, the last few days haven't been so good for us either." That was the understatement of her political career.

With careful directions, and some minor stepped on hands and toes, Lorrie was finally seated and given a drink of water. "Enjoy that, it may be our last water. Each time they bring some down, they tell us no more. We have been rationing it, as best we can." Andrea then introduced the whole group to Lorrie.

Lorrie said hello, then described how she had ended up here with them.

Andrea was startled to hear about the grounding of the Alaska Queen. Lorrie had mentioned in her story, that she had been suspicious of the new engineers mate, Steven, but had forgotten, until he grabbed her.

"What made you suspicious of him?" Andrea asked.

"Well, a few days ago I overheard him in a discussion with a passenger and heard them say something about the bow thrusters, and going aground. That is just what happened."

Andrea was taken aback by this. "Where did the ship go aground?" She had a sinking feeling, when she asked.

Lorrie answered "Right by Douglas Island, where the old mine tailings run into the strait. The bad news is, the stern is also grounded on the other side." Lorrie stopped there.

Andrea thought for a couple of minutes about the impact of that ship blocking the deep-water approach to Juneau. She put that thought aside and continued. "They have managed to isolate Juneau completely, if Auke Bay is plugged with debris from the Alaska Breeze. The airport is the only way in, or out of Juneau at this time. I wonder what happens next." Andrea stopped to consider. "It seems to me that the airport is a likely target too."

Several minutes later Andrea finally asked another question. "Lorrie, did you tell anyone about this man?" She hoped the answer would be yes!

"Yes, I told two people. Another crew member named Joe, and a friend in Juneau that I met this trip. I planned on speaking to the Captain, but never got it done, as events unfolded too quickly."

Andrea hesitated then asked "Why did you tell someone on shore?"

Lorrie smiled and then stated. "I met about the most wonderful man I have ever met and just trust him completely. Just talking to him, made me feel safer and Joe agreed that he was a good choice to confide in. He also knows Joe. He is ex-military, and I think he is the only hope for all of us."

Andrea got a funny feeling in the pit of her stomach. Maybe I waited too long to tell Jim how I feel, she thought to herself. This had to be Jim, Lorrie was speaking about.

Andrea took a deep breath and asked the question. "Are you very close with the man?"

Lorrie thought about it. "Well, I am serious about him, but unfortunately he is still in love with some other woman, who he sees occasionally. He was quite up front about that, but he is so special, I took the chance anyway. I think Joe saw me forced to leave the boat, so my hope is he will tell Jim about me."

Andrea sat back with that.

Lorrie continued. "I think Jim is going to come here as soon as he can. He is that kind of man." Lorrie hesitated. "The only thing is, I hope he is still in town. Just before the grounding, he told me he had an emergency with this other friend of his, and that he would be out of town for a while."

Andrea felt like a great weight had lifted off her shoulders at that comment. "The good news is, I am that other friend, and so if he is out of town, you're right. He is coming here. That's the best news I have had in a long time!"

Peter Ivanovo couldn't hold back any longer. "I think it is great that you both know the same man, but what makes you both think he can help us?"

Andrea considered her response carefully. She knew through her mother, more about Jim than he even suspected that she knew. She thought, "These people need to have hope." "Jim is not an ordinary, ex-military man. He was special operations, for several years and has been involved in a lot of operations in several theaters of war, and some in less-than-friendly countries around the world."

"He has been trained for things just like this hostage crisis. He is an accomplished sniper. I know he can run any kind of boat and has jumped out of more airplanes, than I have flown in. He can save us."

Peter was quiet for a few minutes, then asked "What did you say his last name was?"

Andrea was toying with not telling him, when Lorrie entered the conversation.

"Walters is his last name. He lives on a real nice sailboat, right in downtown Juneau."

Andrea wished for some reason, that she had not shared that information.

Peter took a deep breath. "I have to assume you are speaking of a man that I have heard of, and you are right. He can get this job done. Let's hope he comes sooner than later, before more of us get taken out to feed the bears."

Brenner's Next Move.

Brenner couldn't believe how well everything was going. The idiot scientist, had only required one more bear feeding, to give up all of his research and even let slip, about the ability to help with gold extraction. That little morsel would remain his. He got his men aboard the Hydrofoil and headed out to the chosen location, for the fake call to the Coast Guard. The boat would take quite a bit of time to reach the location, but the helicopter would only take an hour. Brenner had his chopper ready on deck, to fly out before the Coast Guard got close enough to see it. Hard to explain another Coast Guard chopper on deck. Brenner made the fake call himself. He claimed enough people on board, to require the cutter and not just the helicopter. It sounded so good, Brenner almost believed himself.

He had the chopper crew take off, as soon as the call was made. It had enough range to loiter, until the Coast Guard was out of the way. Brenner had his crew dressed in life jackets and survival suits, when the helicopter approached. The crew was updating the boat, as to their expected time of arrival, so everything looked well on deck, except no damage was visible to the boat. The bow, was his best shot? Benson had taken down helicopters with the stinger in three different countries, so this was easy. As the helicopter approached, Benson stepped out of cover, and before anyone could react, he fired. The flight crew never even saw the missile coming. Benson had waited until the open door was not in his line of sight. The missile impacted right at the base of the rotor and the craft was a ball of flame, before it hit the water. No radio message went out. Brenner called his chopper and sent them on their way.

The pilot, in the fake Coast Guard chopper, was ex-Coast Guard, who had served in southeast Alaska, in the past. He knew the proper radio protocol and approach procedures. He contacted the cutter, as soon as he was in the flight path of the downed chopper. He reported that they had picked up a seriously injured victim, but needed to put him on board the cutter, as the helicopter was overheating, and needed to be lightened. As they got close to the cutter, the pilot messed with his engine, to simulate problems and reinforced his need to be quick. He had his man lower the basket with the 'victim' as he approached.

The boat crew was giving him guidance, when the basket was cut loose, and the helicopter sheared off. The pilot dropped the chopper down to the water, and went away as fast as he could. When the basket impacted the boat, there was a huge explosion. The boat was gone from the surface, faster than the helicopter could turn and move back, to check for survivors. Only one life vest was seen. The pilot hovered over the spot, while his men put enough bullets into the body, to sink the vest and all. The entire operation had taken two hours. The Coast Guard was out of the picture.

Andrea talks to Brenner

Brenner could hardly contain his excitement, at how the operation was going. His crew had returned from sinking the cutter, soon after he had docked at the mine pier. He wanted to gloat, so he sent a couple of men down to get the Senator. She would have to do. He wanted to make sure her last few days on Earth, would not be comfortable days.

Andrea was talking to the hostages, trying to keep their spirits up, which was very hard to do in the dark. Not being able to see faces, and get feedback, made it difficult to know if she was reaching them. Andrea could hear the fear in their voices and knew she was losing the battle. The only other strong one was Lorrie. Andrea knew that Lorrie and she would go down together, fighting all the way to the end. Andrea's thoughts were interrupted, when the door opened and two armed-men walked in and grabbed her arm. They pulled her to her feet, and dragged her towards the door. She tried to fight them, but the biggest man hit the side of her head with the stock of his rifle. Andrea nearly fell and was only held up by the gunmen.

The man that hit her, almost laughed when he said, "Listen bitch, Brenner wants to speak to you. Give me any more trouble and I will just feed you to the bears."

Andrea stumbled along, slowly regaining her equilibrium. When she felt in control again, she asked "And just who in the hell is Brenner?" Andrea knew she should recognize the name, but the only thing she could remember about the name, was an off-hand comment from Jim, a few months ago, about his time in Afghanistan. The big gunman just smiled and said "He is the guy that determines if, and when, you all live, or die." Andrea was sure the only question was when. Jim was the only hope. The walk up the drift, was a long, uneventful hike. Andrea was pulled into a side tunnel that lead into a room, with electric lighting. A tall, fairly-distinguished man, turned, as she walked in. Andrea could see right through the good looks and suave mannerisms. The man was a killer.

"Well, well, if it isn't Miss Andrea Warren, whose mother just happens to be the President of the United States of America." The look he gave Andrea, would have scared her, if she was in downtown Juneau, let alone in a mine cave, a long ways away from anything. She took a breath and spoke.

"Yes it is, and if I were you, I would turn us loose now, and you might live to tell about it."

Brenner just walked closer to her and leaned down in her face. "No miss Warren, I'm going to tell you how it's going to be. Your self-righteous mother, who thinks her crap doesn't stink, will rue the day, if she crosses me."

Andrea asked, "Just what do you think you are going to get my mother to do for you?"

Brenner was a bit taken back, by the woman's gall and fortitude.

"Well for starters, she is going to give me one billion dollars to keep me from killing you, and blowing up everyone in Juneau."

Andrea nearly folded, when he mentioned the bomb plans. She was well aware of her mother's policy about dealing with terrorists. It didn't happen. She closed her eyes for a moment, to gather her thoughts, and again confronted the man. "Brenner, you cannot be serious, you are out of your frigging mind. My mother will not deal with you."

Again, Brenner is amazed with the poise of the woman. "How is that Miss Warren?" Brenner paused, then continued "Let me warn you, that my good manners only go so far. So be careful what you say to me."

Andrea knew she was pressing her luck, but what the hell. The man could only kill her one time. "I'll tell you why, my mother has more balls than you will ever have."

Brenner had reached the end of his patience with that comment, and Andrea knew it. The surprise was, he seemed to relax, instead of exploding in violence.

She pressed her luck further. "I have seen a man with balls and you ain't it."

Brenner actually chuckled at that. "I suppose you're talking about your big hero, Jim Walters? Well you can forget that, because he will be dead very soon." Brenner looked thoughtful, before continuing. "I might bring him here, and feed him to the bears, and let you watch. After all, I have been trying to kill him for the last ten years."

Andrea was stunned by that. She had to take a breath, to calm her nerves. "Well you dumb bastard that ought to tell you something about how smart Jim is, and how dumb you are. I guess Jim was right, when he told me that you can't fix stupid."

Brenner began to show anger again. "You don't want to live very long, do you? I have to say, you are living right on the edge of life."

Andrea said "Hell, I knew that when we were put on the other boat. I am not stupid. You are not going let any of us out of here alive. You can't afford to, can you?"

Benner was quiet, for only a minute. "Well that depends on your mother. If she gives me what I want, you might make it out of here alive."

"Bullshit!" Andrea said. "First off, my mother will not bargain with terrorists, not even for me. She will cry over my grave, but she won't give in for me. You can bet on that."

Brenner just raised the stakes. "How about thirty thousand people in Juneau, and the eight thousand tourists I will kill, unless I get what I want?"

That comment took Andrea by surprise. The man knew how terrorism worked for sure. Andrea regained her composure, and rejoined the word battle. "Like I said, she won't deal with a terrorist, but she will hunt you down and kill you, no matter where you go. That much I know."

Brenner realized he was not enjoying this, as much as he would like. "Miss Warren, I don't think you know who you are dealing with. I kill people, just for fun. I have already grounded the tour ship, blown up the airport, sunk a Coast Guard cutter, and shot down a helicopter." He took a breath, then continued. "Walters may know you are alive, but I doubt it. Remember the tour boat was blown up in Auke Bay. Oh, that's right, you didn't know that." Andrea realized that he didn't know about Lorrie, from the cruise ship.

Brenner couldn't resist slamming Walters. "Your superman Walters, and his scum-sucking CIA partner, Choskey are going to die, along with every other person in Juneau, in less than two days. He has always been a day late and a dollar short, in any contest with me."

Andrea said "Oh, you mean that guy you have been trying to kill for the last ten years."

Brenner slammed his hand on the desk and said, "Lady, I would kill you right now, but I want you to know Walters is dead first."

Andrea stayed quiet, as she could see the anger in his eyes. The man hated Jim and Vlad with a passion. "So Brenner, what other horrible things do you want to tell me about, or are we done here?"

Brenner could finally hear a bit of a quiver in the woman's voice. "You smart-ass bitch. I'll tell you, when I am done here. Let me lay out some facts for you: I have cut the power and shut the water supply off, to Juneau. I have taken out the ferry terminal in Auke Bay, and I have bombs in the governor's mansion. The airport is shut down for an extended period of time." Andrea thought he was done, but he started again.

"Did I mention the government plane that is in pieces all over the runway? It was sent there by your ballsy mother, and now fifteen of her best people, are permanent airport residents. So Andrea, you tell me who is in charge here." Andrea was finally taken out of her game. The man was worse than a serial killer.

Andrea could tell that Brenner was enjoying her discomfort. She gathered her wits and asked "If you wanted ransom for me, why not just grab me? Why take these other people? Or is there another reason for all of this that has nothing to do with me?"

Brenner looked a bit startled by her comment, but responded to the question. "Since none of you will leave here alive, I can tell you a bit. Maybe while you wait for the bomb to go off," Brenner hesitated for effect. "Did I mention the large bomb, planted half way down the drift?" Brenner actually laughed out loud at his statement.

Andrea decided to press her luck one more time. "Since you are in a talkative mood, tell me what you have done with Rob Westlake and Amarina Copper. I think Rob was your target from the start."

Brenner was caught unprepared for that question. "What makes you think that?"

Andrea pushed on. "Well Brenner, I am not stupid. He is the only hostage that from day one, has been held separate from the rest of us. I think you took us for a diversion."

Brenner thought about it, then answered. "Well, you are partly right Westlake was the target."

Brenner poured himself a drink, and took a long swig, before going on. "Westlake is in the room to your rear. Unfortunately, your friend, Amarina I think you said, was fed to the bears, to make

Westlake cooperate. I have to say, the bears worked better than any torture I have ever used in the past. You and your boyfriend only make the entire thing that much better. I am getting paid to kill, something I will enjoy, and get the bonus of sticking it to the President. That alone, is worth the entire operation. I just flat-out hate your mother."

Andrea wondered why the man felt so strongly about the President. "What did my mother ever do to you?"

Brenner was quite animated, when he answered. "Well, when she was secretary of defense, she dropped the hammer on my CIA career, and tried to put me in Leavenworth, for the rest of my life. Of course, she had a lot of help from that asshole Choskey, and your lover-boy, Walters."

Andrea remembered something about the incident, now that he had reminded her. Her mother had been the Secretary of Defense, just before running for president. She couldn't resist, so she asked "How did you get out of that?"

Brenner smiled at the memory. "Well, it seemed that the head prosecutor, liked young men, and he did not want others to know that nasty fact."

Andrea primed the pump, "And you black-mailed him into throwing the case."

Brenner said "I don't think it was the black-mail threat, as much as pointing out to him, that he might commit suicide in the very near future that changed his mind."

"Brenner, you are a real peace of work. At least I know your run of murder and killing, will soon end. Jim is going to make sure that, as you put it, you will commit suicide, in the very near future."

Brenner had as much of this, as he could take. He stood up and opened the door to the room, where his men were. He told the two to take her back to the cell. As the men led her out, he said "Say goodbye to all of your friends. Everything ends tomorrow, when I get back." He was laughing, as she walked down the drift.

Chapter Nineteen - Juneau Airport

Jeff Seasons had been an air traffic controller at Juneau, for the last year, and had gotten quite used to the everyday problems of mixing airline arrivals, with the crazy, civil aviation traffic. The float basin alone, landed almost as many flights a day, as a big airport in the lower forty-eight. The challenge was, that many of the civil pilots, didn't have the experience to enter controlled air space, but did it anyway. He had seen an idiot cross the main runway, without calling the airport control tower, and nearly collide with an Alaska air flight. This was not an easy assignment. When he first got the job, he was sure this was a piece of cake location, to break-in at. He now knew different. The good news was, today seemed to be quite slow. He had just landed several small float planes, which kept him from being bored. There were no major arrivals scheduled for an hour, and only two departures. Both had just cleared the runway, when he received a call from an approaching, unscheduled landing. The flight gave a government call sign, and identified itself as a charted Boeing 737.

Jeff had been warned to expect a surprise flight like this, considering the loss of the State Senator, just two days ago. Some investigators had arrived the day after the event, but more were coming in now. He cleared the flight and checked air space, to insure no idiot was trying to sneak in, without clearance. The plane made a picture perfect approach, and had just touched down, when the world changed forever. The plane had traveled about halfway down the runway, when the ground seemed to rise like a volcano. The tarmac exploded under the aircraft, and then the plane disintegrated right on the spot. Jeff pushed the crash signal, but before any emergency crews could get close, two more explosions erupted, splitting the runway and active taxiway, into short chunks. The blast closest to the tower, blew out all of the windows and took the radio antennas right off the building. Everything got incredibly quiet. Jeff was knocked to his knees, but recovered in time to see one crash-truck, drive into the crater in the runway, almost in slow-motion. The rest got stopped, but no one seemed to know what to do.

Jeff was too stunned to even notice that he was bleeding profusely, from several cuts in his face, and noticed that he could not feel his right hand at all. Shock was a great thing for pain control. Jeff moved around the room, checking the other people present. He found two that were dead, with some shrapnel, possibly from the airplane, sticking out of the bodies. He was so numb, he didn't even know who they were at first. Several other men and women, began rising, and moving around, trying to figure out what just happened. Jeff just started to get feeling back in his arm, mostly as pain, when he felt light-headed. Finally, he sat down and passed out.

The emergency services, took several hours to reach and treat everyone. The death toll, was relatively light, since there had been no scheduled flights. The terminal had been almost empty. The crews had not even found any bodies from the airplane and Washington would have to supply a list of passengers, to even find out how many had been on board. This was the single worst disaster in the short history of the Juneau International Airport. The disaster had taken just minutes, but the repercussions would last for years. The strangest revelation to come out was, when the police started checking for missing employees. Only one was reported. An electrician had failed to show up for his morning shift. When the police investigated his home, they found the man dead on the floor, with a bullet hole in his head. The initial findings pointed to a suicide. The police found a lot of cash in the home, and bomb residue in the back of his truck.

Vlad and Jim Get Answers

Vladimir and Jim both agreed, when they heard about the suicide of the suspected airport bomber, it seemed a bit too good to be true. Jim had no doubts who ordered the man killed though. He and Vlad added the new information to the event chart in Vlad's house. Vlad studied the chart, then spoke. "You know, I bet we hear something very soon from Brenner. He has to have some plan to extort more money than the ten million, or none of this makes sense."

Jim considered his words, then said, "You know that the billion will never be paid. The State doesn't have it and the President will not deal with terrorists." He studied the timeline chart, then added, "What if this is all just a cover-up, for getting your scientist?"

Vlad thought, and did a little connecting of the events. "You may be onto something there. This would only make sense, with all of the hostages dead at the end. If Brenner wants to hold Westlake long enough to suck him dry, this thing starts to make sense. We need to know how many bodies were recovered from the boat explosion. I think it is time to actually speak to the CIA." Jim cringed at the thought, but knew Vlad was right. That was the only way they could get the information they needed. Jim spent some time with a map of the area, plotting the explosions he had seen, after the airport. The surprise was, that he knew one cell tower, had not been taken out. That had to be relevant.

Their train of thought was totally interrupted by a series of explosions that seemed to roll around the city. Vlad looked at Jim and said "So much for paying ten million to delay the bombings. This is more of a Brenner operation, the longer we go." Jim looked pained, but couldn't resist saying

"Now I bet you wish you had let me shoot him in Afghanistan, when I had the chance!" Vlad didn't even need to comment on the trite statement.

Vlad got to work on the phone, calling in a bunch of markers. Jim was still staring at the chart, when he had another thought.

"Vlad, how did they set off the bomb, right when the plane was landing?" Vlad hung up the phone and turned to Jim.

"They had to have a man watching, to time the explosion just right." Jim grabbed a map of the Juneau area, and started thinking like the sniper he was.

"I bet Brenner has teams out, observing every movement in the city, as well as at the airport. Jim did a little more thinking. Where would he set up an over-watch site for the city and any other approaches to Juneau? He knew almost instantly, it had to be someone in the tower. He also suspected, that they had eyes on the city itself. Jim explained his reasoning to Vlad, for the tower location, and why he suspected a person watching the city then paused, as a thought came to him. "You know what I think? There is a man, maybe more, sitting up on Blueberry hill right now."

Vlad knew better than to question Jim's guess. Jim had set up too many operations, in a lot of countries, doing similar jobs as this. "So, what do we do?"

Jim looked intent, as he said "You do what it takes to get the information we need, from your buddies in the CIA, and I get into your mine and take out the team on the hill."

Vlad was a little surprised by this idea. "Jim, don't forget we are in the United States and just shooting someone might be taken wrong."

Jim looked at Vlad, and just stared. "This became a personal combat-zone, several days ago. It's time to start evening the odds, and I will deal with the legal side of things, in the future. Maybe I can get a Presidential pardon. These guys are going down now!" He stopped before walking out, and turned to Vlad. "We need to disable the last cell tower that did not blow up. I bet that was left for a purpose!"

Vlad thought for a minute. "You know that would be the best way to set off a delayed bomb, from anywhere. I will get Ling Cod to take care of it. He knows all of those cell tower locations, and has serviced most of them."

Jim walked out and grabbed his .50, along with his spotting scope. Vlad had already shown him how to access the mine, and had given him a very good map. Vlad had electric lights strung throughout the working part of the mine, but Jim took a lamp and a helmet with him. It took Jim a good hour to reach the upper portal, he had identified as the best point to see the crest of Blueberry.

When he had been on the hill, he could see into the mine portal, so he was sure that was his spot. It only took him a few minutes to pick out the hide spot. He watched the site, and finally identified three men. The surprise was, he knew he had looked at least at one of them through his scope before, in the hills of Afghanistan. These were for sure Brenner mercenaries.

Jim continued observing. One man was using a spotting scope, with the other two on over-watch. They were well concealed, but were moving too much. Jim got comfortable and began collecting the information he needed to take a shot. The challenge was going to be the wind, at this elevation. Jim could see several references on the water, for wind direction, and had checked the weather data, prior to leaving the house. The problem was, that the wind up on the hill, could be quite different than down on the water. The distance was exactly one mile. He had used good charts to check distances several days ago, and had recorded the information in his shoot book.

Juneau Gets Hit

Just minutes before Jim was ready to shoot the men on Blueberry Hill, Juneau was rocked by explosions. They seemed to role across the city, from north to south. Every bridge and overpass was gone. The biggest explosion, came when the Juneau-Douglas Bridge dropped into the channel. Jim could see that the man on the spotting scope, was looking at the bridge when the abutments disintegrated, and the bridge span fell into the channel. He knew he had waited a bit long. He got his mind back on the situation and got ready.

Jim thought through several scenarios, but decided he needed a one-shot, one-kill, and could not count on adjusting between the shots. He wanted to take them all out now. He finally decided to pick a known spot, away from the men, to take a shot to check the wind drift. It wouldn't be perfect, but it would do. The best place, was the fake high tower, on the Alaska Queen. The distance was the same and the impact would show up well in the spotting scope. He took his time, and finally sent the round downrange. The shot hit within a foot of his chosen point of impact. He recorded the test shot and figured his adjustments, for the real shots to come. The last thing he did, was to identify each target and chose the rotation of each shot. His final thought, before firing, was that this should have happened in Afghanistan, instead of downtown Juneau.

Jim relaxed and worked out any tightness in his neck and shoulders. When he was ready, he walked through the sequence one last time, he took a deep breath, let it out, and took all three shots as quickly as he could. Only the last man even moved, before the impact. There was a reason Jim loved his Barrett. Three shots and three kills, at a distance over a mile. "Now the war has started," was Jim's only thought. He smiled at his success. He wasn't proud of killing three men, but then he didn't tell them to come here. He had sent them all to hell for coming.

Jim continued to watch the spot and town, to see if anything, or anybody reacted to the shots. He knew that, coming after the explosions, it was doubtful anyone would. Not a thing happened, for over thirty minutes. Jim packed up and left the site. He headed back down to Vlad's. Jim knew this was just the start.

Brenner would now know that he was not going to get everything his own way. What Jim didn't know, was that he had just eliminated every remaining mercenary in Juneau. The rest had been needed for the kidnapping.

Chapter Twenty - The Ransom Note Arrives

Norman was in his office, when the call about the airport explosion came in. The reports were horrible. He sat in his office and cried. How had he gotten himself into this shit? One night without Sue, and he was a wreck. When she was around, he felt confident and totally sure of himself. Now he was dealing with the reality. If things went to plan, he was soon going to be a rich man. If they went badly, he was going to jail for the rest of his life. He was now involved with a mass murder. The report had come back from Washington. There had been ten FBI, seven NTSB investigators, and a five-man crew, on board the government aircraft. That, added to three tower personnel, and one fire fighter. The fact hit him that he had outdone a lot of serial killers. The scary thing was, the count was going up. He waited for the demand note to come in on the internet. This would be a lot easier, if Sue was still by his side.

Norman was unable to eat, or hardly think all day. When his computer announced an email, he didn't know if he should be excited, or run like hell. If he could have run away, he would have. Problem was, there was nowhere to run. He read the note, and finally got the nerve to speak to his secretary.

Norman called Alice into his office, and just handed the note to her. She read the note and started to cry. "What are we going to do? They will blow everything up, won't they?"

Norman didn't have any trouble acting afraid and nervous. "Call the governor for me, and then get that pig, Nate Holland here right away. I want him here when I speak to the press." Alice left and he was alone for a minute, to prepare to speak to his only friend in this town, the Governor of Alaska, Arthur Whiting. Norman thought, as he waited, what a great political name the man had. He had helped Norman get elected to his current job, but had pretty much distanced the relationship, since then. Not much of a friend, now that he thought about it.

Alice soon announced she had the Governor on the line. Norman picked up, then had to wait for the man, several minutes (what bullshit). Finally, the man was on the line.

"Norman, what kind of crap have you started now?" was the first words out of the Governors mouth.

"Listen Bill, the shit has really hit the fan. I think you need to come down off your high and mighty pedestal, and join me for a joint press conference."

Arthur Whiting hesitated, then asked "Why don't we do it here at the Governor's Mansion?"

Norman new this was going to be a shock. "Because the mansion is on the hit list! I just got a demand list, from the people that are claiming to be the one's doing this stuff." Norman rather enjoyed the silence, with that announcement.

"I will be there in ten minutes. When do you expect the press?"

Norman paused long enough to ask Alice. "The local paper is on the way and a local TV crew will be here in fifteen!"

Norman passed the information on to the governor. "Ok, that will give me time to speak to the President." Norman could hear the silly pride in the governors voice at getting to brief the president. He gave Whiting a quick synopsis of the demands, and hung up. His palms were dripping, and he could feel the sweat running down his back. He got up and headed for the private washroom, to dry off before he met the press.

Nate Holland was the first to show up. He looked cool and collected. "How are you going to handle this press conference? You are sweating like a pig, Mr. Mayor?"

Norman could hear the sarcasm dripping from the man's mouth. "Listen asshole, I hired you, and I can still fire you, so help me."

Nate smugly said "The good news is, scared shitless is a good cover for what you are actually, so just act the way you are now. Get this over with and you and I are rich, right?"

Norman looked hard at the man, and imagined him behind bars. What a great thought. He was about to respond, when Alice announced the arrival of the Governor. All talk stopped. Arthur Whiting sat down in Norman's chair, as soon as he walked in. "Let's get our story strait, before meeting the press."

The governor took over all control. "I spoke to the President and she has assured me of every possible kind of support she can supply .I guess the real question, are we going to pay this first ten million dollar payment, or tell them to fuck off?" Norman was a bit shocked to hear the man speak so profanely. Normally, he was almost a prig with language. He realized the word probably came from the President. She had never pulled a punch, or hesitated at saying what was on her mind. It was hard to admit that. He hated her with a passion. Several years before running for Mayor, he had been favored to become the Senator, but she had defeated him in a landslide. That was the end to his planned brilliant political career.

Norman drew as much regal presence, as he could. "I don't think we have a choice. We know, without a doubt, that they will do anything. They've already killed Andrea Warren, and a lot of foreign dignitaries. What would stop them from blowing up the mansion and a few public works facilities?"

The Governor looked at Norman, then shook his head. "I hate to admit it, but this is one time I agree with you. I can get five million dollars by the time specified, how about the city?"

Norman hesitated, but finally nodded yes. "I hoped you would foot the whole thing, but the city can come up with five million. Any chance the President might defray part of the money?"

Arthur Whiting just laughed. "Are you kidding, she wouldn't cough up money, if they still had her daughter alive, to ransom back. Her entire campaign, focused on her tough stance with terrorists, so don't even think she will help us now. The best I got was that, she would not interfere with the first down payment, as long as we had no intention of paying the final billion dollar demand."

Norman looked a bit let down, but just said "Like we could come up with a billion dollars in five days." Alice poked her head in, and announced that the pressroom was full and ready.

Norman walked to the podium and addressed the press. "Thank you for assembling so quickly. As you know, a lot of terrible things have happened over the last few days. I would first like to express my condolences to the families of all the victims. I want to promise everyone, that law enforcement has worked diligently on containing the damage, and they have been working tirelessly, to try and find the crazies that are doing this to us. The Governor has joined us, because the state is in total support of our efforts. I would like to brief you on the events to date, then turn the podium over to the Chief of Police, to answer any questions you might have.

Norman took a sip of water, to settle his nerves, then continued. "Two hours ago, I received a demand list, from an organization claiming credit for blowing up the airport, the boat carrying the fisheries conference delegates, and Senator Andrea Warren. This group, further takes credit for grounding the Alaska Queen, two days ago."

"The bottom line to all of this is, we are totally isolated from the outside world. No large ships can get in, and no aircraft are going to be able to land, for some time. This group has demanded a billion dollar payment, or they plan to blow a lot more up, in and around the city of Juneau." The press was buzzing, with fear and excitement. Norman gave them a couple of minutes to absorb the information, then continued. "We have until tomorrow, to make a token payment, and then a week to come up with the billion dollars. The Governor has agreed to pay half of the down payment, and is in total support of us."

The press room was stone quiet, then erupted in waving hands and shouted questions. The Mayor raised his hands, to get silence. "Let me anticipate some of the questions. The first ransom payment is ten million dollars. Don't doubt this is a ransom. If the money is not forthcoming, the terrorists will blow up several buildings, including the Governor's Mansion and City Hall. We already have significant evidence, that they have no problem blowing things up." Norman stopped talking and waited for the first question. He pointed at the first hand that was raised.

"Is President Warren helping with this issue?"

The Governor stepped forward. "I think I can address this Norman. The President has been in constant contact with me since the first boat explosion. She has agreed to let us make the choice about paying the ransom. She will not assist, since that is against her very public policy on terrorism."

He stepped back. Norman again pointed at a hand, a young lady he had never seen before at a press conference. "Young lady in blue, go ahead."

"Thank you Mr. Mayor. I am from Fox News. Why hasn't any action been taken about the airport employee found dead yesterday?"

Nate stepped forward. "My men have been working the case, as quickly as possible. All indications are, that he did indeed handle explosives, prior to shooting himself in the head. The man in question, was an electrician named Jack Worzel. He had been employed by the state, for twelve years. He had never been in any trouble with the local police, though he had a lot of minor issues in Anchorage, prior to moving to Juneau. He was a bit of a loner and was a heavy gambler. He recently lost a substantial amount of money, and was probably an easy target for the terrorist to enlist."

"There was a significant amount of money found in his home along with more explosive apparatus. That is all we have until the Anchorage crime lab sends us more information."

Norman stepped forward and again asked for quiet. "I know you all have a lot more questions. I will have someone give briefings, as new information becomes available." He turned to go, when a shouted question rang out.

"What about that cute new publicist you hired Mayor?"

He turned, but wasn't sure who had asked. "She is out of town, attending a conference in Washington, at this time. She will be back, as soon as flights resume." He turned and led a charge out of the room.

Back in his office, he turned to Whiting. "When can you get the five million to me?"

Arthur Whiting considered his answer, before speaking. "Explain to me, how this drop is going down."

Norman took a deep breath. This was the payoff. "The Chief here, will take the money up the gondola, to the top of the hill. Someone will meet him and take the money. They didn't specify any more than that. My guess would be a helicopter. No one can get close to that place without being seen, and another helicopter would stick out like a sore thumb. The drop is scheduled for late tonight."

Arthur Whiting looked at Nate. "It seems you are going to earn your money tonight, Chief."

Nate held back the huge grin that wanted to break out. "I will do whatever you and the Mayor need me to. I see this as my duty to protect and serve, mandate."

Norman nearly threw up, hearing Nate prattle on, like some kind of hero. He broke in "Listen, just complete the drop and get back to my house, as soon as it is done. The money will be delivered to this office in one hour, so be ready. I don't want to have to sit on ten million dollars for too long by myself." Norman was quite proud of his shudder, at the thought of being in the presence of so much money.

Governor Whiting looked at both men and didn't feel any relief, but knew he had no choice. "I will be at the Baranof Hotel, if you need me." He had already moved his family earlier.

Nate was in hog heaven, as he left. The entire news conference had gone much better than he had expected. The idiot Norman, had done amazingly well. Once he got going, he was real believable.

Nate returned to his office and made sure to move the morning staff meeting, to an hour before the supposed time limit. He made sure all officers would be in the building, when the real bomb would detonate. He would be long-gone of course, but this would tie up a lot of loose ends, and Sue had agreed to blow the city offices, at the right time.

After grabbing everything he couldn't live without, he left his office for the last time. He made sure to leave the clothing he had been wearing at the press conference, and pored blood (his blood) over the chair he used. He had drawn the blood this morning. There was going to be so much confusion, that he fully expected that to be enough, to get him declared dead. He locked the door on his way out.

Nate drove over to the Mayor's office, in time to pick up the ten million. He and the Mayor opened the case, and lusted over the big payoff. Nate finally grabbed it and closed it up. He made sure no one was listening at the door, and then "Ok, expect me back at your place on time." Norman had trouble letting go of the cash.

"How about we split it up right now!"

Nate was surprised at the Mayor's brashness. "Stick to the plan. Sue has gotten everything exactly right, up to now. I will be at your house on time."

Nate turned and walked out of the office. He was glowing with excitement. "This is going to be the best day of my life," he thought. Killing the pompous ass, was going to be a gift to the city of Juneau, and a real pleasure for him. At his home, he cleared out his personal safe, and grabbed the evidence he was going to plant at the Mayor's house. He quickly checked, to insure everything was ready. He had decided to leave his service revolver in his office, along with his badge, for more evidence. He would miss the gun, but not the badge. He left, with no extra clothes, or any other sign of packing. No rooky mistakes for him. He even left a thousand dollars, in the wall safe. No way for anyone to know there had been twenty there before.

He drove to the Mayor's house, and parked in the back. He calmly walked up to the back door and walked in. Norman was sitting on the one chair, and drinking a large tumbler of what looked like straight booze. "You are a bit early, aren't you?"

Nate smiled, as he put on the rubber gloves, he had pulled out of his pocket. "No, I am right on schedule." He smiled and continued preparing. "I have to tell you Norman, you have given me a lot of pleasure, over the last weeks. Fucking Sue, while she told me how inept you were, has been a real turn-on. The best part of this entire deal, was that I get to kill you!"

Norman was too drunk to move. He had started drinking the minute he had gotten home, and had not stopped.

"What are you talking about, we are both rich. We can do anything we want."

Nate turned at that and pulled out his pistol. "Norman, I have a little surprise for you. I know all about you setting me up, to take the fall for this entire scam. The bad news is, you trusted Sue. She and I have been playing you from the start. Don't worry though, I have all of the evidence, the investigators are going to need, to blame you!"

Norman was slowly realizing that Nate was not joking. The funny thing was, he continued to gulp down his last drink.

"Come on Nate, how about I give you the whole ten million?"

Nate had to smile at that. "Whatever gave you the idea, I was going to share any money with you? I want you to keep drinking that bottle."

He walked to the counter and found an expensive bottle of scotch. "You always were a little on the pompous side, Norman." He handed the bottle to the man. "Drink the whole thing right down." To emphasize it, Nate put his pistol against the side of Norman's head. The Mayor was numb, from the booze and fear. He did what he was told. The scotch burned like fire, all of the way down.

Nate watched the man drink, until he was confident that the he couldn't move by himself. He left him, and went looking for what he needed to set this up. He pulled in one kitchen chair (The only kitchen chair) and set it under the exposed beam, in the entryway. He next pulled a sash cord, he had taken from the drapes in the bedroom. He doubled up the cord, and hung from it, to test the strength. It held his weight with ease. The Mayor was quite a bit heavier, but he would be no problem. Norman was crying in his chair, as he watched his life drawing to an end. Nate would walk past, every now and then and pat the drunk on the head. "Don't worry Norman, this will hardly hurt. I understand that sometimes a man will have an orgasm right at the end."

Nate finished tying a simple slip knot in the cord. He didn't want something complicated.

Nate spent a few minutes checking his arrangements and smudging any surfaces he may have touched, before putting on the gloves. Finally, he was ready. He walked back to Norman "Here is where you have to help me. Think of it as a way to lessen the pain. If I have to drag you to the chair, it will hurt!"

Norman was so numb with booze and fears, he just took the offered hand, rose, and staggered to the other chair. The numbness was total. He knew that there was no other choice. Suicide, was his only out. Even if the Chief wasn't helping him, he would do this himself.

Nate had to balance him, as he stood on the chair. It was a real challenge to get the noose around the man's head. The amazing thing was, no fight from Norman at all. Nate stepped back and waited for the inevitable. Norman actually remained balanced, much longer than Nate had expected, but, finally, the man started leaning to one side, and almost seemed to kick the chair out on purpose. Nate waited, to make sure the rope didn't break. He had killed men before, but this was a new experience. He had to admit it was quite enjoyable, in a sick way. Norman continued kicking for quite a while, but finally stopped. The auto release of bodily fluids, assured Nate that he was gone.

Nate had to hurry, to plant the evidence, and leave the email on Norman's personal computer. He took full blame for everything, including killing the President's daughter. The apology was just as soppy, as the man had been in life. Nate threw in a plea for understanding, from his wife. "Nice touch," he thought. He took one last look at the scene. It was perfect. One shoe had come off and was on the floor. The chair was tipped over. The bottle was on the floor, next to the laptop with the unsent email. Hell Nate believed it. He felt a real thrill, at his professional setting. He left the way he came.

Nate waited, until no cars were close, and pulled out onto the road. He reached over and patted the case with the ten million dollars. When he looked at his watch, he realized he had to hurry.

The gondola had been shut down ever since the cruise ship went aground, but the city was going to run it for him, to go up and pay the ransom. And that was to happen in a few minutes. He arrived on time, and grabbed the case from the left, front seat. He left the keys in the ignition. "Too bad this wasn't New York City," was Nate's only thought. The car would be gone in few a minutes. Here, the thing would still be sitting in a week.

The ex-Chief of Police, got aboard the gondola alone, as that was what the ransom note had said to do. The operator shook his hand, and wished him luck. You would think he was doing something dangerous. Nate laughed at how stupid people in Juneau were. As he approached the top, he saw Sue waiting for him. There was a helicopter in the background, with the rotor turning. He was so excited. He waved and held up the case for her to see. Sue ran up to the gondola as he stepped out. She gave him a huge hug and smiled when he handed her the case, with the money. "How did everything go down there?" She asked. "Baby, it went like clockwork. Norman almost convinced me to pay the ransom during the press conference. I planted all of the evidence and cleaned everything well." He started to walk towards the helicopter.

Sue stopped him and said "Unfortunately, my side didn't go as well." Nate felt his heart start to beat very quickly.

Nate waited for the shoe to drop. Finally Sue took a breath and said "I messed up big-time the other day, when I left town. I left the fake evidence implicating you in this, in my office. I thought it was in my bags. I guess it may work out. The building is ready to blow up." Nate felt like hitting the woman. He should have known she would screw up, sooner or later. He did some quick-thinking and finally said "Okay, I will go back and get the stuff. I can make some plausible story, to keep the operator here and be back in fifteen minutes tops. You be here, or I swear I will find you and end you. Nate squeezed her arm hard enough to leave a bruise.

Sue didn't touch him, or say anything except "Absolutely. There may be some stuff of mine still there also, since I forgot that envelope." Nate started to take the case, but stopped. If he returned down the gondola with the case, he would have to concoct an even bigger story. He finally just got back on the gondola, and pushed the buzzer to go down.

Nate kept his eyes on Sue, as he moved down and away. All he could think about, was what a spectacular woman she was, and how she was going to pay for this unscheduled trip. Sue was almost out of sight, when he noticed that she sat the case down and was holding something in her hand. Sandra blew Nate a kiss, as she pushed the button and watched a small explosion at the top of the car.

It cut the car from the cable and dropped the car a long ways down. If the explosion didn't kill him, the drop was long enough that there was no chance he would walk away. Sandra had decided to do it that way, to insure he was found and identifiable. She didn't even look back, as she climbed into the helicopter. It was airborne, a minute after the explosion.

The pilot turned to her, after she pulled on the head set. "Everything go as planned?"

Sandra thought about that question. "Any better and I would be scared. It did hurt to watch a million dollars drop back into Juneau, but what the hell, easy come easy go!" She leaned back and smiled at her success. Nate had never noticed her slipping the money into his coat pocket, along with other incriminating paperwork.

Taking out the government

The small explosion that ended Nate Holland's grand plans, was drowned out, by what came right after. The next explosions, included the city and state offices, public works buildings downtown, and the governor's mansion. In minutes, the city infrastructure was gone. A few bombs had just wiped out years of progress. The city government, was nearly wiped out. Just a few elected officials still remained alive, along with three police officers, who happened to be off-duty. Nate's plan to take out all of his officers, had been nearly perfect. The ransom had been paid, and the bombs went off anyway. Apparently, ten million didn't buy much. It would take Juneau, months to recover, maybe years. Brenner's plan was still ticking along, like clockwork.

Chapter Twenty-One - Bill's Dilemma

(Days prior to attack.)

After arriving at his hunting camp, Bill spent the first few days piddling around with his airplane. It was a new plane for him, since he recently upgraded from an older Cessna 185 on floats, to the Beaver. This was the plane he had always dreamed of owning, and flying. The new airplane could carry a much larger payload, and in the hunting season, he needed to be able to carry hunters and a lot of gear. Bill had done well with the 185, but it was tired and had needed a lot of upgrading, that would have been expensive. The Beaver had come on the used plane market, from a small commuter airline in Anchorage that had gone belly-up. The paint job was god-awful, and the airframe had a lot of hours, but the engine had just completed a total overhaul. No other commuter service was interested, because of the high airframe hours. Bill had traded the 185 and his old Super Cub on tundra tires, plus a mortgage on his home, to get the new plane. He had to have a good hunting season, to cover his expenses. No way could the tour bus driving job cover them. This train of thought, brought Bill back to thinking about his side-business, instead of his love-life.

Six days ago, he had flown two hunters out to Chichagof Island, for a few days of bear hunting. He was due back to pick them up, in less than a week. Jim was not going to be happy with him, but he knew he better tell him, before going. Bill waited as long as he could, before making the call.

"Hey Jim, I'm up the Taku, like you wanted, but I have a big problem."

"What's that Bill? You've been without for over a week?" Jim knew Bill was addicted to love, but this seemed excessive, even by his standards.

Bill took a deep breath and launched into the explanation. "Well that too Jim, but that's not it. I have to pick up two bear hunters that I left over on Chichagof."

Jim got a sinking feeling, but knew Bill had to pick them up on time.

"Okay, but don't try to come into town with them, since there is a lot of crazy shit going on here." Jim took a moment to think. "Take them down to Sitka, and let them fly out, from there. The word is out in town. You will be arrested on sight."

Bill mulled over Jim's recommendation. The flight to Sitka, would eat up his profit margin in fuel, but it beat going to jail. "Okay Jim, I'm leaving now, because some weather is coming in. I may have to stay in Pelican tonight." Jim knew he would not dissuade the man, and conceded the stop-off.

"Sure Bill. Say hello to Josephine for me." Again, Bill's one-track mind astounded Jim. Even in the middle of possible arrest, Bill still was fixated on an approachable lady. "I know that you will do more than say hello to Josephine, but don't get so enthralled with that huge rack, that you forget to get your butt back here. Don't come back from Sitka, by way of Pelican!"

"Aw Jim, your confidence in me, makes my heart swell." As soon as he got off the phone with Jim, Bill did his flight check, fired up his Beaver, taxied out into the river, pushed the throttle forward, and lifted off into the Alaskan sky. During the hour flight, he struggled to keep his mind on his flying. Part of the time, he couldn't get his mind off his own problems, and the rest was focused on what Jim was so worried about. Since showing up in town, months before, Jim had become a close friend, and not prone to excitement. He was a quiet man, who would help a friend when the help was needed. Bill trusted him, more than people he had known all of his life.

The crazy Russian, was another story. He had known Vlad for a long time, but never felt like he knew the real Vlad. Maybe that was about to change? As he flew along, he watched for his terrain points and after about an hour, spotted Lake Anna. Bill was surprised to see his two hunters on the shore, waving at him. Being a day early, he expected to have to fly around the area, to attract them. Bill made a quick, low-level pass over the lake, to check for any debris, and then put the Beaver down on the lake. As he taxied to shore, he got his next surprise. The guys appear to be packed and ready to go, with no meat sacks in sight. The guys threw their gear in, and told Bill to get them the hell out of there.

Bill got airborne quickly. As soon as he was on his heading for Pelican, he turned to them. "Ok, what the hell is going on? I expected to have to chase you guys around all day, to get you to the plane!"

Both men looked like they had been running for their lives. Bill knew both Mort and Pete quite well. He had been taking them hunting, for several years. He never saw them so hyped-up about anything.

Mort took a deep breath, and with Pete filling in details, gave Bill a quick sketch of the week's hunt. The story was almost too much to believe. Bill didn't know if it was a joke, or what, but he still had personal priorities. "Well boys, the weather is turning to crap, so how about we go into Pelican for the night, and I can get this story straight. We can get a good meal and whatever else you need, except Josephine, she will be busy tonight." Mort and Pete were too happy to be off the ground, to care about anything. If Bill had told them he was flying to Seattle, they would have been good with that also.

Bill landed and taxied to the main dock in Pelican, Josephine and Leroy (an old friend of Bill's) were on there, waiting to meet them. Bill got the plane tied up and they all headed up to the hotel bar and restaurant. As they moved up the ramp, Josephine moved close to Bill. She gave him a smile and a pat on his butt.

"Are you staying overnight? How about dinner for two in your room, and then a lot of snuggle time." Josie managed to rub her huge rack up against Bill.

Bill returned the favor, with a hug and a quick pat. "Darling, I would like nothing better, but we have some very important stuff to talk about, and I want you and Leroy to sit in on this, as you may be of help. I do think a late night snack and breakfast for two, will work out just fine."

Josephine had a contented look on her face, as she said, "I think you are right, big guy."

Bill got all of them together: the two hunters (Pete and Mort), Josephine, and Leroy at the old round table, in front of the big natural-stone fireplace. Bill looked at Josephine and Leroy, then started. "I brought Pete and Mort here, because the weather turned to crap, and to let them tell us what they saw, while bear hunting out at lake Anna. I don't know any two people that know more about this island, than you two. Maybe you can shed some light on this story." Bill looked as worried as Josephine had ever seen him.

"Bill! How many wives, or husbands are chasing you right now? I hoped that you had started to settle down, but I guess that is asking too much. I love you to death, but I won't cry, when someone cuts off your balls. Ok, maybe little bit," she added, but the smile she gave Bill told all.

Bill laughed then started, "Josephine, I'm just going to call you Jo, like I do when the lights go out, is that Okay?"

"Sure is, big guy," she chuckled and gave him another squeeze, under the table.

Bill wished he could just take Jo upstairs, and forget everything for a night, but he knew that was not in the cards. "Okay, go ahead guys; get to what happened out there."

Again Mort started the explanation, with Pete filling in the high points. "After you dropped us off at the lake, we got camp set up. We knew that we couldn't hunt the first day we flew in, so we just hung around camp, ate, and went to bed. Next morning, we started hunting. We see tracks all over the place, but no bears. The more we looked, it became apparent to us, that they were moving out of the area. Pete found several old dens, but nothing else." Mort ran out of steam and Pete took up the story.

"So we started following tracks, and they were going over the hill, toward Kimshan Cove." Bill felt a little like a ping pong ball, as Pete and Mort filled each other's voids. They had spent way too much time together. Again, Mort stepped in. "That's about a five mile hike, and since it was getting late in the day, we went back to camp. The lack of bears was strange enough, but then, that night, we heard a big helicopter, just before dark, way off. We thought it was a Coast Guard chopper, but couldn't know for sure, in the poor light. Next morning, we shag ass over to where we were the day before, and start following the tracks again." Bill was beginning to get impatient, but let the story unfold. Mort slowed for a breath, and again Pete jumped in the void. "The tracks kept going toward Kimshan Cove, but were beginning to look fresh, so we slowed down and started hunting. After cresting a hill, where we could see down to the cove, a big-assed helicopter came in."

Mort resumed the storytelling. "We figured it had to be the same one we heard the night before. It looked like Coast Guard sure enough, but the men we saw getting off, were not Coasties."

Pete couldn't hold himself back and jumped into the conversation again. "These guys were scary, even though we were about three-quarters of a mile from the dock."

Mort jumped back in. "So we hide and start watching with our binoculars. These guys pile out of the chopper and they ain't Coast Guard. They are armed with serious stuff!" Mort was getting more agitated, as the story unfolded.

Pete couldn't hold back and said, "Mort, don't forget the bears!" Mort looked a bit put-out by his friend.

"Yeah, okay, I'm getting to that. We see about six, or seven bears, milling around the dock."

Pete couldn't hold himself back and added "One was a real big SOB. Talk about a trophy bear."

Even Mort seemed to be getting impatient, with the interruptions. "The dock has a fence, to keep the bears away, but there are deer bones, all over the place. We think the bastards must be feeding the bears, to keep them around." Mort ran out of steam and just sat back.

Pete picked up the story. "So we're watching, and this big boat comes roaring up to the dock. They start off-loading a lot of people right away. A woman and a man have a guy between them that is wounded. There was enough blood for us to see from where we were."

Mort interjected, "They get about half-way to the mine opening, when two of the goons, grabbed the wounded guy and chucked him over the fence. It was the craziest thing I have ever seen. The bears tore him to pieces. Then it looked like the woman started screaming at the guy, and he raised his gun and was going to shoot her, but the other guy talked him out of it. You know! That woman looked so familiar to me." Mort looked contemplative. Pete just shook his head in agreement.

Bill got a strange look on his face, and a sinking feeling, then asked, "You guys know what Senator Andrea Warren looks like?"

Pete and Mort looked at each other. "Sum-bitch Mort, I knew we knew who she was, we just couldn't believe it."

"What did you guys do then?"

Pete responded first. "Bill! We beat feet back to camp and waited two days, for you to show up. We didn't even start a fire to cook with. We were scared shitless; ate everything cold, kept our guns loaded, and slept in shifts."

Bill looked at the faces around him and knew he needed to bring them up-to-date, on events in Juneau. "Well, I guess I can explain a bit of what is happening. I know that you have not heard what is going on in Juneau. I will fill you in, but I have to ask you not to say anything to anyone, except two friends of mine that are working to fix all of this."

Pete beat Mort to it. "Sure Bill, anything we can do to help."

Bill glanced around the room at the shocked looks on everyone's faces, but he saw a lot of resolve as well. He took a minute to gather his thoughts, then told them everything he knew.

After they all had some time to absorb the crazy events, Bill said "I was supposed to take you guys down to Sitka, to fly out, but I think I would like to take you back to my place, up the Taku River. I have two cabins there. Are you guys willing?"

"Hell yes, but how come you're up the Taku? Do you have woman troubles again?"

Josephine giggled at the question. "When doesn't Bill have woman troubles?"

Bill got a bit of a pained look on his face. He took her hand and said, "Now Jo, that hurts."

Josephine gave him a quick hug, then said "I love you to death, just the way you are, but you know it's the truth, big guy."

Bill was surprised by the emotion in her words, and in the feeling it gave him. He really cared about this woman.

Bill turned to the last man at the table. "You've been quiet Leroy. What are you thinking?"

Leroy sat up and leaned towards Bill. "Well Bill, from what I'm hearing from Pete and Mort, we are talking about prisoners in the old mine on Chichagof Island, and you know I worked there, until it closed. I think I should go with you, to meet your friends. I think I can help save those people in the mine."

Bill let his gaze wander around the table and settled on Josephine. "Jo, you look like you have something on your mind."

Josephine looked a bit thoughtful, but arranged her thoughts, before speaking. "Well, about two weeks ago, these two guys came in the bar and got to drinking, and I heard them mention the mine; no name, just the mine. They were mean-looking bastards. I will never forget what they looked like. Leroy was there, so I gave him the sign. He was back of the bar, locked and loaded, just in case." Jo paused for a moment, before continuing. Everyone took the opportunity to take a long pull on their drinks. Josephine sat her beer down and continued her thoughts. "They got a call and left in a hurry, and that was fine with us."

Mort decided to jump back in. "Hey Bill, Pete and I got some pictures, but they are too small to make out faces."

Bill thought for a minute. "Give me the film, I know someone that can make them big enough, that way Jo and Leroy will be able to see if those two guys are the ones we're after. So Josephine, that means that you will have to come with me, Leroy, Pete and Mort." Bill wasn't heartbroken when he said that.

"Okay big guy, but only if you and I have the big cabin." The discussion broke up, while Leroy and Josephine made plans to be gone for a couple of days. Fortunately, the timing was good, and it was slow for the season. Josephine's help could manage alone.

By 4:00 a.m., the weather was good, and with everyone on board, Bill got the plane in the air. As soon as he reached cruise altitude, he got on the radio. He adjusted the frequency and keyed the mike, using the call sign Jim had set-up with him. When Jim responded, Bill just said, "The fish will be in the river soon." Everyone looked at Bill, like he'd lost his mind. "What's the problem? Never heard a secret code before?" Bill smiled and everyone was quiet, for the rest of the flight. Too much information to even form good questions, nagged all of them.

As soon as Jim got off the radio, he called Vlad's number. Vlad answered right off.

"What's up Jim?"

"I got the call that the fish are in the river, so meet me ASAP at DP." Jim didn't know whether to laugh, or cry, that all of this cloak and dagger, seemed to be needed. He jumped in his beat-up Ford pickup and headed out. It took fifteen minutes to reach DuPont Point. Vlad already had the lines untied and the engine running on the skiff.

"Since when did I leave you a key to the Boat?"

Vlad smiled, "I thought we were in a hurry and I was closer than you. Nothing is broken."

Jim didn't even bother to comment on the obvious. "That is the least of my worries. Bill needs us up at his cabin on Taku River, right away. I don't think this is about his women troubles. He would have told me if that was the issue."

The conversation continued, as Jim had headed out into Gastineau Channel. As soon as he was clear of the docks and other boats, he opened up the engine. Just like everything Jim owned, the engine on the boat was oversized. The skiff was an eighteen foot hull that jumped on step quickly, with its 150 horsepower outboard. The boat hit thirty miles per hour no trouble.

When they pulled up to the cabin, Bill and the others were just unloading the plane. Jim and Vlad grabbed a load and headed up to the main cabin. Introductions were made and they all sat down to talk.

As the story unfolded, Jim began to relax for the first time since the Alaska Breeze blew up. "Andrea is alive! Now this is a simple military rescue op. This is my strong suit; direct and to the point. No more jacking around." Jim pulled his attention back to the moment. He looked at Vlad and asked "How in the hell are we going to get into the mine and save these people? They will see us coming a mile away."

Leroy was listening and sizing these new men up. He decided he liked what he was seeing and hearing. "Why go in the front door?" Leroy said quietly.

Vlad looked a little put out by the interruption. "I pulled up a map of the mine and it is just one straight drift (horizontal tunnel). A couple of years ago, I looked into the mine to see if it might be a prospect to reopen." Vlad smiled at the looks he got with this information. "There is only one way in."

Leroy shook his head "That's the trouble with you young guys, you look at a map that don't know squat about that mine, and you believe it." Vlad was the one with the look on his face this time.

Bill jumped into the silent moment. “Well Leroy, quit busting our balls and tell us what you know.” Bill was a bit short.

“Well boys, as you know, I worked in the mine from the first day it was open. Long before these pecker-heads took over. Anyway, there is a ventilation shaft that comes in from the side and is hidden by cribbing. If a man knows how, he can get in, without anyone knowing it.” Jim Got excited. This was the break they needed.

“Leroy, where does this shaft come out at?" Vlad asked.

“Well, just about where Pete and Mort were, when they saw all of this.”

Jim did a little thinking, then asked “So if we fly in to Anna Lake, and hike over, we should be able to find the shaft alright?”

“No problem,” Leroy said. “Because, I am going with you.”

Jim looked at the seventy-plus year old man, and shook his head. “Thanks Leroy, but that’s not for an old guy like you. This could get very dangerous, and I can guarantee someone is going to get shot.” The others were a bit surprised by the callus statement of Jim. Leroy took it better than the others. He knew what Jim was worried about.

“Shit Jim, I been walking these hills, long before you were born and I was shot at and shit on, in Nam, long before it became a conflict. I have been in more firefights than your average Alaskan!” Leroy stopped and waited.

Before Jim could respond, Pete was on his feet. “Jim, Pete can’t sit quiet any longer, Mort and I are going with you too. Both of us can shoot, and we can speed you up, because we have been there.”

Jim started to object, but Vlad interrupted. “Okay, here’s what we will do. We go into the lake, and hike over to the top of the ridge. Pete, how many guys did you see?”

“We saw six, and they were all out in the open, not sure if any were in the mine, but these guys all came off the boat, so I’m thinking that’s all of them.”

Vlad made a mental note and continued. “Okay, we will plan on ten, just to be sure. Everyone hikes into the ridge that looks into the bay. We’ll set up an over-watch position there. Mort and Pete will stay there, to give cover fire if we come out of the mine hot. Leroy, I would like you to get Jim and me, to the mine portal, then return to the over-watch site with the boys. Jim, Bill, and I, will go in after dark, unless something changes.” Vlad let the plan sink in, then added, "When this starts, you guys shoot anyone outside. Do you have any problem doing that?" Vlad glanced from face to face. Not a one, looked overly-concerned by the idea (typical Alaskans).

Jim had been thinking, as the conversation continued. "Leroy, how long will it take us to get into the mine?" Leroy thought for a minute and then said. "Well it takes me about a half-hour."

Vlad looked quite intent at Leroy. "When was the last time you went down there? I thought the mine had been shut down since the 80s."

Leroy looked a little sheepish. "Oh, I was in the mine about six months ago." That came as a surprise to all.

"What the hell were you doing down there? I thought there was a full-time watchman on site."

Vlad again surprised the men with his knowledge. Leroy recovered from the surprise of Vlad's knowledge and said. "Vlad, there is a watchman, but he never checks inside the mine, deep enough to get close to my workings."

Bill was staring at Vlad. "I think I would like to know what an average day bum like you, seems to know so much about a lot of stuff Vlad!" Bill noticed the look on Jim's face, and said, "I guess that can wait." Jim broke in, to get the discussion back on track.

Jim was a bit surprised, when Bill didn't argue with him, like usual. He turned to Leroy. "Leroy, you were saying?" Leroy was getting a good feel for the dynamic between Vlad and Jim. He could recognize the military attitude in both. Jim was the action planner, but Vlad was the more strategic thinker.

"Well Jim, you see, I have been going down there since they moved out in 1980, about four times a year."

Jim asked a follow-on question. "What for?"

Leroy felt a bit like he was being questioned by the law. "Well, you don't think I live on the wages I make at the bar, which is slim to none. I have been high-grading gold from the mine, for over twenty years." He sat back to watch the reaction to that.

Bill didn't disappoint. "I thought there wasn't any gold," Bill gasped, then turned. "Josephine, did you know about this?"

Leroy ignored the interruption and continued his explanation. "Not where they looked, but there is, in the ventilation shaft, that we old guys never told them about." Leroy stopped, but then added, "That's why it is hidden behind the fake cribbing."

Everyone was looking at Leroy, in a different light. Bill shook himself and got back to the important topic. "So, when do we go?" Bill asked.

Vlad looked at Jim, then said, "Jim and I need to collect some special gear, from Juneau. We will be back no later than 6:00 p.m. He looked at Bill. "Can you land on the lake by moonlight?"

Bill thought for a minute. "Sure, this time of year, I could land there at midnight. I checked the lake well this morning, so I can come straight in, without an over-flight. It will be quick and easy."

Vlad considered his next move, then "Okay! Jim and I will be as quick as possible, getting the stuff we need. Take Pete, Mort, Leroy, and Josephine, back to Pelican. Then, get back here, fuel the plane, and be ready to go, when Jim and I get back from town. We should be back to Pelican by eight. Josephine, if you could have a quick meal for us that would be great." Vlad stopped, but then added, "I got hold of Willy on the radio, and he is headed for the mine now. Hopefully, he can get there when we have the people ready to move out. You guys get as much rest as you can; this is going to be a long night. Let's plan on takeoff, as soon as we can load the plane; so, be ready. Thanks guys," Vlad added.

After a quick run back to DuPont landing, Vlad and Jim headed towards the parked cars. Before going separate ways, Vlad gave Jim a time to be back, and ready to go.

Jim smiled at him, and said, "Vlad, you get back quick, or I will leave without you."

Vlad smiled, but knew he was serious. "I will not take more than an hour. How may rifles and other gear should I bring?"

Jim thought for a minute. "Since you seem stuck on the idea of involving these civilians, bring a rifle for each one of the men, and a box of armor-piercing for my .50."

Vlad looked thoughtful. "I can also throw in a couple of old law rockets, if you think we might need them?"

Jim looked a bit surprised, but just shook his head. "No! I think the Barrett will do just fine, to stop any boat, or vehicle. The last thing Andrea needs, is a crazy Russian, shooting a rocket at her." On that note, they both headed for their respective vehicles.

As soon as Jim got to his boat, he quickly got to work. He went below, and pulled his weapons out of hiding. The first thing he did, was to assemble the M107, and check for proper functioning. He carefully lubed all moving parts. Then, he checked his carry gun, the .45 auto, and made sure every other piece of equipment, was ready. Jim looked at everything. He should have told Vladimir to bring some concussion grenades, and some smoke. They would have been useful, during the mine assault. Well, he was going to have to make things work, with what they had on hand.

Jim thought about how he would set it up. The other guys would not have to be used during the assault, so their lack of training wouldn't be a problem. Leroy was a real ace in the hole. Just before they left the hunting camp, he had pulled Jim aside and told him he had been a Marine sniper in Vietnam, and was still just as good with a rifle as ever. Jim had worked with a Marine recon sniper team, and knew they were as good as they came. The other guys, would just need to make some noise, to distract the others, while Vlad led the hostages out. As he planned, he felt the old tingling in his arms and legs, that always came before an operation. He was ready mentally and physically.

Vlad drove directly to his home, after dropping Jim. He pulled into the garage, and quickly closed the large door, then checked that all windows were covered, before entering his tunnel. He couldn't keep himself, from thinking about how long his great-uncle, must have taken to build the tunnel years ago.

When he moved in, he had only needed a long vacation (a month) of careful digging, to break into the old workings of the BJ mine. Vlad had spent hours listening to his uncle ramble on, about the mine, and where he thought the best deposits were. He had been right. Vlad had found good color in the first exploratory digging he had done. During the first year, he had extracted enough gold, to support the needed careful purchases of equipment.

Vlad continued to his underground weapons depot. He quickly sorted out what he wanted. Jim had ruled out the law rockets, but didn't say anything about other additional munitions. Vlad could tell how personal this operation was, by how Jim had failed to think about how the two men were going to get the job done. In the past, he would have worried the plan to pieces, and then gone over everything again. As a planner, Jim was the best Vlad had ever worked with. Good planning had kept him and his team in Afghanistan, alive and active. This time, he was thinking too much about Andrea, and not enough about the operation. Vlad knew he would have to be the check and balance guy, this time.

Vlad got all of the arms and ammo loaded in the little electric motor (a small underground mine, train engine, that could pull ore cars, and transport men and equipment) he had personally rebuilt a few years ago. Vlad had learned about the way the motor worked from his uncle, who had been a motorman in a mine on Admiralty Island, for most of his life. It was a good thing he had taken the time to lay tracks and get the motor working, or he would be down here for a day, packing everything out. Vlad chuckled, as he wondered what his CIA contact, would think of his off-duty occupation.

It took Vlad an hour, to transfer the weapons and ammo to his car, and on a last thought, went back down, and got a box of grenades, and some other demo, that might be useful. He realized it was a fortunate thing, Bill had stepped up to the Beaver. It had a gross weight of over 5000 lbs. and could carry over 1800 lbs. useful load.

The reality was, that the plane could pretty much carry anything you could shove through the doors, or tie on the pontoons. That kind of carrying ability, was going to be needed tonight. He set his alarm system, and headed back to the boat.

Jim was on shore, with a two-wheeled cart, to load the stuff from the car. He took one look at what Vlad had, and said "I think we take the big boat. It will take a little longer to get to the plane, but it is going to deal with this crazy load, a lot better, and give us quicker access to it, if we need it."

Vlad nodded and added. "I would have recommended the same choice. The ammo alone, is going to be a load, and besides, I had a late thought and added some other stuff like vests, lights, and some flares. I also brought along a little more firepower than you had asked for." Vlad patted the case he was carrying. "There is an assortment of flash-bangs and frag grenades, plus some smoke. I thought they might come in handy."

Jim looked relieved. "I thought of that after you left. I guess I need to get my personal emotions out of this, and start thinking like a soldier right now!"

Vlad looked at him. "Jim, you at half-strength, is better than anyone else at full, so we are good to go." Without another word, Jim got the boat headed out.

Chapter Twenty-Two - Leroy's Ultimatum

Leroy shared the front of the plane with Bill, on the flight back to Pelican. The load, with equipment and people, would be over what even a Beaver could carry, so Bill was taking the others back. Leroy looked at Bill, and asked, "Bill, why are you are so damn dumb? You are the best pilot, the best hunting guide, and fishing guide, in the entire area, but you don't have the brains to blow up a dingy, when it comes to women."

Bill considered the comment for a minute, then said. "Shit Leroy, why don't you tell me how you really feel?"

"Okay, I will! You treat women like dog crap, and then, when they're about to cut your balls off, you get your buddies to bail you out. It just ain't right."

Bill hesitated for a moment, thinking that he is glad this conversation is on the com, and he and Leroy are the only ones wearing headsets.

"Leroy, you are right. I'm a weak individual. Two ex-wives, who knows how many girlfriends, and I still don't have a relationship that is worth anything."

Leroy looked at Bill and shook his head. "Bill, just cut the bullshit. You are not weak, you're just stupid. You have a beautiful woman that is so far in love with you, that she is almost as stupid as you are."

Bill asked, "Oh yeah, and who might that be?"

Leroy stared at Bill, then went on. "Bill, I am going to tell you the same thing I told you one time, when we were anchored up in boat harbor, and I was trying to teach you a card game. If you remember, you just would not learn, so I told you then, that you cannot be that stupid! I might have been wrong."

Bill finally took the time to think, before he opened his mouth. "I think you must be talking about Josephine."

Leroy rolled his eyes and slapped his forehead. "I am, and you know I'm right! You better think long and hard about her, before we go into this rescue. There is a real chance we may not come home. Do the right thing by her. It's your call."

Bill didn't know whether he should be excited, or scared to death. He had been in love with Josephine since the first time he had met her, but always felt he was not the only man in her life.

"You are right about it being my call, but you know Leroy, I have nothing to offer Josephine. I'm in debt up to my eyeballs and always will be." He paused, then continued. "I have been in love with her for a long time, but just never thought she felt the same. She has been so comfortable with this on-again, off-again relationship, I always thought that was what she wanted."

Leroy looked hard at Bill and slapped him on the shoulder. "You have been the only man in her life for years. It has torn her up every time you come to Pelican, and bragged about all of your stupid conquests. Did it ever enter your pea brain, that she was afraid of scaring you away? The only thing you ever talk about is how bad your two ex-wives were, and how you never plan on tying the knot a third time. As for being in debt, she is a very good businesswoman, and could help you get your life straightened out, if you would give her a chance." Leroy turned away and took off the head set. If Bill couldn't figure it out on his own, he didn't deserve her.

Bill spent the rest of the flight, thinking about his choices and possible outcomes, if he continued down the path he had been following for years. He knew the first two wives left him, partly because of his bad habits, but more importantly, it had been his inability to commit to the relationship. Josephine was too special to do anything half-assed. If he told her how he felt, he would have to go all-in, for the first time in his life.

By the time he taxied up to the boat ramp at Pelican, he had made his decision. After everyone, except Josephine, was out of the plane, Bill stopped her and gave her a real hug and a kiss.

She looked at him and asked "You know I like that, but what is on your mind? You know you have to fly right back to your place, so no time for sex."

Bill smiled and then said "As much as I would love that right now, I have something I need to ask you." Josephine could read the look in his eyes. She just didn't know what the look meant.

Bill took a deep breath and started. "Josephine! I have been in love with you, for a long time. I know I don't have much to offer you, but a lot of bills, and a rundown man, with more bad habits than a convent. Would you put that all aside, and consider spending the rest of our lives together?"

Josephine sat back in the seat and was slightly astounded. "I wonder if you have any idea, how long I have been waiting for you to ask that question!" She took a deep breath and continued. "I have been trying to get you to ask that, for the last two years. Yes! I will spend the rest of my life with you, but let me be clear. I am an exclusive woman, who owns several guns."

Bill grabbed her and looked into her eyes. "Baby, I wouldn't have it any other way." One last hug and she walked up the dock. Bill smiled and pushed the plane out. The flight back to Taku River, went by quickly. Bill had not felt so good, ever. He spent the entire flight, running on auto. "Maybe an old dog can learn new tricks, after all!" he thought to himself.

Vlad and Jim pulled in to the dock behind the plane, right at six. Jim notice that Bill was almost smiling. Something had happened to him, but there was no time to discuss that. All three guys started loading the gear into the plane. Everything was loaded and ready to go by seven. During loading, Bill mentioned that he had over-flown the mine. He told Vlad and Jim, that the cruise boat was gone, but he did see a lot of movement around the mine portal.

"Bill, I hope you didn't fly too close!" Jim was not happy.

Bill quickly shook his head. "No, I was flying the regular offshore route, most people fly, when coming out of Pelican, so no worries."

Jim relaxed "Okay! Let's get in the air, but don't even fly that close on the way back. I want those guys calm and sure they are safe."

The flight to Pelican, took a little over an hour, so they taxied up to the dock, at a quarter-past nine. There was plenty of light to see by, and to load. Everyone quickly got on board, except Josephine.

She was on the dock and arguing. "I can shoot just as well as any of you testosterone-driven pricks! I suppose you expect me to sit here with my thumb up my butt, or something? What exactly am I supposed to do, if I stay here alone?" Josephine was not happy.

"Bill said "I want you to stay by the radio, and when you hear the bears are dead, you'll know that we have the hostages, safe and sound. We will bring them here, so have rooms for them. I am sure a hot meal would be appreciated by all. If you don't hear anything by morning, call the Coast Guard and tell them everything. You are our only backup plan."

Bill gave her a quick hug, and pinch. That seemed to mollify her.

"Anything else?" she asked.

"Yep," Bill added. "Keep the wigwam warm baby." He might have been on the verge of changing his ways, but he still had no class.

Chapter Twenty-Three - THE RESCUE

Bill had to work to get the Beaver off the water, with the weight he was carrying. But, the plane lived up to its cargo-truck reputation, and finally lifted off the water. The down-side to the plane, was the noise level of the big radial engine. It precluded any normal conversations. Fortunately, it was a short flight back to the staging area, where Pete and Mort had their bear camp set up. Everyone pitched in, unloading the gear, then Jim went through a quick familiarization, with the assault rifles Vlad had brought for the men. They were brand new MP5 Heckler and Koch, full auto, or three-round-burst weapons, chambered for nine-millimeter ammo. He had also brought a Beretta pistol for each man, in the same caliber.

Jim had been surprised with the choice, since he knew Vlad had quite a selection. "I chose those, because I thought rate of fire, might be more important than a larger caliber, with more hitting power," Vlad stated when he saw the look on Jim's face.

"You're right, just keeping heads down, is more important than killing people for this operation. Besides, you and I will do the killing, and Leroy will have the Barrett."

Vlad was a bit surprised by that statement. "I didn't think I would ever see anyone other than you behind that gun!"

"Well, Leroy has more kills than I do, and I need to be in the mine. Leroy can set up an over-watch position, and keep anyone from leaving," Jim added. "And besides that, I know he can pull the trigger when he needs to, and will check targets before he does."

Vlad held his hands up. "I didn't mean I disagreed, just that you never let anyone touch that cannon in Afghanistan!"

Jim smiled, "There is a time and place for everything. Don't worry. When Brenner is in the sights, I will be behind the scope. Let's get started." Jim was in full team-leader mode, and did a quick gear check of every man, then looked at Pete and Mort. "Lead out, and remember, these bears shoot back!"

It took until midnight, to get set up on the hill overlooking the mine and the dock. Jim helped Leroy find a good shooting position, and helped him do some figuring for distance and drop. Leroy admitted, he had not done a lot of downhill-shooting since Nam, but hadn't forgotten how.

Everyone moved to a spot on the off-side of the ridge, for the final brief. Vlad didn't even try to inject in this. Jim would have not responded well.

Vlad realized that he was totally on-mission, and not thinking about Andrea. That was a good thing. Jim made eye contact with each man. "I want you each to remember, these men have killed the crew of the tour boat, and maybe a lot more by now. If you have a shot and no hostages are in danger, take it. I promise these mercenaries will shoot you, without a second thought."

Jim paused, to let that sink in. "Stay in your positions. Movement is the only way you will be seen up here. Vlad and I are going to get into the mine with Leroy's help, then give him time to get back here, before we move in. The primary goal of this operation, is to rescue the hostages. Killing a few scumbags is the frosting. Any questions?"

Bill thought for a second then "Yeah. How will we know when things start?"

Jim smiled at him. "When it starts, there will be no doubt in your mind. If anyone comes out of that tunnel, light them up. If a boat comes, after we are in the mine, use your judgment. If there are too many men onboard, head for the plane and call the authorities. If you think you can handle them, do it! Vlad and I have been through some crazy things over the years. We will get out, if things go bad."

Leroy had one more question and response. "You guys get the hostages, we will make sure no one goes down the mine after you. The only question I have is, how we will know when you guys are ready to come out, or are sending out hostages?" Vlad finally stepped into the conversation.

"I will pop a star cluster out of the tunnel, before any hostages come out."

Leroy just nodded his head "Good enough!" He then moved back to his firing position, to check the big gun one more time. He was ready to go, when Jim was.

Jim had Leroy take the point, as they began the careful move to the ventilation shaft. It took about fifteen minutes to find it in the semi-darkness. Finally, Leroy gave a little grunt and Jim moved up beside him. "Are you sure you don't want me to take you down to the main tunnel?"

Jim didn't hesitate. "No, your map and spoken directions, will be fine."

Jim patted him on the back. "I am counting on you to control our guys, when the bullets start flying. You have been there, the rest have not." Leroy smiled.

"Well that is not entirely true. Pete spent four years in the Guard, and did one deployment in Desert Storm. Mort was in the Air Force for a few years, and was a PJ."

Jim looked a bit shocked. "Why didn't they say something?"

Leroy smiled, "I think they were too amazed by all of the events." Leroy put his hand on Jim's shoulder. "You worry about the hostages, and that special lady of yours. We will cover your back."

Without another word, he headed back towards the ridge. Jim knew it would only take him a few minutes going back, so he and Vlad headed into the mine. Jim and Vlad stopped, when they came to the timber cribbing. They could see the simple way to pull them down, to get into the mine proper. Jim got close and spoke low. "Did you know about Pete and Mort?"

Vlad patted him and said "Jim, I know about everyone in the town of Juneau. How do you think I survive? That's my job. Yours, on the other hand, is to make this thing works." Jim looked at him, then turned to the tunnel entrance. He couldn't help but feel a little nostalgic. He could be back in Wallace, sneaking into an old mine tunnel on the hill, behind his family home on Maple street. "A long way to come, for childhood memories. He started pulling out the timbers, as carefully as possible.

Vlad took each one, as they came out, and carefully stacked them to the side. It took ten minutes to open the entry. Jim entered first, and made sure no lights were visible, in either direction. The main drift, slanted down at a constant slope. They were not surprised to see that the tunnel appeared to have been in use, quite recently. The tracks all led down. Only a few appeared to come out. Vlad looked at Jim, and he pointed down.

Vlad scanned the drift, and was interested to see how large the drift was. The best part, was the height was quite good, so they wouldn't have to worry about running into the ceiling. Vlad and Jim each had a helmet, and a mine-light, that threw a lot of light, so they headed down.

This was an eerie assault. No noise and only the mine lights showing anything. After about twenty minutes of hiking, Vlad stopped and checked the map. "By my reckoning, we should be getting close to the underground staging area. How do you want to do this?"

Jim took the map and then said. "You know, this would be a lot easier, if there were more side-tunnels and turns. Since there aren't I think we move as carefully as possible, until something shows. Do these lights dim, or do they only go full-blast?"

Vlad reached up and pointed to an adjustment screw on the battery pack. "You can dim them down, as far as you want, with this knob." He demonstrated on his light. Jim did the same to his.

"Okay, no talking now, until we see the enemy, or the hostages. If we are lucky, there may only be one, or two guys down here. On the other hand, there could be fifty!" Vlad looked at him, with a 'Thanks a lot, stare.

"Well, we better hope for a low number, or we have a real problem!"

Jim smiled, his 'who gives a shit' smile, and added "Don't worry, we are going in, no matter how many there are down here!"

Jim had Vlad stay about twenty feet behind him, and moved on. After another five hundred feet, Jim saw a glow in the tunnel, in front of him. He stopped and waited for Vlad. "Let me move down and see if I can do a little recon." He dropped his mine-light and extra equipment. It took him about ten minutes, to move close enough, to start making out the walls, from the light ahead. He carefully moved close enough, to see the light was coming from a side-tunnel, or room off of the main drift. He carefully moved up, until he could look into the room. There were three men inside, playing some card game. Jim could smell food, and was not surprised to see a bottle of wine on the table. He stayed there long enough, to be sure no one else was there, but the three men.

There was a weapon close at hand, to each one, plus he could see a sidearm on the man with his back to the door. Jim turned and moved back up the tunnel, as quickly as he could, in the semi-darkness. As he got close, he gave the recognition signal (three clicks) so Vlad would know it was him. "We have three armed men in a small room, off the side of the drift, playing cards. It looks like they are pretty secure and bored. Let's take them out, as silent as possible. I sure wish silencers worked, as well as they do on TV."

Jim picked up the gear he had left behind. "We will drop gear, just short of the door. I'll handle the three men." Vlad stopped Jim with his hand. "Are you sure you want to kill them now, instead of sneaking by and continuing?

Jim thought for a minute, or two. "I think we need to insure a safe move, back up the drift. We take them now!"

The move back down the drift, was much faster and they were soon in position. Jim again dropped his extra gear, and Vlad followed suit. Vlad moved to the hinge side of the door, and got ready to open it. Jim was set and gave him the signal. Vlad pulled it open, and Jim stepped in. He fired three short bursts, and all three men were down. Only one man had even gotten a hand on his rifle. Vlad stayed out of the room, long enough to insure no new noises were coming out of the mine, then followed Jim in. With the door closed, Jim and Vlad searched each man and gathered everything they found. Vlad went through each item and was excited, when he opened a small map of the mine that had been in a pocket of the man closest to the door. "Jim! Look at this. It looks like they have the hostages all the way at the end of the drift. That is about a half-mile farther down from here.

Jim looked, then added, "That is good news, but look at the side-room, closer to the entry. It says it is the lab!" Vlad studied the map some more, and then looked at Jim.

"I think we are going to find out that Westlake is there, and not with the other hostages."

They did some quick planning, and decided to get the main group of hostages up to the vent shaft, then work on the lab. They moved quickly down the last half-mile of the drift quickly, now that they knew no one was there, except the hostages. When they reached the locked door, Jim found a light switch by the door and turned it on. Immediately, he heard talking behind the door. He pulled open the door and looked in. He saw Andrea, on the floor beside another woman. When he moved over to her, she finally saw his face. "I can't believe you found us. How long have we been here? How many men do you have?"

Jim finally smothered her questions with a hug and kiss. "One question at a time Senator." He smiled a happy smile, for the first time in several days.

Andrea wouldn't let go of him for several minutes, but finally, stepped back so she could see his face. "I have been telling Lorrie that you would come, but even I was starting to worry. It seems like we have been down here for a month. The only time they come down, is to drop off a little food and water. They always turn off the light when they leave." Jim got a happy expression on his face. "I hoped that Lorrie ended up here, where is she?"

Then he looked down on the floor, as a very familiar blond stood up. He grabbed her, and gave her a hug as well. "You have no idea how glad I am to see you alive. Joe has been worried to death, since he saw that engineer drag you off the cruise ship."

Lorrie had a strange look on her face, as she gave Jim a hug. "I knew you would come, and now, I just realized that Andrea's Jim was the same Jim, I had been talking about."

Jim looked at both women and smiled again. "I guess I am a lucky guy. I seem to be dating the two most beautiful women, for a hundred miles around!"

Lorrie grabbed Andrea's hand and looked at Jim. "No! You are only dating my best friend, Andrea. Get any other bright ideas, and I will cut your balls off for her. Since she is a Senator, and can't do it herself."

Jim smiled and said "Look, I am sorry, but Andrea and I have been beating around a relationship for a long time."

Lorrie didn't hesitate. "Jim, you are the most interesting man I have ever met, and I hope you and Andrea are my friends for a long time!" Jim knew he was a one-woman man going forward, after that statement.

Jim gave each one another hug, and then turned to the rest of the people. "Can everyone walk out okay?" Andrea pointed to a woman sitting down. "Jim, I don't think so. Amelia has a severely sprained, or broken ankle, and Suzuki seems to struggle with any exertion." Jim looked at the two she had mentioned, and asked them, "Can you make it about a mile, with some help?"

Suzuki stood straight and stated. "You lead, I follow. My wife can assist me. My problem is claustrophobia. I feel the walls closing in. If this gets me into the open, I can go several miles."

Jim smiled at that. "What about you miss?"

Amelia considered her answer, but finally, "I will do whatever it takes, to get out of here."

Jim thought about that, then said, "Okay, Vlad will assist you. The first stage, is going to be the worst part, because we will have to use as little lighting, as possible. Once you are all in the ventilation tunnel, lighting can be used continuously. It is about a half-mile to the surface."

Jim let that sink in, then continued. "There are men on the surface waiting, and they can get you all out, to a safe location."

Vlad interrupted there. "Jim, that all sounds good, but what about the scientist?"

"Well Vlad, that's where I am going, as you get the rest out through the vent tunnel."

Vlad tried to think of some better way, that would not leave the shooting to Jim alone, but he knew these people would need his help to get out. "I guess that's the plan!"

As they got ready to move, the sole remaining, secret service agent walked up to Jim. "I am a pretty good shot, and could be that extra shooter you are going to need!" Jim sized him up and was ready to respond, when Andrea spoke.

"Jamie. You have a concussion!"

Jamie looked back at her and continued. "I have been feeling much better the last couple of days, and it's time for me to start doing my job." He looked back at Jim. "Look, where else are you going to find a trained MP5 gunner down here?"

Jim thought for a minute, and agreed. "Okay, you're in. Vlad will hand off his MP5, and you and I will go out the way you came in. I hope you are ready for this. We will not be reading anyone their Miranda rights, you know!"

Jamie smiled lopsidedly (one side of his face, seemed to be paralyzed). "I wouldn't have it any other way, with these guys. Bobby was a good friend and coworker, for a long time. Give me the chance, and I will feed them all to the bears myself!"

Peter Ivanovo had been listening and watching, and finally entered the conversation. "I also have military training, and my man Uri is a trained Speznaz commando. With some weapons, we would like to assist also."

Jim considered, and finally made a choice. "I can use Uri, but I need someone to assist Vlad with the rest of the hostages. If you could help with that, I think we can make this work. There are at least three more weapons in the guard-room that we will pass on the way out. So, let's get going and no more talking, until we reach the side-tunnel."

Jim shut off the overhead light to give everyone a chance to adjust to the dark. After a few minutes, he had them start out. Jim took point, with Vlad next, assisting Amelia Lawson, but Lorrie had stepped up, to help as well.

As soon as they seemed to be moving well, Jim left the group, and headed back up the tunnel, as quickly as he could move. When he saw the lights ahead, from the guard room, he slowed and extinguished his light. He quietly crept up to the door, to make sure no one was there (still alive). He moved into the room and grabbed two of the guards' assault rifles. Surprisingly, they were the same model, as Vlad had brought.

He searched the room for more ammo, and recovered three pistols; all in nine-millimeter. Unfortunately, there was not a lot of spare ammo. He found two full magazines, plus the partials, that had been in the rifles. Jim was almost to the point of heading back down, when he finally heard the movement coming towards him. He flashed his light, to assure Vlad, all was well.

Everyone took a break at the guard house, but Jim didn't want them to get too comfortable. Jim gave the two men the weapons, but saved one of the pistols for Andrea. Andrea took the pistol, and immediately checked it, to make sure it was loaded. Jim smiled and said, "I guess I don't have to show you how to fire it. The safety is a little different. I couldn't tell you who made the thing, but it seems to handle a lot like the military Beretta."

Andrea gave him a hug, and then, "I feel better right now, than I have in a long time. When this is over, I hope you will let me show you how much this all means to me!" Jim got the first real, happy look on his face, since the kidnapping, and just hugged her even harder. Life couldn't get much better.

"Andrea, I have a lot to prove to you as well, so don't make any plans for the next few months!"

Lorrie had been taking this all in, and was feeling a little left out, when Vladimir spoke to her. "I bet that you are a bit disappointed in our man right now?"

She looked at Vlad, and quickly assured him "How could I be unhappy with the man, men I mean, who are saving us?"

Vlad chuckled, "Hard to hide the way you looked, when you saw Jim hugging Andrea!"

She smiled and said, "Oh, I am not going to hide that. I am disappointed, but I knew he was committed to someone-else. I just didn't expect to become best friends with her. I wish only the best, for both of them. Andrea is the most impressive woman I have ever met and Jim, is just special." Vlad gave her a quick hug in the dark.

"When this is over, I will you tell about all of the times he has saved my miserable life. How's that sound?"

Lorrie hesitated for a minute, then said, "I think I would rather hear more about you, and how you came to be involved in all of this."

Vlad thought to himself, "This could get interesting." "That can be arranged as well. Let's get out of here now."

Chapter Twenty-Four - JIM SAVES ROB WESTLAKE

After giving everyone a breather, Jim had them start up the tunnel again. When he reached the ventilation tunnel, he waited for all to get to him. It took several minutes to get everyone into the tunnel and the slider-boards back in place. Vlad would give them a rest, then start out. Jim didn't want them out in the open, until he had time to try and free Westlake. He outlined the plan for the attempt. Since Jamie was still showing signs of the concussion, he would act as the rear security, while Jim and Uri did the assault. They moved up the remaining distance much faster, without the other hostages slowing them down.

Ten minutes, saw them within striking distance of the underground lab. Jim tried to recon the space, but could not be sure how many gunmen were in the lab. He finally decided, that to wait was more dangerous, than just going for it. Jamie stayed at the door, just out of the light, and Uri and Jim crashed the door. Jim went left and Uri went right. They worked so well together, you would have thought they had done this a thousand times, instead of just this once. Jim shot two men, as he breached the door, and turned towards another, but Uri had him down, before he could bring his gun to bear. A quick check, and Jim was sure the room was safe.

Jim moved around and found the door into the lab area locked. He made swift work of the lock (Not designed to stand up to a nine-millimeter). When he opened the door, he nearly got his own concussion. Westlake swung a large bar at his head. Jim grabbed the bar, then said, "Look I am here to help, but if you decide later, I can give you the club back, and let you try to hit me again."

Rob dropped his hands and asked, "Who the hell are you, the marines or what?" Rob was too stunned to say anything more.

"Listen Doctor, call me a Marine again, and I may have to use the club myself!" Jim was smiling, as he said this. "I wish we could stay and gab, but how about we get out of here, before any more crazies show up?" Westlake looked at the man who had rescued him, and added, "The rest of the people are still down the mine, at the end."

Jim was impressed that the man would worry about the others. "No! They are headed for the surface. We got them out first." Jim gave another rare smile, and pushed the guy towards the door.

Jim and Rob moved towards the surface, with Uri and Jamie bringing up the rear. It was a short hike to the portal. Jim stopped, close to the tunnel entry, and turned to Rob. "Do you have any idea how many more men are on the surface? We have taken six out so far. Rob did a quick count in his head, then said,

"I think there may be one more, but they were expecting a bunch more, to fly in tonight. The reason I tried to club you, was that they had told me, taunted me, about the fact that I was soon going to be feed for the bears. At first, the head man had said they would keep me alive for a long time, but that changed when they got the information out of me!"

He hung his head in shame, as he said the last. Jim looked at him, and patted him on the back "Look Doc, I am a trained soldier, and no one can hold out forever, so don't feel bad." Jim was a bit surprised, that he had given them what they wanted, so quickly.

Rob could see the look in the man's eyes. "They fed a woman, the delegate from Australia, Amarina Copper, to the bears and said they would do it to everyone, one at a time, until I gave them what they wanted. Have you ever seen a person eaten by a bear?" Jim realized, how fear-inducing the threat must have been.

"Look, you did what you had to. Let's concentrate on getting out of here. You may still have opportunities to help us with these guys." Jim could tell the man was on the edge of total collapse, and needed to be bolstered up.

Jim was moving towards the entry, when all hell broke loose. As soon as he cleared the portal, he could see a large helicopter, painted like a Coast Guard chopper, on the helicopter pad. Several men were firing towards the guys on the hill. Jim was about to enter the fight, when he saw a man drop, and then heard his .50. Leroy was on the job. Jim made a quick decision and arranged Jamie and Uri, to give him cover-fire, as he moved out, to get a clear field of fire. He aimed the star cluster, and popped it out into the open. He didn't want to catch friendly fire. Jim moved to the left of the landing pad, and was in place, when Leroy managed to take out another one. Jim dropped the last man at the helicopter pad, and moved forward, to check the area.

He was moving towards the helicopter, when a man raised his hands and pleaded to not be shot. "Come out where I can see you and don't think for a minute, that I would hesitate shooting you now!"

The man came out into the open. "I am the pilot, and had no idea what I was getting into." Jim really doubted that, but got the man down and did a quick frisk. No real surprise, he had a pistol in a shoulder harness, the way pilots like to carry. "I guess you forgot about the pistol?" Jim kneed the man, as he stood up, with the thing. He went to clear it, and was surprised to find it empty. "You fly boys never seem to be able to understand how to use one of these things."

Jim was ready to call everyone in, when he heard more firing, starting up on the ridge line. He grabbed the pilot and put his rifle to his temple. "How many are up there?" The pilot knew he was living on thin ice.

"Only three men moved up the hill. The rest were in sight of your men and stayed down here, to attract their fire." Jim got Uri and Jamie out of the tunnel, and was making a plan, when the gunfire ended.

"I don't know if we won, or they did. I guess we will get ready for who comes down!" The men spread out, after securing the prisoner. About five minutes after the last shot was heard, a voice came out of the dark. "Jim, hold your fire, its Bill, we won. He moved out into the open and Jim noticed that Bill had taken a round to his left arm, high up.

Jim wasted no time. "How about the others?"

Bill looked worried. "Leroy is shot bad and Pete got hit as well. We had no idea they were coming up on us. They would have gotten us all, but Leroy saved us. He wouldn't let us move, until he was sure you were okay down here. If we had listened better to him, he would not have been shot. Pete took one early on, but Leroy was shot when they came up on us. He killed two of them, but his rifle jammed. That's when he was shot. We got the last one after that, and headed down to check on you. I'm sorry Jim, we were just not ready for them, when they came."

Jim patted Bill on the shoulder (good arm). "Look Bill, you guys just took out several trained mercenaries, with years of combat experience. You did well!" Jim meant it with all of his heart. He had fought this bunch before. He knew how good they were.

Jim had Bill and Jamie stay on watch at the mine, and he took Uri back up the hill. He left them at the opening to the ventilation tunnel, to help the hostages, when they came out. Jim checked his watch and was surprised as usual, how little time had gone by. He climbed the hill to check on Leroy and Pete.

Mort was working like crazy, trying to stabilize Leroy. He had taken a shot high in the chest, possibly two. Leroy was coughing up blood, and trying to get Mort to stop. Jim took one look, and pulled Mort to the side.

"There was no way to save him, with that chest wound." Mort looked horrified.

"I haven't done this kind of field medicine in a long time, but there is no way to stop the internal bleeding."

Jim sat down with Leroy, and took his hand. "I am sorry for getting you into this. You saved a lot of people tonight. I hope you know that."

Leroy finally looked up and smiled through the blood on his lips. "Listen sergeant, I wouldn't have missed this, for any amount of money. My fear has always been dying alone. I got to go out with good friends, doing something grand." He stopped, as he was wracked with coughing. "I need you to do me a favor though!" Jim leaned closer, to hear what the favor was. Leroy coughed up some more blood, then continued. "Back in my room, at the hotel, is a will. It leaves everything I own to Josephine, and that idiot Bill. Thanks for letting me fight with real warriors, one last time." He lay back and soon expired. Jim rose and was more moved with grief, than he had been in years.

Jim got everyone down the hill, to figure out what to do next. He watched the hostages moving down the hill. Mort had every wound dressed and ready to move, even the one remaining mercenary. Jim was getting ready for a little interrogation, when Rob came over.

"Jim, I think you are missing one bad guy. I don't see the radio operator, and I know he was still at the mine, after Brenner left. Did you find the radio room?" Jim did a quick check on his memory.

"No, I didn't see a radio, or any other communications equipment in the mine."

Rob rubbed his chin, where he had a bad scab, from an earlier altercation. "I know they had communications, and a way to get online. Brenner kind of rubbed it in, when he sent off the formula. He bragged about the money and that he was going to double-cross

PEDEI Corp, as well as the entire United States. We need to find that guy, and the room right now!"

Jim grabbed his weapon, and yelled for Vlad and Uri to follow him back to the mine. When they got to the portal, he quickly outlined the problem and the plan. The last thing anyone wanted, was to lose another man at this point. Jim took lead with the others following. They re-cleared each room and finally found a door, behind the cabinets, off the lab. Jim went through the door fast and ready. A man was sitting at a desk, with a laptop. He turned at the sound of the entry. He grabbed a pistol, as he turned. Jim took no chances, and triggered a burst on the MP5. The man was thrown back against the table, and managed to trigger one shot into the ceiling of the room, before dropping the gun and sliding to the floor.

Vladimir ran to the laptop and realized that the computer was online and in direct connection with someone. Jim walked over to watch. "What do you think? Did he get through to Brenner?" Vlad sat down and was figuring out what to do, when a face came up on the computer screen. It was no surprise that it was Brenner. The surprise was that Brenner was not aware he was not speaking to his man.

"I want to know what the fuck is going on there. Has the tunnel been blown, or not?"

Vladimir looked at Jim and then reopened the line. "Well shit head, I think you can pretty well figure that no tunnel has been blown. The only thing that has blown was your shitty operation."

Brenner looked like he was ready to explode. "Well, if it isn't my favorite Russian asshole. I guess everything has gone to shit after all. I suppose that dumbass sergeant is there with you as well?"

Vlad smiled and added. "The only thing that is missing from all of this, is your dead body at my feet. Your only chance is to turn yourself in right now. Maybe you will get a fun cellmate at Leavenworth?"

Brenner could hardly utter a word through his anger, but finally controlled himself. "If I can't kill you two, I will have to settle for the next best thing. Say goodbye to all of your friends in Juneau. I am going to blow that shit hole off the planet."

Vlad crossed his fingers and hoped Ling Cod had shut down the only active cell tower in the Juneau area. All had agreed that was the most likely way of remotely detonating the bomb. Brenner stayed in front of the camera and dialed a number on the cell phone. He looked at Vlad and smiled, as he entered the last number. He stared at the phone, then dialed again.

Vlad watched him, then said "Hey smart guy, I bet you didn't get through on that phone did you?" Vlad smiled, when he could tell the attempt had failed. Vlad could see Brenner turn towards someone-else. Brenner told the unseen person, to get the boat headed for Juneau. He then turned back to the camera. If looks could kill, Vlad would have gone down right there. Brenner was so red in the face, he looked ready to explode. "You may have stopped the call, but you have no way off the island fast enough to stop me."

"I know the chopper was shot-up on the beach. The best you can have, is some slow, fishing vessel. It is time to blow the city and move on. I have a bunch of money to collect, and a city to blow up."

Vlad tried to stay as calm as possible, to get as much information as possible. "I guess you don't know yet, that your men on the ground are all gone. How about just pulling in here, and calling it a day. Do you really want to be the biggest mass murderer since Hitler, or Stalin?"

Brenner reached towards the computer, but hesitated long enough to say one last thing. "You always think you are smarter than everyone, but this time, I planned better than either of you assholes. I have a backup plan for detonating the bomb, totally separate from my team. Thanks for taking care of the men in Juneau. The plan never included any of them surviving this op anyway. Well, I can't say this has been fun, but it is time to go." Brenner again, reached for the computer. Then, he hesitated long enough to add, "Oh, did I mention that, as I was heading towards the mine, I noticed a piss-yellow airplane on the beach. The boys had a great time shooting it into small pieces." This time, he reached forward and the screen went black.

Vlad turned to Jim. "We are screwed without the airplane." Jim looked thoughtful.

"I wonder how badly the helicopter was shot-up, during the fire-fight." He turned without another word, and ran out of the mine. Jim grabbed the captured pilot and pulled him by the collar, towards the aircraft. "Your only chance of surviving this thing, is if you can get this chopper in the air, in about thirty minutes. Any longer, and you will be a mass murderer!" The guy looked like he would shit himself at that. "Cut me loose, and let me get to work then."

Jim called to Uri "Can you watch him for me? I need to get everything ready to go. That crazy bastard is going to blow up Juneau!"

Chapter Twenty-Five - Saving Juneau

Everyone gathered together, to figure out what to do next. Andrea opened the discussion "I don't have any ideas, but I think I need to try and get hold of Mom. I wonder if a cell phone will still work here. Jim looked at her, reached into his pocket and pulled out his phone.

"You know, in all of the excitement, I didn't even think of trying." He turned on the satellite phone, and was not surprised to get a good signal. "What are you going to tell your mother?"

Andrea thought for a minute. "Well, I can start with the fact that I am alive!"

Vladimir chuckled at that. "I think we need to get some navy support out here, as fast as possible. If Brenner blows the bomb and gets out of US waters, it could be difficult, catching up with him."

Jim let go of Andrea's hand, and added, "I think we are going to be on our own, trying to stop the bomb. If the helicopter will fly, we need to head for Juneau. Vlad, you could drop me at my boat. I can try and intercept Brenner, as he comes into Auke Bay. That will leave you to try and deal with the bomb. I know that is not the best deal in town, so if anyone has a better idea, let me know?"

Andrea took Jim's hand and looked into his eyes. "I think that is our best plan, as long as I come with you. You will need someone to operate the boat, while you are taking care of Brenner!" Vlad looked at both, and just shook his head. "I think I get the good end of the stick on this one. You have no way of knowing how many men are with Brenner."

Peter rose and turned to Vladimir. "I would be much honored to assist you with the bomb. I need to do something to stop this craziness that my country may have aided in putting in motion. I have quite a lot of experience with explosives, and have been trained in disarming devices." Vlad didn't hesitate. "I can use your help. I have been involved with them, for a long time myself, but two sets of hands may make all of the difference." Vlad shook Peter's hand, as he said this.

Andrea took Jim's phone and dialed her special access number to the White House. The phone only rang one time. Her mother answered the phone herself. "I don't know who this is, but you better be very important. This number is only used by two people in the world, and one is dead, and the other is standing beside me!" Listen mom, I am not dead, so don't hang up."

It took Andrea several minutes to convince her mother she was who she said she was. Then, she explained the entire thing to her. Halfway through the explanation, the President put her on speaker, so her father could hear everything as well. Andrea finally got to the rescue, and what was going on right now. "Mom, I am going to put you on speaker, at this end as well. Vladimir Choskey can explain our plan to you, better than I can." Andrea started to hand the phone to Vlad, when her mother asked "Explain to me again, who is Vladimir Choskey?"

"Madam President, I am with the CIA, but have been acting independently, on this operation. It would take way too long to explain how I became involved. We are on a limited time crunch here, so let me get to the point. Brenner has a willing helper within the CIA. That person, needs to be dealt with. If I was to guess, I would also look at his contacts in the State Department. What we need up here, as fast as possible, is some Navy presence, to try and stop Brenner, if we fail on our end."

Vlad had to take a breath, before continuing. "If we can get the helicopter flying, we will try and stop the bomb and catch Brenner."

There was a long pause from the President, then "Okay, I will deal with this side of the issue, and get some kind of naval response ASAP. We have a description of the boat and the top speed." The President paused, then continued. Let me talk to Jim, off speaker please?"

Jim took the phone and walked away from the others. "I am alone at this time Madam President. Jim, you know my name, so no more bullshit!

I have one special request, from me to you." She paused, and then, "I want Brenner dead! Do you have a problem with that?"

Jim let out the breath he had been holding. "No, I was afraid you were going to ask to keep him alive. This guy has slid out of trouble, too many times before. I will take him out, or die trying!" Jim turned the phone off. "Ok, let's get this show on the road."

Jim and Vlad checked all of the injured, then took Lorrie aside. "Lorrie, can you keep everyone together and try and keep spirits up? Willy will be here anytime now, with his boat. He can transport everyone to Pelican, for medical assistance, and a hot bath. I am sure the Navy will be here soon also."

Lorrie looked at Vlad, and asked a simple question. "I know we just met, but when this is all over, do you think we could have a drink together?"

Vlad gave her a hug. "I think more than a drink is in order, at least let me buy you dinner!" Lorrie was smiling, as she turned away, to start organizing the group.

Jim and Vlad headed down to the helicopter pad. Everything hinged on that chopper. They got good news, as they approached. The rotors started turning over, and the engine fired. Jim reached the door the pilot looked at him. "I can't guarantee anything, but I think we can make Juneau. I wouldn't bet much past that though."

Jim smiled and turned to Vlad. "Okay, let's get loaded and hope like hell we can beat the son-of-a-bitch to town."

Vlad added his two cents. "Well we can go straight and faster, than that crazy boat." It took another ten minutes to load up, but then they lifted off.

The flight to Jim's boat, only took forty minutes, but the pilot almost refused, when he found out he had to lift off again. An MP5 poked in the side of his head, got the chopper back in the air. Jim and Andrea wasted no time casting off, and Jim opened up the boat for the first time in sight of the shore. The race was on.

Jim had Andrea on the bow, with his binoculars, watching the sea-ways for any sign of Brenner. It took another fifteen minutes to get around Coglin Island, and within view of Auke bay. Jim had Andrea drop anchor and the wait began. Jim set up his .50 on the top of the fore cabin, and used his spotting scope, to figure some distances to points he could expect the boat to pass through, either coming, or going. He was afraid it would be going.

Andrea asked no questions, until Jim seemed to finally relax. "I don't want to interrupt anything, but how can I help?"

Jim smiled at her, and squeezed her hand. "Andrea, just being here is all the help I need. Keep your rifle handy, in case we have to repel borders." He smiled when he said that, but Andrea knew he was quite serious about the possibility. Jim looked at his watch and did some quick figuring. "I think Vlad should be close to the boat by now. I don't think I could forgive myself, if he dies on this one." Andrea looked at him, grabbed his hand, and pulled him close. No words were needed.

Vladimir kept the gun pointed at the pilot, until he set down, right on the main city cruise ship dock. It was quite eerie, to not see thousands of people around. Apparently, the police had everyone off the streets, during the crisis. Vlad could see people on board the closest ship, staring at him. The entire rail was full of tourists.

Peter looked up, as he came around from the other side of the chopper with his MP5. "I hope we are the only thing these people get to see!"

Vlad shook himself, and got back on task. "There is nothing we can do for them, except find the bomb."

The speed boat was easy to pick out, mixed in with all of the fishing and sport vessels, so they headed for it. As they got close, Vlad saw the last thing he wanted to. Brenner was just jumping in a small boat, tied up to the stern of the bomb boat. He ran around and tried to get a shot, but had to take cover, when Brenner opened up on him. The small boat was quickly out of range, so Vlad and Peter ran to the boat and carefully boarded. "Peter, we probably have at least twenty minutes, I would guess. It will take that much time to get to a safe distance, and Brenner is not the suicide-bomber type."

Vlad went below decks, while Peter started searching the deck and helm area. Vlad found the detonator right off. "Peter, get down here, we have a serious problem."

Peter ran down and joined Vlad in the aft cabin. Peter took one look and just said. "Oh shit!"

Vlad sat down and asked, "I was hoping you had a better idea than me, on this one. There is no way to shut this thing down." Peter took a breath, then took a closer look. He could see that the detonator was quite simple and easy to understand, just impossible to disconnect, or turn off. He ran several alternatives through his mind.

"I see that you recognize the device, as well as I do. It is a military detonator, made in France, and there is no way to dismantle it, without setting off the bomb. We could try and separate the bomb from the detonator charge, but it will take hours to pull all of the fertilizer, out of the forward cabin. And even then this charge, would do severe damage to the city."

Vlad was brainstorming ideas in his mind, and finally said. "What if we scuttle the entire boat, bomb and all?" Peter thought for a minute and then,

"I think that is our only choice. We need to get as far away as possible, and into the deepest water we can, in the next ten minutes, and get this thing headed for the bottom."

Vlad wasted no time. He just headed up to the helm and hotwired the boat. He was just casting off, when GoGo Joe walked up the dock. Vlad wasted no time, he just told Joe to get on board. He knew Joe would know the deepest spot in Gastineau Channel. As the boat pulled away, Peter started opening every scupper he could find. He then grabbed an ax, and headed forward, to chop another hole in the bow. That got the water flowing in, at a good rate.

Joe never asked a question. He looked too surprised, to even form one. Vlad looked at Joe and said, "I need the closest deepest spot in the channel that we can reach in ten minutes, or less." Joe thought for a minute, and took the helm. He didn't know what was happening, but he could do a job. Vlad left him, and joined Peter in his effort to scuttle the boat. When he felt they had enough water coming in, he grabbed Peter and headed for the deck, to figure a way off for them. They found a dingy on the stern, and quickly rigged the outboard and got it over the side. Vlad ran back up, to see how Joe was doing.

"This is as good as it gets. There is close to one hundred feet, under us right now, and as it drifts, it gets deeper," Joe added.

Vlad shut the engines down and pulled Joe with him, towards the rear. "I think it is time for us to go." Peter was in the dingy and had the engine fired, by the time they reached the stern. They dove in, and Peter turned and opened up the outboard. Vlad checked his watch and was glad to see the boat sinking rapidly. He looked at his watch, as the bow rail went under. "It could blow any time now. Let's hope Brenner, was a bigger chicken than I thought!"

Peter never even turned to watch. He concentrated on going away, as fast as the small outboard would allow. They were actually pulling into the dock, when the explosion came. Peter continued running the boat towards shore and ran up the launch ramp. All three were thrown down, but glad to be alive. Vlad watched the explosion and had been amazed by the water spout. He was staring at the water, when he realized things were not over yet. "Oh shit, hold on." Peter finally turned, then threw himself down and grabbed on. A miniature tidal wave was headed for them. It picked up the dingy and them, and headed inland. When the boat finally came to rest, Vlad and the others stepped out in downtown Juneau.

Waiting for the Shot

Jim was becoming quite frustrated, when he saw a large boat coming around the point from Auke Bay. He was on the scope, right away and identified the hydrofoil. He had to wait until the boat was out in the open, and past them, to be able to see inside the cabin. Brenner was at the helm, with a woman beside him. Both appeared to be quite happy. Jim waited until the boat was passing one of his known points, and took a shot at the exhaust ports. The starboard engine began smoking.

Jim tried to hit the port engine, but couldn't get a reaction out of it. He shifted to the helm and took his time, lining up his final shot. The boat was moving too much to hope for a head shot, but even in the body with a fifty would do. He lined up his shot and took a breath. He squeezed off the most important shot of his life and missed! Just as he shot, there was enough movement in the boat that his shot impacted right on the back of Brenner's head. Jim tried to take a shot at the woman, but she ducked out of sight, and his heart wasn't in it, to just start shooting. The Navy could pick her up. (Everyone makes a mistake occasionally).

Jim pulled the anchor and got headed back to Auke bay. All thoughts were on Juneau and his friend Vlad. Andrea helped Jim get his sniper rifle back under cover. Jim then had her take the helm, while he picked up his brass and deep-sixed it. They were just tying up, when the explosion came. It was much muffled and not anything like he had expected. "Vlad and Peter must have been at least partly successful. There is no way Brenner would have messed up a bomb that way."

He grabbed Andrea and hugged her, as tightly as he could. "I think we may live after all. How about a long cruise, just you and I, for a month, or so, with no one else around to interrupt?"

Andrea kissed him and just looked into his eyes. "I thought you would never ask. How about somewhere warm, with no guns or bombs?" she added.

"I think that can be arranged!" Jim's smile could have been seen from the lower forty-eight. It took several minutes to secure the boat, and then find transportation into Juneau.

Since Jim knew that the terrorists had blown up the Brotherhood Bridge, a car was out of the question. He checked the remaining boats, and picked a flat-bottomed river boat. It was sixteen feet, and had a jet drive. Jim helped Andrea down to the boat, and then hotwired it.

"I wonder what my constituency will think about me stealing a boat." Andrea was chuckling, as she asked it.

"I think that should be the last worry of the most famous Senator alive!" Jim poked her in the ribs, as he ran the boat past the airport and through the shallow end of Gastineau Chanel. Andrea had a thoughtful look on her face, when she responded.

"I am afraid my mother will be pushing me to run for higher office with this kind of notoriety, but she is in for a surprise."

Jim looked at her. "What kind of surprise?" Andrea looked resolute.

"I'm done with politics. She can capitalize all she wants. I think I am ready for that real commitment you have always spoken about, if you still want me?" Jim would have stopped right then, to hug her, but not until he knew the fate of his friends.

When they approached downtown Juneau, they could not believe their eyes. The boat harbors were gone, and there were boats, and sections of docks, clear up on Eagan Drive. Jim commandeered a car, and they spent the next hour, looking for their friends. Finally, they found GOGO, Vlad, and the Russian, Peter Ivanovo, working with other volunteers, rescuing trapped people. The amazing thing was, all were fine. All three had simple bumps and abrasions. Unfortunately, the city was a real mess. The miniature tidal wave, did do some surprising good. Several of the buildings that had been blown up, had been burning since the explosions. The tidal wave had put out all of the fires. It would take a lot of work to repair the damage.

Chapter Twenty Six - The President Cleans House

The first day, after the explosion was averted, saw the city begin to climb out of the fear-induced trance, the entire population had been under. The infrastructure of the city, was in sad shape. First, all of the bombs had taken power, water, and most communications offline. Ling Cod stepped up, and started organizing repair crews, for the water and electricity utilities. Most of the more senior, city employees, had all been killed, or wounded, when the municipal offices had been destroyed. The Governor's Mansion had been damaged, but not destroyed. Only three police officers were lucky enough to have been outside of town, when the rest were dispatched to buildings that were now gone.

The Chief had been quite successful in his plan, to kill all of his officers. Alaska State Troopers, were flown into town, to supplement the three remaining law enforcement officers, and to begin the investigation. Vlad and Jim dove in and assisted wherever they were needed, while Andrea essentially took over the overall management of the city. The City Clerk was the one remaining city elected official, and after being discharged from the hospital, for her minor injuries suffered in the explosion of city hall, was sworn in as the acting Mayor.

The surprise of the entire event, was that the small tidal wave had done more good than damage. It had extinguished several fires in the downtown area and caused enough tide change in the channel, to allow a fast-thinking captain, to refloat the grounded cruise ship; made easier with the damaged bow-thrusters repaired. The Alaskan tenacity and character was tested, but as usual, won out. The final bill was going to be incredible. The Governor declared Juneau a disaster area, and the President did the same, insuring federal aid.

The biggest surprise came, when a big move was made to take this opportunity to officially move the capitol to Anchorage. The attempt wasn't the surprise. But, the Governor refusing to even contemplate it, was. He had, in the past, been a big advocate of the move, but stated that no terrorist would push an Alaskan out of town. No mercenaries were found alive, but eight bodies were eventually recovered. This included the men on Blueberry Hill, Jim had taken out. No pardon would be needed. They were officially recorded as being killed in a shootout with law enforcement.

The Navy cruiser had been successful, in running down the damaged Hydrofoil (Northern Lights). The bad news was, that when they boarded the boat, they only found three bodies. Sandra was not onboard. The one body found by the helm, had to be identified by finger prints. Jim's shot, had removed Brenner's entire face, and most of his head. No tears were shed. Jim personally explained the events to the President. Five days after Jim and Andrea stopped Brenner, the rest of the kidnapped dignitaries, and the injured rescue team, arrived in Juneau. Willy had to fight constant engine troubles, but finally limped in, to find himself quite a local hero. Andrea made sure that Jim and Vlad, were not mentioned (at their request). The others, were the talk of the town. Officially, that was the story, but the truth did slip out, eventually.

The airport was returned to limited operation, a week after the bomb explosion. Several loads of emergency supplies, had been flown in already. The investigation, would last for months. Vlad, Jim, and Andrea, were put on the first flight out of Juneau, headed for Washington, DC. They were joined by Robert Westlake, who the President was looking forward to meeting. He was not as excited as she was. He had spent hours with the FBI investigators, and had been assured that PEDEI Corporation, would not walk away free and clear. The President wanted blood.

President Warren

President Warren had not been off the phone more than a minute, before calling for her top advisors, and the director of the FBI. She took long enough to hug her husband and then put her game face back on. No one dared even question any directive from her. Everyone knew she was a no-nonsense person, but this incident had sharpened even that. The staff meeting was small, and only included the Secretary of State, the FBI director, the director of Homeland Security, and the head of the State Department. When the president walked in, all got quite. "I am not going to beat around the bush. We have a problem in the CIA, and the State Department!" Heads jerked, when she included the State Department. "This crazy Brenner, had help from both departments. I want the FBI to find the guilty, as quickly as possible. If you can do it quietly, that is fine, but let me be perfectly clear! I don't give a damn about protecting anything, or anybody, on this one. I want names on my desk by tomorrow."

The President gave her staff, time to absorb what she said, then continued. "I know that the CIA, is not going to be as cooperative as they could be. You will just have to work with what you have."

When she hesitated, the FBI director finally got the nerve to ask a question. "Can I ask why Director Smith is not here?" The President thought for a minute, then she said,

"I cannot be certain about him, until you tell me he is not involved. I will call him and tell him he needs to open his doors to you. As far as I am concerned, we are looking for a treasonous bustard, and no one is above question. Frank! I also want you to drop every investigation you have, and focus all of your resources on PEDEI Corporation. I have no doubt they are the instigator of this whole thing, but I don't want Bismarck, or anyone slipping out of the noose." She paused after that and added, "I expect answers tomorrow, and warrants to be served, starting the day after!" President Warren turned on that, and left the room.

Frank Brown, director of the FBI, summed up everyone's thoughts, by simply saying, "Shit, she's pissed." Everyone quickly got up and left.

The President had her preliminary report by the next day and was able to call in her CIA director John Smith (great name for a spy). He was brought up to speed and the investigation was kicked into overdrive. The day Andrea and Jim arrived in DC, President Warren knew most of the names of the people who had been assisting Brenner with intelligence, and who had supplied actual aid. After considering all options, it was decided to leave them in place for the time being, to find out how they were dealing with Brenner, and if anyone-else was using the same people.

It took several weeks, to finally begin to close the books on the Juneau terrorist attack. A lot of heads rolled, by the time the President was confident all had been found out. Every cabinet meeting, seemed to have some new faces, each time they got together. Not that they had been involved, but in most cases, that they had not been aware. The CIA director retired and the director of Homeland Security stepped down, after the failure of her department, to even have any idea about the entire episode. The entire debacle, had finally been released to the press, with the exception of the State Department mole.

The FBI, with direction of the President, was using him as a conduit, to get the head of PEDEI, Grant Bismarck. The FBI was having no luck, finding enough evidence to tie him directly to the operation, though the security chief of the corporation, had agreed to testify for some leniency. Unfortunately, without cooperation, his testimony would be tainted. The break came, when Robert Westlake called the FBI contact he had been given. Leah (Westlake's fiancé and executive secretary to Bismarck) had finally arrived in DC, to be with him. She presented him with a large file, containing photos, tapes, and office documents, proving that Bismarck was the primary conspirator.

The President had called a quiet meeting, with Choskey and her future son-in-law, and explained the situation to them. The documents Leah Swain had produced, were not going to be admissible. The President proposed an alternate approach, involving Jim and Vladimir. Jim was not happy, but agreed to the plan the President had.

The worst part of the entire thing, as far as Jim was concerned, was that she had found a way to put him back on active duty, with a promotion to Captain, while he and Vladimir closed the book on Bismarck. All anyone heard for several days, was Jim mumbling about never wanting to be a dammed officer. Soon after the meeting, Jim and Vladimir disappeared from DC, for several weeks.

After weeks in the desert, Jim and Vlad were ready for some nice quite time. They would have to explain how they got the great tans. "Did you ever imagine that Andrea's mother, would be quite so decisive in her actions Jim?" Vlad asked.

"Well, I knew she could scare the shit out of me, every time I met her, but, no." Jim leaned back against the seat and looked thoughtful. "You know, I was beginning to get worried that that scum would not do the deed, there at the end. He should have been getting pretty dehydrated by the third day."

Vlad smiled. "Well, did I forget to tell you, he had several small bottles of booze in his coat?" Jim sat up and looked at Vlad.

"Why didn't I think of that? It is even better now. I figured he got delirious, and just walked out! That would have been too easy for that slime ball,"

Vlad exclaimed. "He needed to know what he was doing. Even then, it doesn't make up for what he did and caused."

Jim patted Vlad on the shoulder. "You're right, but it comes close, so take a nap, it's a long flight to the states." Jim sat back, and like any good soldier, was asleep almost before his head hit the chair.

It took three days for Jim and Vlad to reach the Juneau Airport, after a quick stop in DC. When they walked off the government airplane, Rob and Leah were the first to meet them. Vlad handed the case to Rob, and said, "I believe this belongs to you." Rob looked a little surprised. Jim smiled and simply said, "This was all we could think to get, for a wedding present." Rob opened the case. There was a pile of cash, all of his missing notes, and the copy of the formula he had given to his kidnapers.

"I think you forgot to remove the cash?"

Vlad just started walking away. "What cash?"

Epilogue - SANDRA MAKES HER ESCAPE

Sandra was in shock, when Brenner's head disintegrated, right beside her. One minute he was talking, and then nothing. No sound, no nothing. He just pitched forward, and fell lifeless, to the deck. She had heard, what sounded like bullet strikes, hitting the back of the boat. Brenner had tried to keep the engines running, but one stopped. Right after that the shooting seemed to stop, Brenner's head disappeared, and he dropped. She realized it had to be another shot, and instantly dove to the deck. She waited for several minutes for another shot, but it never came. Sandra finally rose and started thinking what to do next. She was on her own.

Brenner had shot the other two men that had been aboard, right after leaving Auke Bay. Sandra had an idea of where to steer, but the boat was only running on one engine and would not deploy the hydrofoils. Sandra was a survivor and did not plan on going out on this note. She had the account information, for Brenner's big stash, and had over a million dollars in cash on board. She just had to figure out how to survive. There was no evidence of her, back in Juneau, so she just had to get off the boat and back to civilization.

Sandra was almost beginning to relax, when she saw a large ship approaching. She turned the boat and steered away. There was no question that she would be caught, if she stayed on board, so she had to get off.

After setting the auto helm, she donned a survival suit and stuffed the money inside. She knew that the Navy, or Coast Guard would miss the dingy and the primary survival raft, but there was a small inflatable on deck, that Brenner had used, that had no fixed location for storage. She got it over the stern and loaded some supplies aboard. The first island she came to, that got her out of sight of the approaching Navy ship, gave her an opportunity to run in close and go over the side. She was able to reach shore and hide the boat, before the navy cleared the island. Hopefully, the chase would take a while. Sandra hid on shore for several days, until her limited supplies were running short. She then attracted a passing fishing vessel, headed out. It wasn't hard, for a woman like Sandra, to convince the two-man crew to take her with them.

The End

Unfinished Business

LOOK FOR THE NEXT BOOK 'POOR CHOICES'. Coming soon.

Chapter One - Vladimir

Vladimir walked out of the bank, a happy man. The CIA had broken into the bank records and gotten the code for the account, but had found that the money could only be moved, or accessed directly, so he had flown down to do it. The President had already promised, that any money recovered from Brenner, would go to Juneau, to help pay for recovery. This ten million would be a big help. As he walked out, he did notice a woman across the street, looking at him. Now, he was a pretty average-looking guy, so this got his attention. She was wearing sun glasses, but there was something about her that made him look twice. The second time, she was speaking to a man and Vlad decided he had imagined the first look. He got his mind back on the game at hand. "Damn. If Lorrie saw me staring at another woman, she would drop me like a rock," he thought to himself. He totally dismissed the woman and continued on to the taxi he had waiting, to take him to the airport.

Several hours later, he was sitting in the oval office, with his director and the President. He handed the wire transfer information to the President. She just smiled and said. "Why don't you take that back to Alaska, and give it to the new mayor."

Choskey took the paperwork back, and smiled. "I would be honored. I guess, I wasn't sure you were serious, but thank you very much."

The President took a drink of her coffee and then asked, "What are your plans now? Are you staying on with the CIA, or going to enjoy your fame in Juneau?"

Vlad thought for a minute and looked at the director. "I guess, I hope I can continue work, like I have been doing."

The director of the CIA had watched and listened, but now he stepped into the conversation. "Vlad, since you are the President's favorite spook, who just saved her daughter, I think you can write your own check."

Vlad smiled and added, "Right now, I need to get back to Juneau, and help with the recovery, and see what is left of my own properties. Besides, Juneau needs all of the help it can get, to return to normal any time soon."

At that, President Warren stood up and shook the director's hand, and gave Vladimir a hug (which didn't thrill the secret service men in the room). "Thank you again for saving my daughter, and be sure to pass that on, to all of your friends, that helped. I will be in Juneau, to present awards to all of your helpers in a month."

Vlad and the director, took the action as a dismissal, and headed for the door. Vlad had to go through several more hours of debriefing at Langley, but was finally allowed to fly back to Juneau in the morning. The entire money recovery, had taken him half-way around the world, and ended as it began, in Juneau.

During the flight back, Vlad remembered the woman he had seen in Nassau. The more he thought about it, the more certain he became, that she had been looking at him. There was something about her that reminded him of a woman in his past (Sandra Brown)!

He had met her on an operation in Europe, right after he joined the CIA. He had fallen for her, against all advice from wiser men. She was a contract employee, who was used any time an agent needed to be compromised. Vlad spent a lot of time with her, and had seen her working. She could change her look from a street walker, to princess, just in the way she acted and moved. Clothing only enhanced her ability to be anyone. The woman across the street, had a figure just like Sandra, but the face was wrong. The more time he thought about it, the more confident he became, that he just wasn't sure, one way, or the other. The reminder of Sandra, did make him think about the last time he saw Brenner, motoring away from the Juneau dock, just before the explosion. There had been a woman with him, and the more he thought about it, he was sure that it had been Sandra.

Vlad passed the information on to his boss, as soon as he got off the plane. Maybe with a name, she could be picked up, but knowing her as well as he did, he really doubted she would be found. The only question was, did she know he had been involved in getting Brenner? Vlad thought back to the encounter, and was sure she had. She had glanced back, as the boat pulled away from the dock. He had been totally exposed at the time. The more he thought, the more convinced he was. She had always been able to remember faces and simple gestures of everyone she met. Vlad couldn't remember a single time, when she had been stumped by a disguise.

Sandra always saw through them. Vladimir called Jim, as soon as he got to his home in Juneau. "Jim, I have some bad news. While I was doing that little chore for the President, I was reminded of a person from my past." He paused for effect. "I don't think you ever met an operative named Sandra, but I worked with her several times in the past, and I believe she was on the boat with Brenner, when you blew him away."

Jim remembered a story Vlad had told him one night, in Afghanistan, about an agent he had been involved with. It had been a typical soldier story (Beautiful woman with no morals and a crazy desire for sex, in strange places). "Vlad, are you talking about the same woman you told me stories about?"

Vlad had to nod, yes. "That's the one. I know she left our relationship, and had begun working for Brenner, while he was still CIA. Knowing her as well as I do, that means they were sleeping together as well. When Brenner left Juneau, after setting the bomb, I saw a woman with him, and you said you thought there was a woman in the boat, when you finished him. I am sure now, it was her. I have to tell you, she was a vindictive bitch, when I knew her and capable of anything. If possible, I would think she is better now, than she was then. The only good note about her, was she was never a planner, or deep thinker, but that did make her a great assassin."

Jim thought about this, and then asked. "What is your point? I would assume you gave this information to your friends in the CIA and the President!"

Vlad hesitated and then added, "I did pass the info to my boss, but the President was not told, as far as I know. I don't have any positive proof, but I am sure."

"Well, why tell me? I am no investigator, or even a spy!" Jim was a little confused by the entire conversation.

"Look, I am telling you, because she is a real piece of work. She loves killing and is quite good at it. She was talented, even before the CIA trained her. She is not going to be too happy about Brenner being dead, and all of the money gone. I still don't know how I got out of the relationship alive, before. She told me then, I should watch my back. Jim. She only sees things through her eyes. She can screw you and stick an ice pick in your brain at the same time. Finish the sex without you, and feel great. There isn't a remorseful bone in her perfect body. And the thing is, I think I may have seen her in Nassau, by the bank, when I transferred the money."

"I know you and Andrea are planning on a vacation trip, as soon as you wrap up business in Juneau, so just watch for anyone who pays too much attention to you, and keep a gun close!" Jim hung up the phone and did what he always did, when thinking. He got out his pistol and checked it. He dismissed most of Vlad's worry, as overreaction. Vlad had always been a worrier, when in a combat zone. Jim did chuckle as he thought that. He knew he would watch for a good-looking woman, paying any attention to him, or Andrea. He did do a little thinking and remembered the look of the woman in the boat when he shot Brenner. He had scoped her, just before sending the round into Brenner's head. It had been the best lucky-shot he had ever made (Long-range, on a moving boat, while he had been on another boat himself). "Too bad I wasn't aiming for his head," he thought to himself. He had aimed center mass, but the boat had hit a swell, just when he fired. The fifty caliber bullet had removed most of the head.

Jim tried to sleep then, but finally gave up and called Andrea. She was in Anchorage, for a meeting with the Governor. He was not in any hurry to return to Juneau, and was trying to use some of the government's emergency money, for other projects, instead of in Juneau, where it was earmarked for. Andrea was spending more time, flying between Juneau and Anchorage, than anywhere else.

She finally picked up on the seventh ring. Jim didn't mention the information from Vlad. There would be plenty of time for that. Her secret service personnel had been replaced, so Jim was confident they could handle everything. Andrea had tried to refuse the two agents, but her mother had been adamant. Andrea still blamed herself, for the loss of one agent, and the serious wounding of the other. Jim finally hung up. Andrea would be back in town the following day, and he would be able to protect her himself. His last thought, before drifting off, was how much he missed her, when she was gone. She had already informed the Governor, that she would not be running for reelection. Her mother was trying to talk her out of walking away from the family business, but was not trying very hard. That thought put a smile on his face and he was finally able to fall into a fitful slumber.

About the Authors

MELVIN G. BROWN is the author of the autobiography, The Sanctamooja and me. Mel was born in 1940. He grew up in Eastern Washington, and spent a lot of his young life on a small homestead in Northern Idaho, with his grandparents. He has amassed a lifetime of adventures and experiences. Mel is able to bring a bit of down-home feel, to everything he writes. Mel lives and writes on the coast of Oregon, near the city of Waldport.

SCOTT S. WATTS was born, 1950, in Wallace, Idaho. He joined the United States Air Force in 1969. He served eight years, then received a commission in the United States Army. He served another four years active duty, then spent another sixteen years in the Army Reserve. Scott graduated from the University of Idaho, with a degree in Clinical Psychology. Much later, he completed a Masters Degree in Psychology, from The University of Phoenix. Scott presently lives in Northern Idaho, and works in social services.

You may contact Melvin Brown if you would like at melvinbrown@peak.org or Scott Watts at scottwa241@gmeail.com